CW00524085

Bestselling author **Merryn Alli**
family and spent her childhooc
it gave her itchy feet, and in
unloved secretarial career to work as cabin crew and see the
world. The arrival of marriage, children and cats meant a
more settled life in the south of England, where she's lived
ever since. Having gained a PhD, she taught university
literature for many years and loved every minute of it. What
could be better than spending one's life reading and talking
about books? Well, writing them perhaps.

Six Regency period romances followed, then those itchy
feet kicked in. The Regency was abandoned and *Daisy's War*,
a wartime trilogy, found its way to the top of the Amazon
charts, followed by the Summerhayes books—a saga of
romance and intrigue set in the Sussex countryside during
the summers of 1914 and 1944.

But itchy feet never rest and in 2020 she finally went over
to the dark side! The crime series, the Tremayne Mysteries, is
set in locations around the world and features Nancy, a feisty
1950s heroine, turned amateur sleuth.

Keep in touch with Merryn via the web:
Website: **https://www.merrynallingham.com**
Facebook: **http://www.facebook.com/MerrynWrites**
Twitter: **http://www.twitter.com/merrynwrites**

Other Books in this Series

The Dangerous Promise (2020)

Venetian Vendetta (2020)

Caribbean Evil (2020)

Cornish Requiem (2021)

RIO REVENGE

Merryn Allingham

RIO REVENGE

This novel is entirely a work of fiction. The names, characters and incidents portrayed in it are the work of the author's imagination. Any resemblance to actual persons, living or dead, events or localities is entirely coincidental.

First published in Great Britain 2021 by The Verrall Press

ISBN 978-1-8382742-6-9

Cover art: Berni Stevens Book Cover Design

Chapter One

Rio de Janeiro, February, 1957

The staccato sounds of a heated argument filled the corridor as Nancy Tremayne stepped out of her hotel bedroom. She glanced to her left. A man and woman faced each other, their figures tensed and hands gesticulating. As she watched, the man appeared to move even closer, towering over the small woman in a threatening manner. Nancy walked towards them making for the lift, hoping her presence might calm the situation, but it wasn't until she had drawn almost level that the shrill torrent of Portuguese came to an abrupt halt. The woman wore a badge, pinned to the lapel of her brown uniform—Vitoria. Our chambermaid, Nancy thought, most likely on turn-down duty.

As she passed the grey-suited man, a swift glance at *his* badge told her he was Diego Ramos, Under-Manager. His face seemed familiar. His photograph, she recalled, had been on a staff board in the hotel foyer when they'd arrived, and it was a face that stuck in the memory. In the photograph, as now, his expression had been unsmiling, almost frozen, with lips slightly pursed and eyes that lacked warmth.

Nancy gave a brief nod in their direction and walked into the waiting lift. The woman's face had flushed red and there were traces of tears on her cheeks. Looking back, as the lift doors closed, she saw that Vitoria had disappeared into one of the bedrooms, but the man remained where he stood, his face set and a sheen of sweat on his forehead.

The incident had been oddly upsetting. It was the man's menacing attitude, Nancy supposed, too reminiscent of the threats she'd once suffered herself. Or perhaps it was simply that she was still tired from the long overnight journey from London. The travelling had seemed endless, with stops for refuelling, first in the Canary Islands, then Buenos Aires, and finally landing at Rio de Janeiro. No wonder they had slept for hours since arriving at the Tivoli.

Her husband had gone ahead to find a taxi to take them to an event that neither was looking forward to. But it was an important evening for their host, Francisco Silva. A gala reception held in honour of an important city official whom, for business reasons, Francisco was keen to impress.

The Tivoli, an elegant hotel on the prestigious Avenida Atlantica, was Francisco's pride and joy, along with a wine-growing estate south of Rio. Winemaking was a hobby, he'd told Nancy, one he'd loved for years, but it was mining that was his true passion, the means by which he'd made a fortune large enough to buy a hotel like the Tivoli. He owned a number of mines in the neighbouring province of Minas Gerais and, most importantly for the Tremayne family, he was now the proud owner of Wheal Agnes, one of the few working tin mines in Cornwall.

'Good timing, sweetheart.' Leo was waiting at the lift doors and greeted her with a hug. 'The taxi has just arrived.'

Despite their broken night, her husband looked dapper in a dark grey suit and crisp white shirt, his hair a distinguished silver. Nancy had always considered him a handsome man and when he was dressed for an event like this evening's, he came into his own. But his face was too pale. He had had a wretched winter, of course, one bout of bronchitis following another.

'*Buffet Bonito,*' Leo told the cab driver, reading from the scribbled note that had been left for them at Reception, and in minutes they were speeding along the broad tree-lined avenue, car lights flashing, horns sounding.

Tonight would be their first real sight of the city. *Marvellous City*, according to its inhabitants, Nancy had read. It hadn't looked that marvellous in the small hours on the lengthy drive from the airport. There had been little to see: a dusty thoroughfare fronted by rundown houses, some little more than shacks, and what looked to be open sewers lining either side of the road. It wasn't the image Nancy had expected or seen replicated time and again in the guide books.

Until the moment, that is, that travelling through a final tunnel, a circle of dawn sky had appeared ahead, and then opened fully to the most wonderful panorama of city and sea.

Crescent-shaped bays stretched for miles, their waters glinting golden in the early morning light. Small boats bobbed crazily on the rolling waves and buildings of every colour clustered around white sand. Behind them, tall mountains of deep green thrust their way into a peach-coloured sky that was already turning to its daytime blue. Paradise, Nancy had thought, and felt her heart give a small jump at the sight of such astonishing natural beauty.

The scene she'd left behind this evening, though, wasn't at all beautiful. The raised voices, the menacing atmosphere, the image of a woman, threatened and cowed, was still with her. Paradise could be easily lost.

'You're very quiet,' Leo said. 'Are you feeling all right? The journey was exhausting, I know.'

'I'm fine,' she said, turning towards him and trying hard

to sound bright. 'And so I should be. I've been sleeping for hours.'

'It will take a while for our bodies to catch up with the time difference,' he said sagely.

If anyone would know, it was Leo. He frequently travelled abroad—to value paintings for private clients, attend conferences, open galleries. Or rather, he had travelled frequently, until this winter when he'd been so unwell.

'I would much rather be doing something else on our first night here,' he said. 'You, too, I imagine.'

Nancy sighed in agreement. 'I guess we owe it to Francisco to attend. He's been so very generous—inviting us to stay at his hotel, promising to take us sightseeing and act as our escort to Carnival.'

'I'm not sure how much escorting he'll manage. When I spoke on the phone to him last week, he mentioned how busy he was at Minas Gerais. It was good of him to be around to welcome us, but I doubt we'll see a great deal of him in the next week or so.'

Even if they didn't, Senhor Silva had been more than kind. As soon as Perran, Leo's elder brother and now manager of the Cornish mine, had mentioned to Francisco how ill his younger brother had been, the response had been immediate. Francisco had insisted that Leo and his wife visit him in Rio de Janeiro as guests of the Tivoli to enjoy the holiday of a lifetime. *Carnival,* he'd said, *that's the time to come. The weather will be fantastic. You can swim and sunbathe, eat and sleep, as you will. And dip in and out of the festivities. Parades, parties, open-air performances*

Nancy leaned her head against her husband's shoulder. 'He didn't say much about his guest of honour tonight. I gathered he's an important man, but not much more. Do you know his name? Francisco must have told us, but I can't remember.' She wrinkled her nose in an effort to recall.

'Senhor Minaro, Monaro? He's an official in the city government.'

Monaro? The name was familiar. Where had she heard the word? Recently, she was sure. Very recently. Then she remembered. It had been in the hotel corridor less than an hour ago, a name repeated several times in the argument she'd witnessed. Nancy had no Portuguese, but because the word had been so heavily emphasised, it had fixed in her mind.

'Monaro has just been elected as one of the city mayors,' Leo said. 'There seems to be a lot of them. Elected corruptly, according to Francisco. But the man wields power. He sits in the Câmara Municipal which passes laws, and that could include who gets to explore which bit of land.'

'And that's important?'

'It is to Francisco. Mining licenses are part of their remit. Apparently Francisco is keen to expand his business and now that Wheal Agnes is turning a profit at last—the money he's spent on extending the under-sea workings is a gamble that's paid off—he's looking elsewhere. Somewhere nearer to home. Not Minas Gerais, but a new area. He'll need a licence to develop the land, but he has a lot of competitors. Hence the need to persuade Senhor Monaro by funding what I imagine will be a very expensive evening.'

The taxi swooped to a stop outside an expanse of white stone, flaming torches on either side of the grand entrance. From the open doorway came the clink of glasses and the swell of music—a full orchestra, it seemed. Once inside, they were directed towards an immense banqueting hall, so bright Nancy had to half close her eyes. Reflections were everywhere, doubling, tripling, bouncing off the highly polished wooden floor and the glass walls that made up three sides of the room.

Sheltering behind those walls was what appeared to be an imitation forest.

Lights in the shape of flower blossoms hung suspended from the high ceiling and artificial bushes lined the room's perimeter. More lights shone from each table, this time in the shape of tree branches. On the one solid side of the room, a twenty foot table was laden with a gargantuan buffet.

'Impressive,' Leo murmured, while Nancy smoothed the skirt of her blue silk, relieved she'd worn her best dress and taken the trouble to pin up chestnut waves that had gone haywire during the journey.

Francisco must have seen them arrive and was steering a path through the crowds towards them, a warm smile on his face. For a moment, his way was barred by a waiter carrying a tray of champagne, but Nancy was quick to take a glass and the man moved on. Champagne, though, was the last thing she wanted to drink.

'The reception seems very well attended,' Leo said, glancing around the crowded room.

'Yes, I am most happy. In Carnival there are many other interests, but a good orchestra and this place.' Francisco gestured to the banqueting hall. 'It has done the trick.'

'And your guest of honour?' Nancy asked. 'I hope he's turned up.'

'Alvar Monaro? He's over there—in that small group people. I must introduce you.'

And before either she or Leo could excuse themselves, Silva was cleaving a path through the chattering crowd, clearly expecting them to follow.

Monaro turned as Francisco approached, breaking off what he was saying and stretching his mouth into a smile. He spoke in Portuguese, causing his host to take a hurried look at his watch.

'It is almost time for your speech, Senhor,' Silva said in English, his tone reassuring. 'But not quite. First let me introduce my friends from England, Professor Tremayne and his wife, Nancy.'

The man facing them was stocky and middle-aged, with a stomach that threatened to burst open the frilled evening shirt he wore. He offered them his hand, arranging his face into another smile that didn't quite reach his eyes. The hand Nancy took felt soft and cloying.

'Ah, that English mine of yours, Francisco.' He spoke with a heavy accent, using, Nancy noticed, their host's first name. It was hardly respectful.

'Professor Tremayne is a world expert on Renaissance art,' Silva said determinedly.

Alvar Monaro looked blank, his eyes expressionless. A man with no interest in art, Nancy thought crossly, remembering the wonderful paintings she had left behind in the London studio. To come to Rio, she'd had to take an overdue holiday from the art restorers where she was nearing the end of her apprenticeship.

Not that getting away hadn't had its attractions. After the wretched winter Leo had endured, he'd needed the sun, and to be truthful, she'd needed a break, too. The worry over his health and the situation with Leo's assistant, was wearing her down.

She had hardly seen Archie since that forbidden evening in Cornwall last year—he'd moved out of Cavendish Street into his own flat almost as soon as the three of them had returned to London, apparently with Leo's blessing—but the not seeing him was as bad as having him close. When Francisco Silva had issued his invitation, Nancy hadn't been averse to going. A change of scene had been welcome, away from the house Archie had once shared and the streets he still walked.

'A world expert will have travelled the world.' Monaro's lips had tightened into a sharp, thin line, and Nancy detected a sneer in his voice. 'Naturally, you have been to Rio before?'

'Sadly, no,' Leo answered amicably, 'but I'm very much looking forward to my stay.'

'You must see all the sights.' The smile that wasn't quite a smile was back. 'The beaches—Copacabana, Ipanema—the Sugarloaf, the Corcovado. You will find the statue the most inspiring sight in the whole world.'

'The Corcovado? That's the figure of Christ, isn't it?' Nancy tried to join the conversation.

'Indeed, dear lady. You will have seen it from your aircraft.'

She had been so punch drunk from tiredness that she'd seen nothing, but it was easier to ignore being called a dear lady and agree.

'I'm looking forward to a closer look,' she said.

'You must let me take you there,' Monaro said suddenly. 'Yes, I will take you there myself.' The man puffed out his chest a little. 'A special trip. How would you like that?'

She would have much preferred to see it alone with Leo and hesitated, but her husband stepped in quickly. 'That is extremely generous of you, Senhor,' he said.

The man nodded absently. 'I will be in touch… Francisco, it really must be time now for your speech.' Funnelling a pathway between a scattering of small tables and white-draped chairs, Monaro headed towards the stage at the far end of the room, Francisco hurrying to catch him up.

'He's very eager to hear himself praised,' she said.

'Senhor Monaro is not the most entrancing specimen, I grant you, but we best keep him sweet for Francisco's sake.'

He hadn't been entrancing, not at all. Nancy had thought him vain and ignorant. But there was more. Something abhorrent in the softness of his hand. Something glacial beneath the manufactured smile. The mirrored eyes, the cruel mouth, suggested a nature that would not bear too much light.

Chapter Two

Nancy was looking forward to the day ahead. Scanning the clothes that yesterday she'd hung in haste, she pulled from the wardrobe a sundress that was marginally less creased. It was one that happened to be a favourite, and today the bright yellow chiffon and its ruched sweetheart neckline seemed to embrace the optimism she was beginning to feel. The holiday would be a success, Leo's health would improve, and she would return to London refreshed.

She was pulling a hairbrush through a tangle of waves when there was a tap on the bedroom door. 'I'll go,' Leo said, collecting his wallet from the bedside table.

There was a murmur of conversation before he called out, 'The maid is here to clean, Nancy. Are you ready?'

'Just about.'

Fixing a headband quickly into place, Nancy grabbed her bag from the bed and followed him out into the lemon-scented corridor. The chambermaid waiting behind her cleaning trolley was the same woman she had seen yesterday in fierce argument with Diego Ramos. It prompted a hazy memory in Nancy as she hovered in the doorway. She felt sure she'd seen the man again after that argument. But where? She had been so tired last night she barely remembered the taxi ride back to the hotel from the *Buffet Bonito*, but it was there that she'd seen him, wasn't it? His face in the shadows. He'd been standing half-hidden behind one of the grand pillars that guarded the entrance to the building, waiting. But for what? For whom?

'Leo,' she called after her husband, who was already halfway down the corridor, 'I think I'll take a scarf. You go on—I'll be down in a moment.'

Leo turned a surprised face to her but, with a nod, walked on. Immediately, Nancy darted back inside the room where Vitoria had begun to change the bed.

The maid looked up. 'I finish?' she queried.

'Yes, do. I came back because I wanted to ask you... are you all right? I mean after yesterday?'

The maid looked puzzled.

'The argument—with Mr Ramos,' Nancy prompted.

Vitoria's face darkened at the name and her lips compressed.

'You were crying,' Nancy went on, touching her eyes in dumb show. 'You were very upset.'

Vitoria nodded. 'He no let me go.'

'Go where?'

'Sister.' The maid paused, evidently trying to find the English for what she wanted to say. 'Little girl missing. I want go help. But Ramos no let me go.'

'A little girl is missing?' Nancy thought rapidly. 'Your sister's little girl?'

When the woman nodded, she said, 'But how awful. When?'

Vitoria sank down on the half-stripped sheets, holding up two fingers. 'Two day.'

'Have you told the police?'

'Police. Hah!' The woman almost spat.

'But the little girl—could she have had an accident and be in hospital? A bad leg, a bad head.' Nancy once more resorted to mime.

Vitoria shook her head fiercely. 'No, no. Livia took when she go school—she eight year old. I pay money for school,' she said proudly.

'You pay for your niece's education? That's very generous. But what do you mean—she was "took"?'

'Many *crianças* took.'

'Children? Children abducted?' Nancy could hardly believe what she was hearing. 'Is your sister rich then?' A ransom could be the only explanation, otherwise it made no sense. 'Much money?'

Vitoria gave a crooked smile. 'We poor. I work at Tivoli. Sister make dress, skirt, *blusa*.'

'She's a dressmaker? If there's no money, why abduct… why take Livia?'

The maid rubbed her thumb and finger together. 'Little hand. Girl hand. Good to steal.'

'Pickpocketing?' Nancy couldn't keep the scepticism from her voice.

The maid was not discouraged by the doubt she must have heard. 'Bad men,' she said. '*Crianças* took, made steal. Two years now.'

'And no one is doing anything to rescue these children? No help?'

'Who?' was the sole answer. 'Girls good to take. They steal and when grow…'

She didn't need to finish the sentence. Nancy knew exactly what she was suggesting. A group of young girls trained to pickpocket and, when they grew too noticeable amongst the crowd, used in other, even worse ways. How truly dreadful. No wonder this poor woman was distraught.

'And Mr Ramos knows of this? Knows why you want to go to your sister?'

'He know.'

She was finding it almost impossible to understand the situation. A young child was missing—according to Vitoria, many young children—people in authority knew, but no one had lifted a finger to help.

Nancy stood for minutes staring at the wall, then realised the maid had begun again to strip the bed. Strands of yesterday's argument drifted back to her.

'Yesterday with Mr Ramos,' she said, 'you mentioned a name. Monaro. What does he have to do with what's happened?'

Vitoria roughly bundled the sheets into a large linen bag. 'Monaro big man. No speak.'

'I met him last night. I can see he is an important man, but why did you speak of him to Mr Ramos?'

Vitoria stopped her bundling and looked at Nancy, her dark brown eyes judging, trying, it seemed, to gauge how trustworthy this inquisitive guest was. 'Bad man,' was all she would say. Then turned back to the bed.

It was impossible to press her further and, remembering to collect her scarf, Nancy hurried to the lift and down to breakfast. She hadn't liked Monaro and was willing to believe that in Vitoria's words he was a bad man. But bad enough to abduct young girls from the street? And powerful enough not to be held to account?

And then there was Ramos. He had been angry with the maid, more angry it seemed when she'd mentioned Monaro's name. Diego Ramos had been hanging around *Buffet Bonito* last night. Had he been waiting to see Monaro?

No, she told herself, she mustn't get caught up in this. It was too loathsome even to think of. They were in Rio for a holiday and for Leo to relax and rest. It was what she must do, too.

When she joined her husband at the breakfast table, he had a guide book open and a map of the city spread before him.

'Ah, there you are!' He looked up and smiled. 'I thought you might be sewing the scarf!'

Nancy slipped into her seat and looked around. Only a few tables remained vacant—breakfast was obviously a popular meal with the Tivoli's guests. Bowls of sweet cereal had been delivered to a neighbouring table, along with a plate of exotic fruits and another of small, unfrosted cakes.

She felt a sudden hunger. 'Have you ordered yet?'

Leo nodded. 'The works. Hope you have an appetite.' He poured them coffee from the pot the waiter had left.

'We need to get a taxi to Praia Vermelha—red beach in English,' he said, his finger marking a route on the map. 'The cable car to the top of Sugarloaf goes from …' He bent his head to look more closely. 'An Avenida Pasteur. Apparently it's also a charming residential area, *with an architectural mix and beautifully landscaped gardens.* We could go for a stroll there before we buy tickets.'

'Maybe decide on the walk after the cable car?' she suggested. 'I'm thinking the earlier we go, the better. It could get very hot towards midday.'

*

It was already very warm when they emerged from the hotel entrance.

'You were right about going early.' Leo passed a handkerchief across his forehead. 'Let's get a cab quickly.'

For a moment, Nancy didn't move, amazed at what seemed to have happened overnight. 'Leo, just look at the street—was it like this when we went out last evening?'

Bunting had been strung between lamp posts, and

garlands and glitter were everywhere. On the walkway that fronted the beach, a small parade of people in fancy dress danced and twirled to a samba rhythm. A brightly decorated truck had pulled up directly opposite the hotel entrance and its owner was serving a line of customers.

'Beer,' Leo said. 'Ice-cold Brazilian beer.' He mopped his forehead again. 'I can see the attraction.'

'When I spoke to Francisco, he said that Carnival doesn't open for two days. Not officially. But they seem to be celebrating already.'

'Starts five days before Lent, I think—very Catholic—though the samba doesn't feel too Catholic. It's a mixed culture, I guess, a blend of African and European.'

Leo waved his arm in the air and a taxi slid to a halt beside them. 'Great timing,' he said, opening the rear door for her, 'though there's no rush. The cable car runs all day and there are cars every twenty minutes or so. At least, that's what the guide book says.'

The guide book proved correct. A ten minute ride deposited them outside the cable car station where a small queue had formed at the ticket office. Quickly, they joined the line for the next car that arrived in minutes and, once full, was swung immediately into the air. There were no seats and being compressed into such a tight space was uncomfortable, but it hardly seemed to matter. The ride was over almost as soon as it had begun.

'Is this it?' she asked Leo, as their fellow travellers streamed from the cable car.

He delved back into his guide book. 'It says here that the ride to the top of Sugarloaf is in two sections. Where we are now is Urca Mountain. From here you have to take a second car. Let's look around first.'

It was certainly worth the look. At nearly a mile high, Urca

Mountain offered incredible aerial views in every direction. Nancy peered over her husband's shoulder, tracing the landscape on the map he held. 'That must be Guanamara Bay. We saw it when we came from the airport. And this bay here,' she pointed down at the map, 'that's Copacabana beach.' Shading her eyes, she searched the distant crescent of sand. 'I can't make out the Tivoli from here—but it has to be among that mass of white buildings.'

'And look!' She grabbed Leo's shirt sleeve. 'Just look over there, to the west. To the other mountain. The statue of Christ the Redeemer. It must be huge if we can see it so clearly from here.'

'Nearly a hundred feet, I read. He's the next must-see on our list.'

Monaro's invitation, the conversation she'd had with Vitoria, crept unbidden into Nancy's mind and the day seemed suddenly darker. She had to forget what she'd heard, she told herself, but how did she? How did she forget a child taken by force for goodness knows what terrible purpose?

'Senhor Monaro offered to take us there,' she said gloomily, unable to shake off the hovering cloud.

Her husband's face fell. 'I'd forgotten that. I guess we'll have to go with him. For—'

'For Francisco's sake,' she chorused, then fell against him laughing. It made her feel a little better. 'Did he leave for Minas Gerais today?'

'He mentioned he was going straight after the event last night. Goodness knows, what time he arrived there, but hopefully it means we'll see him back here tomorrow. Come on, let's get in line again.'

Leo fished their tickets from his pocket and within minutes, it seemed, they were stepping out of a second car and onto the top of Sugarloaf. A row of souvenir shops confronted them, stacked high with carved wooden animals, copper bowls, painted plates, tiny sculptures, and rack upon rack of postcards.

'No,' he said firmly. 'You can look later.'

'I wasn't— 'Nancy began.

'I know your delight in woodcraft.' Taking her hand, he steered her away from the stalls, at the same time avoiding an ice cream vendor approaching at a rapid rate.

'Let's enjoy the view first, then we'll make for a restaurant. There looks to be several.'

The view was once again magnificent. A three hundred and sixty degree perspective of mountains and city and sea.

'A bird's eye view almost,' Nancy said. 'Or maybe a monkey's.' She looked down at the animal she'd heard chattering at her ankle, a hopeful expression in his eyes.

'Don't feed him, whatever you do,' an American voice warned her. 'They're cute but mighty aggressive.'

'I bet they are.' Leo smiled at the passer-by, and took her hand again. 'Let's get out of the sun. We can enjoy the view from inside.'

At the nearest restaurant, a waitress bustled towards them, notepad swinging from her hip.

'What drink do you recommend?' Leo asked her, when they'd been ushered to a table by the window. 'Something Brazilian perhaps?'

The girl gave a nod and returned a few minutes later with two fat glasses of lime-coloured liquid. '*Caipirinhas*,' she offered. 'Nice and cool.'

'And what exactly will we be drinking?'

'Lime juice, sugar and cachaça.' When Leo looked questioningly at her, she said, 'A kind of rum. Very Brazilian. Like the samba.'

'Just like the samba.' Nancy took a sip and, glass in hand,

leaned back in her chair against a pillow of warm air. She felt her limbs loose and easy.

'Enjoying yourself?' Leo asked.

'Immensely. And you?'

'I love it. The natural beauty of the place is staggering. Rio is probably the most beautiful city I've ever seen, and I've seen some. I must make sure and brag to Archie when we get back. At last, I've been somewhere that he hasn't.'

The name had her half close her eyes. She rarely saw Archie these days and spoke to him even more rarely, but he was always in her mind. And in her heart. Leo had never asked why his assistant had suddenly decided to quit Cavendish Street, where for years he'd happily occupied the top floor, to move to a far less agreeable lodging in the East End. Nancy had a bad feeling, though, that her husband suspected what had happened between them.

Banishing the image of a wry smile and startling blue eyes, she took another sip. 'This *is* nice and cool.'

She must relax, she told herself. She wouldn't think of Archie and she must forget the lost child. There was nothing she could do to help, and Leo would hate her to interfere, to begin her poking and prying as he called it. He was in Rio to enjoy himself and she must as well.

When a few hours later, they returned to the hotel, there was no sign of Vitoria, though Nancy looked for her, and in the evening another chambermaid appeared on turn-down duty. Vitoria must have been given leave to go to her sister after all. Nancy was comforted by the thought.

Chapter Three

London, February, 1957

Archie pushed aside the papers he'd been working on and walked into the adjoining bedroom to find another jumper. It was a cold February and his flat had virtually no heating: a couple of two-bar electric fires that were expensive to run. The place was a bit of a dump, to be honest, not a patch on his old flat. He missed the top floor of the Cavendish Street house, having lived there a fair time and put thought into making it comfortable.

But he'd been right to move out. It was better than being constantly on edge, wondering if he'd see Nancy, wondering how they'd act around each other. And he liked living in the East End. There was always a decent breakfast to be had at *Charlie's.*

He rummaged in his wardrobe and pulled out an old fishermen's jumper, one he'd had since he was fifteen. That was when he'd left school and joined the crew on the *Morwenna*, his brother's fishing boat, only to find he suffered an acute sea sickness that wasn't going away. Even now, the thought made him grin. The youngest son of a fishing family, and he couldn't cope with the kind of seas his big brother, Rich, faced every day of his life.

Even wearing the heavy cable jumper, he couldn't get warm. Maybe he'd abandon the work a while, and go for a walk. Leo had left him plenty to get on with, but everything would be finished right and tight before his boss returned. His life held little else of any interest.

Nancy wouldn't be shivering, that was certain. He looked at his watch. In Brazil, it would be two in the afternoon, and he wondered what she was doing right now. He shouldn't think of her so often, but he couldn't stop himself. He hoped she was getting some enjoyment from the trip, though if he knew Nancy, and he thought he did, she would have much preferred to stay in that studio of hers.

It was for Leo, he thought wryly, that she was thousands of miles away. Why his boss had to travel so far to enjoy a few weeks of recuperation, Archie couldn't fathom. Leo had been pretty sick these last few months and it was true he needed sun and rest, but the long journey to Brazil—how good a choice was that? Francisco Silva had been insistent, though, and Leo had always wanted to see the famous Carnival. Over the years, in all the trips he and Archie had made to South America for work, they had never once visited Rio.

Carnival, by all accounts, was pretty wild, and now that he wasn't around Archie could only cross his fingers that Nancy wouldn't find trouble—she had a nose for it. But it was right that he wasn't there and right that he'd moved to this flat. The months since their return from Cornwall, even living separate lives, had been difficult enough. Neither of them could forget what had happened in Port Madron.

It had been building for a long time. Really, ever since they'd met. She had been Leo's wife for a mere hour when he'd first set eyes on Nancy. He'd been away, seeing his folks in Cornwall. For how long? A week maybe, that was all. But when he got back, it was to find his boss had married a girl fifteen years younger and one he hardly knew. Leo had been the white knight riding to Nancy's rescue—and she had needed rescue. The bloke she'd been engaged to had more than one screw loose, Archie thought, the memory still vivid of how Philip March had traced Nancy to Cornwall last year and begun his terror campaign all over again.

It was all water under the bridge now, over, done with, and he had to move on. She did, too, and they were both trying. After that evening together, he'd looked for another job. It was the only decent thing he could do. But though jobs were more plentiful now, it was twelve years since the war ended and employment was looking up, he could find nothing that would pay a decent wage. So he'd done the only other thing he could, and that was move out of Cavendish Street, let husband and wife sort out their marriage in peace.

Sometimes when he caught Leo looking at him, he wondered how much his boss suspected. Not a word had been said, but neither had Leo questioned his assistant's decision to move out. And that made him uneasy. At one point, he'd half expected to be given the sack, but he'd been spared that ignominy. Why the restraint, he'd wondered? Leo was already an eminent man when he'd rescued Archie from a miserable future—deadening, casual work was all that was left after the war for a common soldier—and what Leo had given, he could easily have taken away. But maybe he'd felt too strong a loyalty, to Archie and his family, coming as they did from the same village. Or maybe it was longstanding gratitude that it was Archie's action on a Normandy beach to which he owed his life.

Whatever it was, it made Archie determined that he would harm the man no more. When he had work to deliver to Cavendish Street, he made sure that Nancy was away from home, working at the studio. Only very occasionally had their paths met and they'd barely spoken this last year. It was as though they both feared any conversation might burst the bubble they'd made for themselves. Still, he would have liked to know how she was, whether she'd caught up yet with her oldest friend, Rose, whether she'd made contact with her parents at last, now that hopefully she'd seen the last of March. Even how her apprenticeship was going.

She must be nearly qualified now. Leo had never liked her working, expecting her to fit his view of where women were happiest—at home, looking after house and children. The baby thing hadn't worked out, and Leo hadn't managed to make Nancy into a housewife either. She was too independent to bend to a husband's will, too determined to carve her own path through life. His boss had eventually swallowed the apprenticeship, but when it came to the future, when it came to her taking on a permanent job, there were likely to be fireworks. At least, Archie wouldn't be there to see them.

Chapter Four

Rio de Janeiro, February, 1957

The telephone rang while Nancy was still in the bathroom. When she emerged from the shower, hair dripping, Leo was replacing the receiver. 'That was Francisco. He's just back from Minas Gerais, and keen to say hello.'

'At breakfast?' she murmured, discarding a fluffy white bath towel.

'Before breakfast, I'm afraid.'

She shrugged herself into a clean shirt and a fresh pair of trousers. Pedal pushers— that's what the store assistant had called them—in dark blue cotton with turquoise cuffs. More daring than Nancy's usual choice, but in this flamboyant city, they felt right.

Leo looked her slowly up and down. 'Very fetching! Though I still prefer you in a dress.' He walked over to the bedside table to collect his wristwatch and wedding ring. 'Francisco has a meeting at the Town Hall at ten—it seems that it's essential he attends, the mining license he's pursuing is up for discussion—but he wants to see us first.'

'He's waiting for us now?' She picked up the towel again, scrunching it vigorously through long waves.

'Afraid so. He's keen to take us on a tour of the hotel. Can you cope without eating?'

'If that's the only problem the day brings... Give me a few minutes and I'll be ready. I'm sure I saw a hairdryer in one of the drawers when I was unpacking.'

*

Francisco Silva was at the reception desk talking to a man that Nancy recognised from the staff board as the hotel manager. His deputy, Diego Ramos, hovered in the background, clearly listening to their conversation. She imagined the man would be keen to ingratiate himself wherever possible, and knowing what passed between his immediate boss and the Tivoli's owner would be valuable.

Francisco turned as he heard them approach. For a man who had travelled a considerable distance on what must have been very little sleep, he looked remarkably rested. Smart grey trousers and a short-sleeved shirt that was pristine in its whiteness created a business-like impression. The brightly striped jacket on his arm, though, hinted at something more extravagant.

'My friends! How good to see you again! I am sorry I could not say a proper goodbye at *Buffet Bonito*—my guest was, how can I say, a little demanding?'

'It was fine, Francisco,' her husband said easily. 'We climbed into a taxi and were whisked back to one of the most comfortable hotels I've ever stayed in.'

Their host beamed. 'You are enjoying the Tivoli, then? That is good to know. It was not always as comfortable as this.. Not by any means. That is why I wanted to take you on a tour of my hotel—show you the improvements I have made. And all those I would like to make. But I am so sorry that I cannot be with you for the rest of the day.'

'You have work to do, old chap,' Leo said. 'We're the ones

on holiday.'

Francisco beamed again. 'Come with me. We will start with the cellars, I think, and work our way up to the roof garden. That will be a splendid place for breakfast, but it is there I will have to leave you, I am afraid.'

'To the cellars, then,' Leo said cheerfully.

Nancy was delighted to hear the lightness in his voice. After only two days, he was looking so much better. Leaving behind her work in the studio had not been easy, particularly at this moment. Her apprenticeship was coming to an end and she was desperate to impress her mentor sufficiently to be offered a permanent post. Connie's was a small restoration business, known for its high quality work, but there were few openings for new staff. It would be the best prize ever if Nancy were taken on, but seeing Leo looking and sounding so relaxed, she couldn't regret her absence.

The winter months had been an anxious time, watching her husband's health deteriorate from one bout of bronchitis to another. And all the time, feeling the heavy weight of guilt. Guilt that she didn't love him as she should. Guilt that he had rescued her from a dangerous situation and she had repaid him by loving another man.

She gave herself an inner shake. She wouldn't think of it, and wouldn't think of Archie six thousand miles away.

'We have extended the cellar space very much,' Francisco Silva was saying. 'Now we can store double the amount of wine than we could at first. The hotel is attracting more and more guests every year, and those guests like to drink! Brazilian wine is very good, too—and the wine from my own estate the very best.'

'Does your estate supply the hotel?' Nancy asked.

'It does. But *A Fortuna* cannot provide enough and I must buy from elsewhere. The wine estate is a *passatempo*, you know. A special interest. A place to find calm when business is hard. If you had more time, I would like to take you there to see for yourself.'

Nancy smiled. 'I'm sure I'd love it, but Rio and Carnival will probably be more than enough.'

'On this trip, yes. But you must come again and see more of Brazil. *A Fortuna* is south of Rio in the Vale dos Vinhedos. Many, many wineries and most of Brazilian wine produced there. Very green, very hilly—like the foot of the Alps in Switzerland. This is what I am told.'

The lift had taken them past at least one more floor below the foyer, Nancy reckoned, and she could feel immediately the atmosphere was different. The cellar space was cool and dark, smelling of damp, wet earth. There was another strong odour, too. The *smell of* wooden shelves and a great deal of cork.

She looked around. A double layer of arches filled three of the walls that stretched far into the distance and, in each of the arches, bottle after bottle sat one atop the other. The fourth wall sported a line of kegs, stacked horizontally.

'The barrels over there,' Leo said, pointing to them. 'How are they different?'

'They are used to store our house wine. See,' their host wagged a finger at the taps attached to the end of each keg. 'It is still excellent wine, but a good deal cheaper for the customer. And good for us, too—each keg holds well over twenty bottles.' He broke off suddenly. 'But what is that?' He was looking across at the row of kegs. One had been left slightly to the side, and was standing vertically and seemingly with a half-closed cover.

Muttering to himself in Portuguese, Silva walked towards the rogue barrel. Nancy saw him come to an abrupt halt. His hands flew up into the air, and an anguished cry came from his lips.

'*Oh deus, oh deus!*'

'Whatever is it?' Leo hurried towards him, Nancy close behind.

Their host had a stricken look on his face, and after that one desperate cry he seemed to be struck dumb. He pointed a shaking hand at the open barrel. And then Nancy saw for herself.

A figure was crammed into the keg. Sunk deep into the wine. A woman's figure. She forced herself to look more. She had an uncanny feeling that she knew whose figure it would be. And she was right. Vitoria Dias.

The woman's body had been pushed fiercely down to fit into the keg, the white frill of her maid's pinafore floating gently on the surface. Her head was tilted back, her mouth open, her eyes glassy and staring. Nancy turned away, sick to her stomach.

No wonder she hadn't seen the chambermaid last night. Poor, poor Vitoria. She hadn't been given leave to help search for her sister's child. She'd been absent from her duties because she was here, in this cold cellar, drowned in a barrel of wine.

'I must telephone the police immediately.' Silva had at last come back to life. 'I am sorry, my friends, I cannot...'

Leo took hold of the man's arm. 'Go, Francisco. Go now. We'll find our own way back to the foyer.'

Their host rushed towards the lift, his body as stiff as a tin soldier set in motion.

'Your jacket,' her husband called after him—Francisco had dropped the garment in his haste to leave—but the words barely sounded, swallowed whole by the cavernous space. Leo slung the jacket over his arm. 'We best take it with us, I guess. Francisco can collect it later.'

He turned and put a gentle arm around her shoulders. 'What a dreadful sight, darling. I wish you hadn't seen it.'

He bent his head to look into her eyes and what he saw there must have prompted him to hug her closer. 'No, Nancy. Don't think about it! The police will be here very shortly and they will deal with the problem.'

Maybe they will, Nancy thought. But Vitoria hadn't trusted them, so why would she? Was it likely they'd discover who had taken this woman's life so brutally? She doubted it would be their most pressing concern. Vitoria was poor, a lowly worker, and maybe, just maybe, she had stepped out of line. Was that why she had lost her life? For daring to suggest that Alvar Monaro was in some way behind the abduction of the missing child? Did he employ people who did this kind of thing? It was more than likely.

Yet who would have told him of Vitoria's suspicions? One of the hotel staff? They were likely to be the maid's closest contacts, people to whom she might talk during her working day. In her mind, Nancy wandered through the names on the staff board. She had almost committed that board to memory by now. Diego Ramos! Of course. It had to be him. He had spoken to Monaro the evening they'd gone to the reception at *Buffet Bonito*. The evening the under-manager had quarrelled with Vitoria. That's why he'd been at the restaurant, lurking in the shadows. Waiting for Monaro. Waiting to warn him.

'The police might want to speak to us,' Leo said, breaking into her thoughts, 'but until they get here, we can't do anything. Do you still feel like eating?'

Nancy shook her head. The image of the drowned woman wouldn't leave her. 'I think I'll miss breakfast, but you mustn't.'

'If you don't think it's too cold-hearted?'

'Of course not. I'll see you back in the room.'

'I won't be long. I'll forget the roof garden today and breakfast down here.'

In place of the appetite she'd lost, Nancy's anger had begun to simmer. How could a hard-working woman like Vitoria have lost her life for something she'd said? It was grotesque. Crossing to the lift, she waited some minutes for it to arrive. It was a busy morning, floor numbers flashing by in swift succession without the lift ever making it to the foyer. She would be best to climb the stairs. It would be hard going but she needed distraction.

The staircase, when she found it, appeared to travel down as well as up. Down to the cellars, she wondered, made uncomfortable by the thought. As she hesitated, a bell-boy appeared on the lower steps, adjusting his uniform cap before he began the climb to the foyer. Had he come from his room? From a floor between her and the cellar, the floor they'd passed in the lift? It must be where the staff were accommodated. It was then Nancy made a decision. Her husband might have warned her, but Vitoria was owed a debt.

As soon as the boy had walked past her and into the foyer, she padded swiftly down the same staircase to the lower floor, seeing straightaway that she'd been right to assume it was used for live-in staff. The labels on the bedroom doors made it plain. Hurrying along the stone corridor—how different from their own luxurious floor—she glanced at the names as she passed. She needed to be quick. It wouldn't do for her to be caught here. Her only possible excuse was that she'd become lost, but that was unlikely to be believed.

Vitoria's room was halfway along the corridor on the right-hand side. Very carefully, Nancy tried the door. She had no idea if anyone from the hotel, even Francisco, might have checked or be checking right now on the maid's room. But the door opened easily and the bedroom was empty.

Closing the door softly behind her, she let go of her breath. She'd made it here without detection but, with little sense of what she should look for, a search would be a daunting task. Anything that might give a clue as to who was behind the woman's murder, Nancy supposed, but looking around, it seemed unlikely she would find it. The room was small and bare: a single bed, a shabby wardrobe, a small cotton rug, and a solitary wooden shelf where Vitoria had kept the few nicknacks she possessed. A tiny vase of artificial flowers, a delicate wooden box and a single photograph in an elaborately decorated frame.

Nancy reached up for the photograph, taking it to the small slit of light that came from a window high on one wall. She recognised Vitoria straightaway. She was standing beside another woman, her sister, Nancy presumed, and between them, holding their hands, was a little girl. Livia. The child was evidently in her best dress, a pale pink cloud of organdie with a deeper pink sash, and a deep pink bow in her dark curls. A pretty child with a sweet smile. Nancy felt a tangible shudder at the thought of this small innocent in wicked hands.

There was a deeper resonance, too. She had no children of her own, nor was she likely to. Since her miscarriage two years ago, she had given up any idea of having a baby. It had seemed pragmatic to accept the situation—pregnancy was a danger for her—and although Leo had initially been the one to want a child very badly, he rarely mentioned the possibility these days. He'd had too many other problems to contend with. But looking at the photograph gave Nancy an unusual pain, a deep sense of loss, of what might have been.

Shaking off her melancholy, she scolded herself into action. She should be in and out of this room as quickly as possible. But where to search? The suitcase beneath the bed was empty, the room possessed no drawers and, when she looked into the wardrobe, there was nothing hung there but a newly pressed maid's uniform and a floral dress with a matching cardigan. At the bottom of the wardrobe, a pair of black lace-up shoes — part of the uniform, Nancy guessed — and a tired pair of cream sandals.

The maid's life in the hotel had been narrow and a little sad, so different from the colour and vigour just outside its doors. Except for the photograph, there was nothing to suggest that Vitoria *had* another life. Nancy glanced up at the shelf again and this time she took down the wooden box. It was plainly made, but the wood had been polished and shone brightly. Evidently, a much loved keepsake. She lifted the lid. There were several letters inside. She had no wish to pry, but in any case she would understand not one word. The signature at the end of each letter, though, was always the same. Ester. Was Ester Vitoria's sister? It was a reasonable conclusion. Did she know yet of the dreadful end her sister had met? Would anyone, in fact, bother to tell her?

Nancy looked through the pages, searching for the writer's location. There was no address on any of the first three letters, but the last had a few lines scrawled at the top. Perhaps that was when Ester had moved to a new home and wanted to let her sister know where to find her. Nancy rummaged in her handbag for a notebook and carefully transcribed the address. The house was in an area called Santa Cecilia. And that seemed to be the street — *Rua Augusta*.

Tucking the notebook away, she made for the door. It was definitely time that she wasn't here. Once more, she was lucky. The corridor was empty and she was able to reach the staircase to the foyer unseen. If her luck held, she would make it back to the bedroom before Leo had finished breakfast.

The bell-boy she'd noticed earlier adjusting his cap was standing by the lift. On impulse, she said to him, 'Do you know a place called Santa Cecilia?'

He appeared to understand little English, but at the mention of the place, he gave a definite jolt backwards. Had she mangled the word? It would hardly be surprising. She tried again. 'Santa Cecilia,' she said slowly.

He shook his head at her. 'No, no, madam. Not go.'

'But why?'

'Bad place. *Favela*.' Then when Nancy look puzzled, he said with an attempt at English pronunciation, 'Favella.'

She had read about the favellas in Leo's guide book. Shanty towns, slums really, climbing the mountains that circled the city, poor communities that had settled on land no one else wanted. As more and more refugees had come from Europe or people migrated from the Brazilian countryside, the lack of housing and mass transport had forced Rio to grow vertically and the favellas to spread.

The same guide book had warned that such places could be hotbeds of crime. But that wasn't going to stop Nancy.

Chapter Five

She reached the bedroom, flushed and slightly breathless, only minutes before Leo appeared in the doorway.

'It was a good breakfast,' he said, 'but how are you feeling now? You looked quite ill downstairs.'

'Better, thanks. I just needed to rest.' It was only a white lie, she told herself. 'Do you know if the police have arrived?'

'Not yet. I met Francisco in the foyer, waiting for them. It looks as though we'll have to hang around for a while in case they want to speak to us. I'm afraid it's messed up our morning. I was hoping to stroll along to the next beach. I'm told it's much quieter than Copacabana.'

It would be difficult not to be, Nancy thought. The crescent-shaped bay opposite their hotel, its wide sands protected by two headlands, stretched for miles, yet there was rarely more than a foot of it unoccupied. For the Cariocas, the name she'd heard given to the city's residents, the beach was a second home: from early morning to late at night it was the centre of intense social activity. Watching from her balcony, Nancy had been fascinated by this lively outdoor life. A daily migration of bathing suits, beach shoes, parasols and deck chairs, streamed across the Avenida Atlantica from the neighbouring apartments. People splashed around in the sea's shallows or braved the deep, rolling waves, fearsome in their strength. If you didn't swim, you could run, walk, cycle. Play beach tennis or volleyball—both had clearly demarcated courts. And at the end of the day, you could take a stool at a row of kiosks on the promenade that sold beer and juice and finger food—eating and drinking and talking with friends. It was a world in itself.

'We can explore the beaches later and I'm happy to wait. I've brought a good book with me—Daunt's recommended it—the bookshop in the High Street? *My Family and Other Animals*. We could read on the balcony until the police call.'

'It could be too hot for me, but I'll give it a go. I've still several journals to read. Archie has typed me extracts from articles I might find relevant, but really I need to study them properly.'

*

It was several hours before Francisco Silva telephoned their room. Leo had become increasingly uncomfortable as the sun rose high in the sky, and had moved to sit in a shady corner of the bedroom. From time to time, Nancy could see him fan himself with the journal he was reading.

'That's a relief,' she heard him say, when he answered the phone. Then, 'We'll be up in ten minutes.'

'You'll be pleased to know that the police won't need to speak to either of us,' he told her as she came in from the balcony. 'Apparently Francisco has given them all the information they need. He's very apologetic that this has happened on our holiday.'

Nancy's forehead wore a deep crease. 'But Vitoria? What of her?'

'Vitoria?' Leo looked puzzled.

'The maid who was drowned,' she said more severely than she'd meant to.

'I don't know. He didn't say. But he's invited us to lunch on the roof terrace—a special lunch, he said, to make up for our bad experience.'

She felt a hard knot form in her stomach. Vitoria was nothing to Leo, of course, nor even to Francisco, but there was an inversion here of what should be important. No one seemed to care that this poor woman had died. And not just died, but been murdered in the most horrific fashion. All that seemed to matter was that she and Leo enjoyed their holiday and ate well. But she said nothing, washed her hands, brushed her hair, and walked with her husband to take the lift.

'This is my latest innovation,' Francisco greeted them, as they emerged onto the roof terrace. 'The space has always been here, but I hope I have made it a little more special.'

He had, Nancy thought. Very special. The large expanse had been split into two distinct areas with a protective glass barrier enclosing the entire space. Hard landscaping had been softened by clusters of green bushes interspersed with huge flower arrangements. The area nearest the lift sported a small pool with reclining sunbeds and striped umbrellas. Cabins for dressing and undressing were discreetly hidden against the wall of the building.

'We eat over here.'

Francisco held out his hand to guide them to the second area where a long bar, flanked by a profusion of greenery, lined the whole of one wall. Large squashy sofas with small tables filled the remaining space. Nancy noticed that several had been pushed together to provide a large enough surface for what appeared to be a huge lunch. She still had little appetite but crossed her fingers that she'd wouldn't let her host down.

Francisco waved them to their seats. 'Let me get you drinks. Something cool? It is going to be a very hot day, I think.'

To Nancy's mind, it was already a very hot day and she looked anxiously at Leo who was once more wielding a linen handkerchief. Since his illness, the heat seemed to affect him far more than she remembered. He'd coped well in the weeks they'd spent in the Caribbean, but he wasn't coping too well now.

'Will you try a *caipirinha?* It is Brazil's national cocktail. Or maybe you prefer coconut water?'

'The coconut water, please,' she said.

'Me, too,' Leo echoed.

They'd enjoyed the *caipirinhas* they'd been served on Sugarloaf, but today the temperature had risen dramatically and drinking spirits in such a heat was unwise.

'While we wait, let me explain the food we have. Naturally, we serve an international menu in our restaurant. The Americans, for one, do not take kindly to foreign cuisine. But I have tried to tempt you with some Brazilian delicacies. To start, we have a shrimp and yuca bowl, or if you would prefer soup, the chef has made chicken and rice.' Francisco raised an eyebrow questioningly. 'No. Then we will have the shrimp bowls. They are very light. Plenty of room for the small pies. I ordered them with cream cheese and prawns... I hope that goes well. Also cassava and shredded chicken that has been battered and fried. And there is Brazilian cheese bread to soak it all up. To finish we have *brigadeiros* —chocolate fudge balls. What do you think?' He spread his hands wide, waiting for their verdict.

'It looks splendid, Francisco.' Leo was the first to recover from the roll call of food. 'I only hope we can do justice to such a feast.'

It was Nancy's hope, too, though she doubted she would make it to the *brigadeiros.*

'Did the police keep you long?' she asked, as their drinks

arrived at the table.

'An hour maybe. Inspector Alvarez was quick, but I must introduce him and his men to members of my staff and that took time. The morning has gone, I am afraid.'

'What did the inspector want to know?'

'Please—have a small pie, Nancy. They wanted only very simple things. My movements this morning, who I was with and when, where we were when we found the lady, and at what time. Then his men questioned the night staff—that was difficult. For the most part, they were asleep. But no one had seen anything. No intruders. Nothing out of place. A chambermaid remembered seeing Vitoria Dias around six o'clock last night on her way to her room. When she did not appear for her evening duty, the housekeeper asked another maid to take over.'

'Did no one check on Vitoria when she didn't turn up?' Nancy pursued.

'But, yes, of course. The housekeeper went to her room but it was empty.'

'What time was that, do you know?'

'I think she said about nine o'clock last evening. After the maids had reported that no one was doing turn-down duty on floor six. She was very cross with Vitoria.'

'So Vitoria Dias simply disappeared—until we found her this morning?'

Leo frowned. Nancy knew he wanted her to stop asking questions.

'It is a mystery. There was a suggestion—from one of the policemen—that maybe the woman was not happy in her mind. They ask Diego Ramos whether she has problems. I think that maybe they think, well ...'

'Suicide? Surely not. Only consider the way Vitoria died.' The image of the dead woman crammed into the keg, her eyes sightless, her maid's pinafore afloat, still had the power to make Nancy feel unwell.

'No, indeed. But there were no problems. The housekeeper decides the rotas but Ramos is in charge of the staff. They come to him if they are in difficulty.'

'And he said the maid had no problems?'

Francisco nodded. 'Not that he knows.'

Clearly, Ramos had lied. He'd been well aware how desperate Vitoria had been to search for her missing niece. But why had he lied? So that he wasn't exposed as an unfeeling boss? Or to make sure he kept as much distance as possible from any enquiry into the maid's death?

Nancy felt her husband look at her, his eyes clearly signalling she should keep silent. 'I don't suppose you managed to get to your meeting?' he asked their host, evidently keen to change the subject.

Francisco spread his hands again. 'It was unfortunate. By the time the police leave, it is too late. But the matter is not completely lost. The meeting today is only the beginning. There will be others.'

'Leo said you are hoping to gain a licence to mine in a new area. Where is that?' Nancy asked, between forkfuls of fried chicken.

'It is somewhere called Rodonia. In the north-west of the country. Over two thousand kilometres away.'

'That's a huge distance,' Leo remarked.

'It is the distance that is one of many problems, my friend. But the area has such potential! Minas Gerais has been known a long time for its minerals, but Rodonia will be even better. Cassiterite was discovered only a few years ago. By a prospector, quite by chance. It is all very new and very exciting. But you will understand that it is a remote region. You can only reach it by small aircraft or by boat on the Madeira River. Also it is a territory of thick tropical rain forest and this makes exploration difficult and expensive. But for anyone who can find the money to begin, the amount of cassiterite—tin dioxide, you will know the term, Leo, from your family's mine—it promises riches.'

'So distance and money. But I take it, that's not all that's hampering you.' Leo helped himself to a chocolate fudge ball as Silva gave a small sigh.

'No. There are licenses to be granted. And this is a political matter.'

'Which is where Senhor Monaro comes in?'

'Exactly.'

'But if the area is so far away, why is a man like Monaro involved?' Nancy asked. 'How does he have the power to grant a licence for a place so many miles distant?'

'Senhor Monaro has authority. Rio can be a rough city, many immigrants, many different people, but Monaro is mayor for a wealthy quarter. This gives him much power. As for Rodonia, he comes himself from Porto Velho which is the main city and has kept much influence there. The meeting today was for people to declare an interest. The cartel have banded together—they will share a bid—as I say, it is a very expensive project. There will be much discussion, but who gets the license will be Senhor Monaro's decision finally.'

'Is this the cartel that employed Tomas Almeda?'

Almeda had been Francisco's right-hand man until he'd discovered the man plotting against him, taking money from rivals to scupper his chance of buying Wheal Agnes from the Tremayne family.

Francisco's face darkened. 'That man! I am glad to say that he has found no job—not even with my enemies. They pay him to do me harm, but when he is no longer useful to them, they drop him—bang!'

He didn't suggest those same enemies might still be working against him, Nancy noticed. Might, if it wasn't too fanciful, be in collusion with Alvar Monaro.

'We must wish you good luck then,' she said, drinking down the last of her coconut water.

'Thank you, Nancy. Now, may I order coffee for you both?'

'That was a magnificent meal,' she said. 'I don't think I could eat or drink another thing.'

'Nor me,' her husband echoed.

'Then if you will excuse me, I must leave. I must return again to Minas Gerais for a few more days. I come back today only for the meeting, but thank goodness I am here. The police know where to find me if they have more questions. I promise, they will not bother you.'

Nancy *was* bothered, though. It still rankled that Vitoria's death was being swept to one side by everyone involved, but she tried hard to subdue her feelings. It was plain that Francisco was doing all he could to give them, as he'd promised, a holiday to remember.

He stood up, glancing hurriedly at his watch. 'I must go immediately. A small aircraft will take me to Minas Gerais this afternoon, and I must not keep the pilot waiting.'

There was a general shaking of hands, a round of good wishes, and he was gone, almost running towards the lift.

'Damn!' Leo looked after him. 'I meant to give Francisco his jacket, but I left it in the bedroom. How stupid.'

'You can return it when he gets back,' Nancy soothed. 'He's hardly going to need a jacket in this weather!'

Chapter Six

On their way back to the room, Leo mentioned again walking to the beach, though this time the suggestion seemed half-hearted. 'Ipanema, that's the name of the place I had in mind. We could still go. We've the whole afternoon ahead.'

He sounded weary and Nancy could see that he was feeling the heat badly. No wonder—at this time of day, the sun was a ball of fire, blazing down from a cloudless blue sky.

'Maybe we should rest a while,' she said. 'We've eaten a big lunch.'

He looked grateful. 'If you don't mind… we could take a walk later perhaps? When it's a little cooler.'

She doubted it would be cool until late in the evening and, though she'd heard nothing to suggest that Ipanema was unsafe, she was hesitant to walk there at night. Beaches by moonlight could be romantic—she was quick to suppress the memory—but they could also be disquieting, even Copacabana so close to the hotel. Last night, when she'd walked out onto the balcony, she'd heard the waves pounding, seen shadowy figures in the distance, and puzzling small lights scattered across the sand.

It proved a good decision not to go: Leo was asleep almost as soon as he'd fallen on the bed, arms and legs spread across the white counterpane. Taking up her book, Nancy sank into one of the room's easy chairs. Reading was far from her mind, though, and when Leo began to snore gently, she put the book down, slipped on her shoes and collected her handbag. In case he woke before she returned, she scribbled a brief note to say that after all she'd decided to go for a walk.

Avoiding the Reception area, she stepped out into the broiling afternoon. A taxi appeared, seemingly out of nowhere, and in a few minutes she was on her way to Santa Cecilia. The cab driver had shown much the same reaction as the bell-boy when she'd told him her direction, but he'd shrugged his shoulders and pulled out into the stream of traffic.

It didn't take long before they were at the foot of one of the mountains that circled the city and, looking through the taxi window, Nancy saw a warren of narrow lanes, alleyways stepped by rough stones that wound their way up the hillside. The houses appeared a kaleidoscope of different materials — some made of brick, others from cinder blocks and sheet metal, a few from wood scraps patched together, all sitting one on top of another.

'Santa Cecilia,' the driver said gruffly. 'You go.'

She wanted to ask him if he recognised the address she'd copied into her notebook from Vitoria's letter, but was unsure that the words, in fact, spelt a favela street name. She had no way of knowing and, in any case, the driver was keen to be away.

A small boy was watching her as she climbed out of the cab, his eyes following the vehicle as it reversed and took off at great speed. Nancy went up to him and showed him the words she'd written on the paper.

'Do you know this street?' she asked, and then felt foolish. The child probably couldn't read yet, let alone understand English.

A woman appeared behind the boy and called to him. Her eyes held suspicion when she looked at Nancy, and she started ushering the child back into the house.

'Please,' Nancy called after her. 'Do you know this street?' She waved the notebook forlornly in the air.

The woman turned. She seemed to think for a moment, then came closer and peered at the page Nancy had open. Tipping her head back, she pointed a finger to indicate a narrow alleyway that zigzagged upwards to the top of the hill.

'Up there?' It seemed an uncomfortably long way.

The woman nodded, then abruptly swept the small boy into her arms and disappeared into the wooden building.

It was a vague direction, but at least it was a direction and, bracing herself for the trudge ahead, Nancy started to climb the pathway the woman had indicated. It was stunningly hot, the hill was very high, and an open sewer appeared to run the entire way to the top. Climbing ever upwards, the path, always dirty and occasionally smeared in animal excrement, twisted and turned in a dizzying fashion.

As Nancy climbed, she realised that what had appeared an empty hillside from below was teeming with life. Passageways on either side of her path were filled with people at work, people selling, buying, running errands. A variety of shops were tucked into whatever space offered: a bakery, a chemist, a store with racks of cotton clothing. And everywhere dogs, panting in any shade they could find.

Halfway up the hill, she braved another question, this time asking an elderly man who sat sunning himself in the middle of a patch of uncut grass. Again, the direction was unclear, his hand simply pointing upwards. Finding Ester was not going to be as simple as Nancy had hoped. The streets were largely

MERRYN ALLINGHAM

unnamed and if she ever arrived at the right house, it would be by chance.

She climbed on, though, the path becoming ever narrower and had almost lost hope when she saw a woman emerge from a ramshackle porch, a bundle of washing beneath her arm. This had to be a last chance.

Once again, Nancy opened her notebook to show the address, this time mentioning the woman she sought. 'Ester?' she asked. She had only the first name and there could be many Esters.

The woman's face was expressionless and in desperation, Nancy said, 'Ester sews. Clothes.'

Taking hold of a handful of the cotton skirt she wore she shook it, then mimed the action of a sewing machine. The woman at first looked bewildered, but then her face cleared and she pointed a little way along the road to a small house that was painted bright yellow.

'Obrigada.' Nancy gave her a heartfelt thank you and walked towards the yellow house. A sign hanging from a tree branch announced *Barreto* and, since she was pretty sure that people in Santa Cecilia didn't name their houses, she assumed this was Ester's last name.

Her tentative knock brought a youngish woman to the door, and Nancy knew her immediately: the resemblance to her older sister was striking. The woman wore a faded pinafore, her hair scooped back from a tired face into an even more faded headscarf.

There had been a look of eagerness on Ester's face when she first opened the door—had she been hoping for news of her little girl, Nancy wondered?—but the light quickly disappeared and the lines of her face folded back into unhappiness.

'Ester Barreto?'

The woman nodded.

'My name is Nancy Tremayne. I'm staying at the Tivoli hotel,' she began. 'Your sister...'

Had Ester learned yet what had happened to Vitoria? Somehow Nancy doubted it. But the poor woman needed to know that something bad had happened. At least, then, she could make her own enquiries.

The mention of the hotel seemed a magic talisman. Nancy was ushered inside the small wooden building and given the best chair in what was a tiny and slightly bedraggled room. An ancient sewing machine stood on the only table, along with a number of bales of material. Cotton mainly but silk, too. A bird cage hung in the corner and a macaw, beautifully feathered in deep blue, cast a watchful eye on Nancy. Apart from this room, there appeared to be only one other, a bedroom perhaps, with a small passage to one side that housed a sink and a cooker.

'Coffee?' Ester asked her. She spoke with a heavy accent and it was clear that she had little English. But then why would she? Nancy fumbled in her handbag for the pocket dictionary she'd begun to carry.

'Thank you. *Obrigada.*'

'Sister?' the woman reminded her, turning towards the passage.

'I'm afraid Vitoria has had an accident.' It was the best Nancy could do. '*Acidente,*' she said. 'At the hotel.'

'Vitoria?'

'I'm sorry. *Eu sinto Muito,*' Nancy said, trying to pronounce the phrase she'd looked up. 'Maybe you go to the Tivoli?'

It felt wrong not to tell Ester the dreadful news right now, but without the language, Nancy was at a loss. The dictionary could only take her so far and she was fearful that whatever she said would come out wrongly.

'*Vitoria. Acidente.*' Ester nodded. Anxiety had joined fatigue in ridging her face. 'I go now?'

'*Em breve.* As soon as you can.' Nancy's heart went out to her, knowing what awaited. She wanted to do something for this woman, however small.

When Ester returned with small cups of dark coffee, she said, 'Vitoria told me about your little girl. About Livia.'

The woman jumped up at the name and went over to the table. From behind the bundles of cloth, she produced a photograph and handed it to Nancy. The same smiling face that had sat so proudly on Vitoria's shelf looked up at her.

'A beautiful child,' Nancy said. '*Bonita.*' She remembered the word from Francisco's party.

Ester gave a sad smile, then took hold of Nancy's hand and led her into the second room. A small bed, its patched covers scrupulously clean, lined one wall, while on the other side of the room, a camp bed signalled where Ester herself slept.

Her hostess pointed to the desk which stood adjacent to the bed. 'Livia,' she said.

The desk was bare but for an open exercise book, a sharpened pencil, and what looked a very old textbook. Two pictures had been carefully taped to the wall above: one of a youngish, good-looking man and the other, incongruously, a female Catholic saint.

Ester must have been aware of Nancy's gaze, because she touched the crucifix she wore around her neck, maybe trying, Nancy thought, to say they were a religious family.

'And this is Livia's father?' she asked, making a guess at the other picture. '*Padre*?' she tried.

'*Pai,*' Ester corrected. Whatever had happened to him must remain a mystery. The language barrier was just too great.

She followed Ester back into the sitting-room and to the

cups of coffee that were waiting for them. Taking up Livia's photograph again, Nancy asked, "Have you had any news yet? *Notícia?*'

Ester shook her head, then held up three fingers.

'She's been gone three days?' Nancy correctly interpreted. 'Have you any idea who might have taken her? *Quem?*'

'Bad men,' the woman managed.

'Senhor Monaro?' she questioned, sipping a coffee so strong she thought her hair might stand on end. 'Is he the bad man?'

'Monaro!' the woman said in a voice of loathing, and clicked her fingers angrily.

Her suspicions could be right, Nancy thought. But what if they were? The man was a powerful politician, newly elected. Maybe corruptly, but he'd have supporters, henchmen, no doubt a pack of brutal men to do his bidding. She remembered her stay in the Caribbean, the way that Jackson Garcia had employed such men to do his dirty work. What could a lone woman do against that?

She looked down at the photograph still resting in her lap. This little girl, though, was in jeopardy and no one was fighting for her. Her mother was too poor, too powerless, to call Monaro to account. Vitoria may have tried and been killed for the attempt. It was up to her, Nancy thought, to do what she could. Or at least try. Monaro was supposedly taking her and Leo to the Corcovado any day now and it would be an opportunity for her to tackle him head-on. What good it would do, she had no idea, but at the moment it was her only resource.

'May I take...' she had begun to say, thinking that she would need a photograph if she were to confront the man, when a voice called from the open doorway.

'Ester. *Sou eu.*'

'Jessica...*entre*. I make,' her hostess explained, pointing to the bale of silk spread across the table.

The young woman who entered could have modelled for a fashion designer. Tall and slim with long legs and a skin that was creamy caramel. Her face was a beautiful heart-shape and her long dark hair hung straight and shining to her waist. The bright red lipstick she wore seemed to illuminate the dim space of Ester's room.

The girl looked at Nancy, her beautifully arched brows slightly raised.

'Nancy Tremayne,' she said, jumping up from her chair and offering her hand.

Jessica granted her a half smile and a handshake soft as a marshmallow. 'And why do you come here?' she asked in a clear voice. There was the slightest trace of an American accent. If she had lived in the United States, it would account for her good English.

'I've come from the Tivoli hotel. I'm staying there. It's where I met Ester's sister.'

It didn't seem much of a reason to account for her presence here, but Nancy hoped it would do.

The arched brows rose a little higher. Evidently, Jessica thought differently. '*I* am here to be measured.'

She expects me to leave, Nancy decided, but she wouldn't go just yet. This woman could be helpful.

'Did you know that Ester's daughter is missing?' she asked.

The woman gave a small moue. 'Everyone in Santa Cecilia knows.'

'You live here then?' She couldn't keep the surprise from her voice.

Jessica looked aghast. 'Of course not. I live in Leblon. You don't know Rio?' She didn't wait for an answer. 'Leblon is the most expensive quarter in the city. My house is the most expensive in the road.'

'How pleasant it must be.' Nancy kept her tone amiable. She was already lining up her next question.

'As you say, very pleasant. I am surrounded by mountains and I face a beautiful lake, with a thick forest behind me,' Jessica said proudly. 'It is magnificent. There is a balcony around the whole building, so wherever I am, I can enjoy the view.'

Nancy went to speak, but Jessica had not yet finished her eulogy. 'Now I am building a spiral staircase—the house already has chimney pots! Pink chimney pots—so when my staircase is finished, it will be a fairy tale house.'

Was it worth continuing this conversation? Nancy was becoming tired of the woman's boasting. She must try, though.

'Have you any idea what might have happened to Livia?'

'Why would I?' Jessica pouted her bright red lips. 'Children disappear all the time from the *favelas*. Particularly little girls. You will know what I mean.'

'I'm afraid that I don't.'

'You are from England, Senhora Tremayne? Maybe things are different there. But here, there is only so much work for a woman. You sew or you clean or you do what women have always done.'

Nancy frowned. The inference was unmistakeable, but surely the woman could not be suggesting such a thing for a child. 'Livia is eight years old,' she said, her voice shaking with indignation.

'She will grow and in the meantime she can steal. Little fingers. An innocent face. She can earn money for herself.'

'Are you saying that she left home willingly?'

'What else? There are hundreds of little girls like Livia in every *favela.'*

Ester had been looking anxiously from one to the other, the English too rapid and too complicated for her to follow. Nancy could only be grateful. This dreadful young woman was suggesting something so terrible no mother should ever hear it.

She could feel Jessica's hostility permeating the air, but decided to risk one more question.' Do you know a Senhor Monaro?'

'Why do you ask?' Jessica snapped back.

'Only that he has promised to take my husband and myself on a visit to the Corcovado.' She schooled her voice to sound bland.

The young woman's shoulders relaxed. 'How nice. But he is a good man. You will enjoy your trip.' And with a barely perceptible movement, she glided to the door and stood there. 'Ester will need to get on,' she said sweetly.

Nancy had no option but to get to her feet, sliding the photograph into her pocket as she did. She looked across at Ester who had seen her do it. Her hostess must have understood the unspoken message because she nodded very slightly and hurried to show her guest to the door.

Walking back along the path she'd taken earlier, Nancy's mind was filled with the recent encounter. What a dreadful woman this Jessica was—to say that Livia had left her mother of her own free will to become a pickpocket, and eventually a prostitute! How could Ester bear to work for her? But she wouldn't have the choice, Nancy concluded sadly.

As she rounded a bend in the track, a bright red shirt came into view. It belonged to a young man, a handsome young man, cigarette in hand and propped against a fence that had seen better days. Nancy was unsure which one of them was doing the propping. He gave her a lazy smile as she passed, continuing to smoke but saying nothing. Something about the scene gave her pause. The men she had seen in Santa Cecilia so far had, in one way or another, been at work, or in the case of the elderly chap from whom she'd asked directions, too old to labour. So why was an able-bodied young man hanging around, doing nothing? He was waiting, it seemed, but for whom? It was possible... but perhaps that was a speculation too far.

Walking downhill proved a good deal easier than the journey up, but even so it was another quarter of an hour before Nancy reached the main road. Taxis here were nowhere near as numerous as on the Avenida Atlantica and it took a while before she could hail a cab on its way to the city centre.

Leo was just stirring as she closed the bedroom door behind her. Hastily, she scrunched up the note she'd left him and took up her book.

'You put me to shame,' he said, half opening his eyes and stretching himself in a star-shape across the bed. 'All that diligent reading.'

Nancy felt a surge of guilt and could only hope he wouldn't spot that her bookmark hadn't moved a page.

'I'm glad you managed to rest, you must have needed it,' she said, as much to soothe herself as Leo. 'And don't forget, Carnival begins tomorrow. We'll need every bit of energy we have—by all accounts it's pretty exhausting.'

After the afternoon she'd spent, Nancy knew the feeling.

Chapter Seven

The joyous rhythm of samba woke her early the next morning. She slipped from the bed and walked out onto the balcony to take a look.

A large crowd was below, milling around a convoy of slow moving horse-drawn floats, laughing, cheering, dancing shoulder to shoulder to the music filling the air. A pirate gyrated along the black and white cobbled pavements, a cow girl on one side of him and an angel on the other. A crab sporting a headdress of pink shell looked up and waved at Nancy. Each costume, sprinkled with armfuls of glitter, flashed in the early morning sun, their brilliant colours making Nancy's eyes pop.

Leaning her arms on the balcony's wrought iron, she felt the sun warm her face and smelt the lemon of the citrus trees. Their perfume encircled her.

'Goodness, how warm it is already!' Leo joined her on the balcony, sliding his arm around her waist. 'I'm glad now that we decided against buying tickets for the Sambadrome. I know it's vast and open-aired, but I don't think I could cope with the heat and the crowds, if this is anything to go by.' He pointed to the swaying, laughing dancers below. 'Unless you really wanted to go? If you did, we might just wangle the odd ticket. It will be a spectacle, that's for sure—the costumes are said to be amazing, and I know the samba schools spend months in preparation.'

'I'm happy to stay put.' Nancy nestled against his shoulder. 'It's going to be another very hot day and we'll need the sea breeze more than ever. We have the spirit of Carnival, don't we, just feet away?—the floats, the costumes, the music. One of the receptionists told me there are huge numbers of parties like this going on everywhere.'

'Then we better go and find some!'

*

They were crossing the foyer, sunhats in hand, when the concierge glided over to them, an indulgent smile on his face. 'Professor Tremayne? You have a telephone call at the desk.'

Leo exchanged a surprised look with his wife.

'Who could it be?' she asked.

'There's only one way to find out.' He followed the concierge back to his desk.

Nancy plumped herself down to wait on one of the sofas that lined the foyer, half hidden by an array of potted palms. A minute or so later, the police inspector Francisco had spoken of—at least, she assumed it must be him, accompanied as he was by several uniformed men—walked through the hotel's revolving door. She was disappointed. To her mind, Alvarez didn't seem much like a policeman. His shirt was rumpled and his trousers bagged at the knees, pooling around a pair of scruffy loafers. Nancy saw him looking across the foyer. He was evidently here to meet someone.

On the spur of the moment, she jumped up and walked over to him. 'Inspector Alvarez? I am Nancy Tremayne,' she introduced herself. 'I was with Senhor Silva when he found Vitoria Dias.'

'Ah, yes.' The inspector had a droopy moustache which

he stroked constantly. There were flecks of dandruff on a tie that had seen better days. 'You must not worry, Senhora Tremayne. We do not need to speak to you.'

'I wanted to speak to you, though,' she said, with her sunniest smile. She was grateful the man spoke English since a dictionary would have been hopeless in the situation. 'I wanted to ask you how the investigation was going.'

The policeman looked blank.

'Vitoria Dias—have you made any progress in discovering her killer?'

The inspector's hands and shoulders rose in the air in an almost choreographed movement. To Nancy, it appeared a gesture of dismissal.

'It is too early. And maybe we will not be lucky. A casual thief is difficult to find. There are many entrances to the hotel, and he could have used any one of them.'

'To go to the cellar? Why would he do that?'

'Who knows? Maybe he explores the hotel before he begins his stealing.'

'I see. And what did he steal?'

Alvarez looked uncomfortable. 'So far there are no reports by the guests of anything that is missing.'

'So nothing was stolen by a person who broke into the hotel specifically to steal?'

'The man may have become nervous and left with his pockets empty.'

'After he murdered Vitoria?'

'Yes, that is it.' He sounded grateful.

'It seems there were two people in the cellar who shouldn't have been.'

The inspector looked puzzled.

'The chambermaid? Why was she there? Her job is cleaning bedrooms. Unless, of course, someone asked her to meet him there. But if that were the case, the attack wouldn't be random, would it? The killer would not be a casual thief. He would have to know her.'

Nancy was improvising, but it was clearly an oddity that Vitoria had been found in the one area of the hotel she would not be expected to visit.

'I am afraid there are all kinds of wickedness in the world, Senhora Tremayne, though in this city we have little murder. Maybe a fight over women where honour is involved, but usually it is gambling or stealing. It could be that Senhora Dias was working with this person. Told him of the hotel guests and their possessions, encouraged him to steal. But then perhaps they quarrel and this bad thing happens.' He gave another expressive shrug of his shoulders.

Nancy was astonished. He was suggesting that Vitoria was a criminal, almost that she deserved to be killed. If Alvarez was already so prejudiced, how could he properly investigate her death?

She decided to try another tack. 'Did you know that Vitoria's young niece has gone missing?'

The inspector looked blank again and pulled at his moustache.

'Livia Barreto.' Nancy pulled out the photograph that, with Ester's blessing, she had slipped into her pocket. 'The child is eight years old and has been missing for days. Are the police looking for her?'

'I have not heard of this disappearance,' he said gravely.

'There may be a connection with Vitoria's death,' Nancy pursued, hopeful that if the inspector thought so, he would start looking for the child as well as the killer.

'Where does the girl live? We can make enquiries.'

'Santa Cecilia.'

'The *favela*?' The shoulders rose even higher. 'Children

from the *favela* go missing all the time.' It was an echo of Jessica's comment. 'These places are *imoral*. Children are hungry, there is no money, so they are told you must steal.'

'Who would tell her such a thing?'

'Her mother, her father... whoever cannot feed her.'

'So where, in your opinion, would Livia have gone?'

'I do not know the child or her family, but I would guess she has joined other children. They band together, roam the streets, and pick the pockets. They steal as a gang and are very successful. One of them distracts the tourist with a little song and dance, or a story of how poor they are, while another has their hand in a pocket or in a bag. That way they eat. And they cost their parents nothing.'

His easy assumption that such a young child had fallen into a life of crime was utterly shocking, but Nancy wouldn't be put off.

'Where exactly do they live, these gangs of children?'

'Anywhere and everywhere. There are plenty of places for them to stay out of sight. Tunnels, arches, old shacks where the owner has died, old warehouses no longer used.'

'An eight year old would live in this manner?'

'This is not England, Senhora Tremayne,' he said gently. Then catching sight of someone behind Nancy, he gave a nod of his head. 'Please excuse me, I must leave now.' And with a small bow, and another stroke of his moustache, he disappeared, his companions in tow.

Nancy turned to look after him, catching a glimpse of the man the inspector was meeting. It was Diego Ramos.

'What was that all about?' Leo asked, appearing at her shoulder.

'I asked the inspector if he'd made any progress with his investigation into Vitoria's death.'

'And has he?'

'No,' she said, briefly. 'Who was that on the telephone?'

'That was... I can't remember her full name. Emilia someone. She is Monaro's very own personal assistant. Apparently he has charged her with organising our trip to the Corcovado.'

'I wondered if he might have forgotten.'

'Not so. It's set for Tuesday—we have a couple of days' grace. Monaro and his limousine will pick us up at two in the afternoon. Emilia left me in no doubt that we are exceptionally honoured.'

Nancy didn't feel honoured. She'd been eager to visit the enormous statue of Christ that dominated the city of Rio—she'd been reading an interesting feature in the *National Geographic*—but now the trip felt more like a penance. The thought of spending an entire afternoon with the slimy Monaro was wretched, her only comfort that she might have the chance to question him about Livia. She clutched the photograph tightly before slipping it back into her handbag.

'If you're ready,' Leo said. 'Time to take the plunge!'

*

Three hours later, after a morning of weaving a path through noisy crowds, with their toes regularly trampled and the occasional dousing from a shower of beer, they chose a café at random and sank thankfully down at one of the shaded tables. The smell of coffee floated towards them.

'I don't think I'll ever walk again,' Leo said, half easing his shoes. 'Flowing alcohol and excitable crowds make for a rowdy time—you need to enjoy a good party to survive this.'

Nancy smiled broadly. 'It's quite an experience but I've loved every minute!'

The explosion of sound and colour had been tiring, it was true, but at the same time enormous fun. Every street

MERRYN ALLINGHAM

had been **alive with the sounds of samba and the smell of** *caipirinhas.* Huge themed floats had drifted by, their wildly dressed occupants swaying to the hypnotic beat of cymbals and trumpets and steel drums, while thousands of people wedged themselves tightly together, shouting, cheering, at times singing discordantly, and always, always dancing. Carnival had opened Nancy's eyes wide. *Utterly immodest,* she could hear her mother say. The throbbing heat, the vivid, feathered costumes and the exotic sensuality of the samba, was something she had never before encountered.

Leo, though, appeared unmoved by the atmosphere. It was lunch that most concerned him.

'How about rice fritters to begin with?' He put down the menu he'd been studying.

'To begin and to finish with. All I want is drink. Gallons and gallons of ice-cold coconut water.' She turned to the hovering waitress in her white uniform and white cap. 'A very large glass, please!'

'For me, too,' Leo said. 'And two plates of rice fritters.'

'Two?' she queried, when the waitress had left.

'You might decide to eat, once you've cooled down.'

She began to disagree, but then became aware of a disturbance on the other side of the street. 'What do you think is going on there?'

A crowd had begun to form, the moving stream of people coming to a halt. Nancy tilted her head so she could see better. An entertainer was juggling what looked to be makeshift fire torches. The crowd began to cheer and a rhythmic clapping started. But as more people stopped and joined the group, armed policemen appeared out of nowhere. To Nancy, it seemed a harmless enough gathering, but then a page from Leo's guide book came to mind. Fire, it said, could be a potent symbol of unrest in Brazil.

The police surrounded the juggler, clicking open the safety catches on their machine guns. There was an immediate silence and, for a few tense seconds, everyone appeared to hold their breath. But a lowering of the guns signalled the police considered the man harmless after all and the festivities snapped back into motion. *Caipirinhas* were drunk again, feet once more danced to the beat and the street vendors resumed their strident calls.

'That was scary,' Leo said.

'This is not England, Senhora Tremayne,' she quoted. 'That's what the inspector told me when I questioned him about Vitoria.'

'He's right. It isn't and it's as well to remember that. Brazil has a kind of democracy—Francisco called the country a populist republic when we spoke of it—but the military are always in the wings, always exerting pressure. It's a recipe for political instability and for rough dealing on the streets.'

She wondered how a falsely elected Senhor Monaro fitted into such a scheme, what part might be played by the "bad men" that both Vitoria and her sister had spoken of. But she kept her thoughts to herself, saying only, 'It certainly looked rough,' and turning to thank their waitress who had arrived with plates filled with rice fritters.

Leo delved in immediately, despatching several in quick order. 'Won't you try some? They're very good.'

He put his fork down and she felt his glance measuring her. 'You mentioned the inspector just now,' he said. 'You shouldn't have accosted him in the foyer. You ask too many questions, Nancy. Always. You promised me that you'd stop.'

She held up her hands, as though surrendering. 'I have stopped. Honestly!' Hoping to distract him, she helped herself from one of the plates. 'I think that after all I could manage one or two of these.'

In the end, Nancy found she could manage more than one or two—the fritters were excellent. She was wiping her hands on a paper napkin, when she caught sight of a face she knew, almost hidden in the crush of the crowd. Jessica—what was her last name, she wondered? Nancy wouldn't have noticed her, but for the bright red dress. Was that one of Ester's creations? The girl seemed to be enjoying herself, dancing nimbly from pavement to road, road to pavement, and throwing her head back in laughter, long tresses of hair flying to the tune of the samba.

Perhaps she had misjudged the woman. Today, Jessica appeared unaffected, happy with the simple pleasures of Carnival. And she had a partner. It might account for the difference in her mood. She had her arms around him and they were dancing body to body down the street. Nancy looked again. The young man dancing was the very same person she had passed on her way down from Ester's house, leaning against the fence, smoking and waiting. Waiting for Jessica, it seemed.

'Penny for them,' Leo said.

'I was thinking that maybe we shouldn't party any more today. It's stifling hot.'

'I'm glad you said that. The heat has been getting to me for the past hour and the Tivoli is beginning to look blissful.'

They paid their bill and had begun to wander back towards the hotel when the sun suddenly disappeared. Nancy looked up at the sky, transforming itself as she watched from deep blue to an angry, molten grey.

'What do you think?' she asked. 'Will we make it back in time?'

Before Leo could answer, there was an almighty peal of thunder and a flash of lightning that rent the sky apart, then zigzagged its way into the sea. A second stroke illuminated the crowd, still dancing, still cheering. Nancy caught sight of the red dress a short way ahead. Jessica was dancing on with her partner, unperturbed. It was then that Nancy saw someone else she knew. Diego Ramos. His head was bobbing up and down, as though he was looking for someone and, as Nancy watched, he strode purposefully into the crowd, directly towards the red dress. He'd found what he wanted. He'd been searching for Jessica and, by the look on his face, wasn't happy to have found her. What was his relationship to that expensive young woman from Leblon?

'I think we're going to get very wet,' Leo muttered. 'Can you run?'

'Of course, I can run. Watch me!' she taunted, taking to her heels, with her husband in pursuit. The rain began to fall almost immediately. Heavy, thudding, drenching. Tropical rain. By the time the hotel was in sight, water was dusting their eyelashes and streaming from their hair.

Leo pushed open the revolving door. 'That is quite a storm.' His shirt was plastered to his chest and Nancy's sandals had buckled beneath the onslaught.

She laughed. 'It hasn't dampened the crowd's enthusiasm.'

'It's certainly dampened mine. But we can always return to the fray after the storm has passed. How about a walk on the beach after dinner tonight?'

Nancy frowned, unsure it was wise.

'Are you worried the beach isn't safe? You shouldn't be. There are hotels running the length of the Avenida Atlantica. Wherever we are on the Copacabana, we'll be in full view of a hundred people.'

'Still...' she hesitated.

'Nancy!' He put his arms around her. 'What could possibly go wrong?'

Chapter Eight

In the aftermath of the storm, the temperature had dropped considerably, and eating dinner on the roof terrace, Nancy felt an unaccustomed chill.

'If we're going walking by the sea,' she said, 'I think I'll grab a cardigan. How about you?'

'A jacket, definitely.' Leo rubbed his bare arms to warm himself. 'Amazing, after those steaming temperatures this morning!'

She got to her feet. 'I'll run down and fetch them while you finish your wine.'

'And very good it is, too. I'll have to congratulate Francisco on his vineyard.'

Nancy was away only a few minutes. Buttoning her cardigan as she walked from the lift, she handed her husband a brightly striped jacket.

He shook his head. 'Not mine, sweetheart.'

'I know, but I couldn't see anything suitable in your wardrobe—you don't seem to have brought a casual jacket with you, and you're about the same size as Francisco. I'm sure he won't mind you borrowing it for an hour.'

'But a striped jacket—think of my reputation as a suave man about town!'

When Nancy went to take the garment back, he laughed.

'Only teasing. It will be fine. I shall look a true Brazilian.'

After they had crossed the busy Avenida Atlantica and were strolling along the beach, she was very glad of the extra layer. Not that it was truly cold, but after the intense heat of the last few days, their bodies had yet to make an adjustment.

The evening was still magical: the night air clear, the waves beating out their thunder and the warm sand soft beneath her feet. It felt good to be walking with her husband. Their sudden marriage a few years ago hadn't always been easy, but it was Leo whom Nancy had to thank for her rescue from an escalating danger, and it was something she would never forget. He hadn't married her only to save her. He'd married her because he truly loved her—and she'd always tried hard to love him in return.

At times, she found him autocratic, forceful in his wishes, and determined that his was the only way. The issue of her working, for instance. It had been a constant battle between them, the arguments wearying and deeply upsetting, before she had won the right to continue her apprenticeship. Then there was the baby they had lost—Leo had reacted very badly to her miscarriage, blaming her for something she couldn't have prevented. And later, being cold and unforgiving, when she'd told him it was unlikely she would ever bear a living child, that she didn't want to put her body through such a dreadful experience again.

But he could also be kind and gentle. A generous spirit. And excellent company, too, like tonight. She enjoyed being with him, walking together, quietly, companionably. It was true that he'd never stirred in her the passion she was capable of, but she loved him and, since his illness this winter, they had grown closer.

'What a view!' Nancy stopped and turned full circle, admiring the line of shining hotels on one side and, on the other, the moonlit sea, calmer now but its waves still restless as they toiled to shore.

'I knew you'd enjoy this walk. Mind you, it would be hard not to—the scenery is breath-taking. But you must agree, there's not too much to worry about. See, the beach is empty. The locals have gone home, I guess, and the tourists are too busy eating and drinking.' He waved a hand towards the line of hotels curving their way around the bay.

An empty beach? Maybe. As Leo was speaking, Nancy had sensed a movement in the shadows, where the sand finished and the road began. She turned her head slightly to look, but there was only darkness, except for a scattering of lights dotted around the sand.

She pointed to them. 'Those small lamps... don't they suggest there could be people here?'

'I imagine they've been lit for some time.'

'What are they for, do you think?'

'I'm not absolutely sure—we should ask Francisco when he gets back—but my guess would be that they're religious shrines.'

Nancy looked at him in surprise. 'Catholic shrines?' Brazil, she knew, was home to a large Catholic population.

'Somehow, I don't think so, but Catholicism isn't the only faith here. You find Afro-Brazilian practices prevalent in the cities. They seem to be a mix of Catholic belief and the old African religions. In Rio, it's something called Umbanda that's the most popular.'

'And is it okay to be a follower of Umbanda?' To Nancy, the lights suggested a faith that was covert.

'Generally, I think, though there might be some hostility still. Suspicions it's a front for witchcraft. But Umbanda appears pretty innocuous. It teaches a peaceful life, one based on charity and on respect for people and nature.'

'And it came from Africa, you say?'

'From African slaves forcibly shipped here. The original inhabitants had died in large numbers from the diseases Europeans brought with them and the Portuguese needed labour for their new colony—to work on the plantations.'

'That must be have been a long time ago. The religions have lasted well.'

'They have, but it's not that long ago. Brazil was the last country in the Americas to end slavery—and they've only just got round to putting it into law. Over four million men, women and children were transported here before slavery was abolished.'

'It sounds like another Malfuego.'

'The same sad story,' Leo agreed. 'Umbanda came from West Africa. There was precious little the slaves could bring with them. Just their songs, their stories, their spiritual beliefs. And being enslaved, it was sensible to mix their own festivities and rituals—dancing, drumming, chanting to the spirits— with those of their owners' faith.'

Nancy walked towards one of the small lights. 'But why these?'

'Followers leave offerings in public spaces—offerings for the spirits. Food, candles, flowers. The beach is a good place, don't you think?' They had walked closer to the sea and the sound of the surf muted Leo's voice.

She put her arms around him and hugged him tight. 'How good it would be to paddle! It's probably not the best time, though.'

'We need a beach day—tomorrow perhaps? Then you can have a proper swim, not just a paddle. The sea looks too dangerous at night to go anywhere near. Watch those waves, they're still crashing in.'

Nancy stopped again to look out over the ocean. Even

when the air was still, as it was tonight, the Atlantic was ceaseless in its thunder.

There was a sudden crack behind her and she turned abruptly. A hint of movement, a slight shift of shadow. Gone now. But Leo! He was prostrate at her feet, spread-eagled on the sand.

'What?' she asked frantically. 'What happened, Leo?'

There was no reply and she dropped down on her knees, cradling his head, repeating his name over and over. It was then she felt it. A stickiness on her fingers. Lying him gently back onto the beach, she peered at her hands in what light there was. Blood. It was blood! Leo had been hit on the head. He was unconscious and bleeding badly.

'Help!' she cried, in a forlorn attempt to attract attention.

But they were alone. Or maybe not. Was there someone standing in the darkness, ready to hurt again? Whoever the attacker was, had come from those shadows, and dealt Leo a terrible blow. Maybe killed him. Nancy bent down again and put her fingers against her husband's neck. She could feel a pulse, but it was faint. She had to get help, even though it meant she must leave him lying here alone.

Steeling herself, she clambered to her feet and ran as swiftly as she could towards the road. The evening saunter along the black and white cobbled promenade had begun and she rushed up to the first couple she saw, desperate they would speak English.

'My husband has been hurt,' she gasped, unable to get her breath after the fierce run. 'He's down there, by the sea. He needs an ambulance.'

'Gee, that's terrible. What happened?' It was an American voice, and she thanked whatever God was listening.

'I'm not sure, but can you help? Can you ask our hotel—it's the Tivoli just behind you—to telephone for an ambulance? I need to get him to a hospital immediately.'

'Sure thing, lady. Bets, you stay here,' he said to his wife, 'and I'll go get the hotel to make the call.'

'Thank you so much.'

'I'm going with the lady,' Bets announced. 'She needs someone with her. Who knows when the ambulance will get here?'

It was a thought Nancy was trying to suppress, but she was glad of the woman's company. Bets was cheerful and encouraging, keeping Nancy's battered spirits from failing completely. In the event, they waited no more than ten minutes, but it was the longest ten minutes of Nancy's life.

The ambulance men were kind and efficient, sliding Leo on to a stretcher and hurrying him up the beach to their waiting vehicle. Nancy had only time to thank Bets and her husband, before she climbed into the back of the ambulance, and they were away, sirens blaring.

*

It was a nasty wound, the doctor told her, when finally she was allowed to see her husband.

'He has been hit with something heavy and sharp,' he went on. 'It has cut deep into his head—very deep.'

'And?' She held her breath.

'And we do not know yet if his skull is fractured. We must x-ray, but first he needs to recover a little. We have stopped the bleeding and made stitches. The brace will keep his neck and spine stable, but he is still unconscious. Once he is awake, we will find out how bad is the injury to his head. For now, he has been given something to help with the pain.'

'I can stay with him?'

'But, naturally. You may stay as long as you wish.'

Nancy took a chair and moved it closer to the bedside. A

thick bandage swathed most of Leo's head, an ominous red stain showing faintly beneath. His eyes were closed and his face a ghastly colour. The brace around his neck made him look stiff and inert, as though he had already died. She took his hand, talking quietly to him, hoping he might hear her.

'Leo, it's Nancy. You've suffered a bad injury. On the beach. But you're in hospital now and they're looking after you. You're going to be fine. I'm here and I'm staying. I'll be with you through the night.'

There was no response and she settled back in the chair, her mind in turmoil. Why had Leo been singled out for the attack? She had been left completely untouched and nothing had been stolen from either of them. Who could have done it, and why? She felt a horrible qualm, deep inside, that she might be to blame. That she had shown too much interest once too often. The visit to Ester—a thousand eyes must have seen her in the favela. The questions she'd asked about Vitoria's death. Perhaps someone had overheard her speaking to Inspector Alvarez or, even more dreadful to imagine, the policeman himself had instigated the attack to keep her quiet. But then why Leo? To warn her, that if she didn't stop, she would be next? And meanwhile, she could watch a loved one struggling to live.

During the night, a nurse came to carry out checks, scribble notes— two or was it three times, Nancy couldn't be sure—but apart from her visits, they were left alone. Dozing in the chair, she felt herself falling in and out of sleep, her body aching and her eyes raw. It was around three in the morning when she was woken from the uncomfortable doze she'd fallen into. Was it Leo who had made the noise? Or the nurse again? She leant forward and took his hand. It moved slightly. Then he opened his eyes and a spurt of joy rushed through her. He had regained consciousness. He was going to be all right. But then she remembered the x-ray to come and what that might show.

'I'm here, Leo,' she said gently. There was a minimal squeeze of her hand. 'Don't try to speak. Just rest.'

'Archie,' he croaked.

'Archie?' What was Leo thinking of? Why mention Archie?

'Must come,' he said slowly and painfully.

'But he's in London, Leo.' Her husband's mind must have become scrambled in the accident.

Leo moved his eyes slightly as though to acknowledge her remark. 'Telegram... plane,' he said. 'Archie... must come... important.'

Then his eyes closed and he lapsed back into unconsciousness.

Chapter Nine

It was a different doctor who walked into the room early the next morning, just as one of the junior nurses handed Nancy a welcome cup of coffee.

'How has he been?' the doctor asked.

Nancy put down the cup, her face intent. 'He woke for a few minutes in the night, but then lost consciousness again. I mentioned it to the nurse when she came in to check, but she said he was doing well.'

The doctor unhooked the chart hanging at the end of the bed. 'Heart rate, blood pressure, temperature—all good. We are checking the level of oxygen in his blood. The results will come soon.'

'Professor Tremayne.' He shook his patient gently. 'Can you open your eyes, please?'

Leo must have heard him because his eyelids twitched. Nancy could it see it was a struggle for him to wake.

'Let's take a look.' The doctor shone a torch into his patient's half-open eyes. 'Hmm,' he said non-committally. 'Now, how well can you move your arms?' Leo managed a few feeble movements. 'Good,' the doctor encouraged. He pulled back the bedcovers. 'And your legs?'

The man nodded, seeming satisfied with what he saw. 'He will go to x-ray during the morning, Mrs Tremayne. Unless that shows anything bad, I would say your husband is out of danger. If I can suggest… you should return to your hotel for a while, eat breakfast, have a few hours' sleep.'

She was about to reject the suggestion, when she saw Leo nodding. 'Go,' he croaked.

It was sensible advice, she supposed. Once the hospital discharged him, Leo might have a long recovery ahead and she needed to stay fit. Then there was the telegram she'd been asked to send, though she was still in two minds whether or not to contact Archie.

'I *will* go,' she bent to kiss Leo on his forehead, 'but I'll be back very soon.'

She had reached the open doorway when she saw the figure of Francisco Silva striding along the corridor towards her.

'Nancy!' He opened his arms in a wide embrace. 'What terrible news. They tell me at the hotel when I arrive and I come straight here. Who were these bad people? What did they steal?'

'I don't know,' she said dully. 'I never saw them. Whoever it was, took nothing. They attacked Leo, then disappeared.'

'But that is extraordinary.'

Should she mention her fears that she was to blame? For trying to discover what had happened to Vitoria's niece? She was still pondering whether to make a clean breast of it when she realised that Francisco was staring into the room, a deep frown on his face.

'He looks bad, I know,' she said, trying to reassure their host, 'but so far the doctor seems reasonably happy with him. We'll know more when they've done an x-ray.'

'The jacket.' Silva pointed at the garment, his finger trembling.

Last night after the nurse had undressed Leo, Nancy had hung the jacket on the back of the single chair. Surely

Francisco wasn't angry that her husband had borrowed it?

'It is mine.'

'I know and I'm very sorry. We borrowed it, but... it wasn't harmed in any way.' Her voice trailed off. Francisco's unfamiliar meanness was making no sense.

'You don't understand, Nancy. It was not Leo these people attacked. It was me.'

She gasped, realising what he was saying. 'You mean they thought Leo was you?'

'Yes, yes,' he said, a trifle desperately. 'It must be so. We are the same size and it is dark on the beach at night. This jacket is special, too. It is well-known in Rio. People know it is mine—my *fraca*. My fun. It must be they want to hurt *me*. Otherwise, why attack Leo? Unless you wish to steal—and there are other of ways of stealing that are more gentle. That do not attract such bad punishment.'

'But who would want to injure you?'

Francisco shook his head sadly. 'There are many. The cartel, if you remember.'

'But would they...?'

'It is possible. Then there is Tomas Almeda. He has much hate for me. When he failed to stop me buying Wheal Agnes, the cartel punished him for it. He bears a bad grudge. Maybe he works for them again, though I did not think so.'

A nurse was approaching with a trolley filled with medicines, and they had to step to one side. Once she had passed, Francisco started to move towards Leo's room, but Nancy laid a detaining hand on his arm.

'What exactly is this cartel? Who belongs to it?'

'Three or four men who own mines in Minas Gerais. They have agreed to fix a price for their tin. A high price which makes them a profit but bankrupts those who buy it.'

'And you are not part of it?'

'They try to force me, but I refuse. It is not the law. But most of all, it is not right.'

'So they are your enemy?'

'I believe so. And it is why they wish to stop me from making my business larger.'

'They are the men competing with you for the licence you need?'

He nodded.

'And you think it's possible that one of them attacked Leo?'

'Not one of *them*. Of course, not. They pay criminals to do it.'

Nancy took a while before she spoke again. She was trying to make sense of what Francisco had told her—this was a world of which she had no experience.

'And this group of criminals, this gang,' she said slowly, 'will attack any person if they're paid to do so?'

'Naturally. It is how they make their money. They threaten, they wound, they kill.'

'Is that how Monaro was elected mayor?' she asked, in a sudden realisation. 'Did he pay for other candidates to be threatened or hurt in some way?'

'I am not sure but more than likely.' Francisco's lips twisted. 'And now he is elected, I must smile at him.'

'That is sickening. So who exactly does Monaro pay? Who does the cartel pay?'

'I would say a man called Sousa. Leandro Sousa. He is very powerful, head of a criminal mafia that makes much money from illegal gambling. You have heard of the *bicho*— the animal game?'

Nancy shook her head.

'It is very popular here. It is also against the law. The bosses who run it make very large fortunes, then they pass this bad money through different businesses. Good businesses. Sousa owns many of those, also he owns land, and he has houses everywhere.'

'He lives in Rio?'

'In Leblon. A most expensive area. The house he has built is more like a palace.'

The mention of Leblon reminded Nancy of the woman she had met at the favella.

'Does this man, Leandro Sousa, have any family?'

'But yes. It is how it works. Father to son to nephew to cousin. All are involved. And in public, it is all respectable. A wife, children—at least one child.'

'A daughter?'

'Maybe. I am not sure. All I know is that this family is very bad.'

Nancy felt the stirring of a deep fear. 'And you are in their firing line.'

'As you know, I wish to bid for the new license in Rodonia and the cartel is determined to stop me. Maybe, if they break my head, that will do the trick.'

'And now they've broken Leo's head instead.'

'I am so sorry, Nancy. I invite you here so that your husband can be better—and look what happens.'

She laid a gentle hand on his arm. 'It's hardly your fault. You have been a superb host, and it was our choice to go walking on the beach at night.'

Francisco gave a small tutting sound, evidently determined to take the blame. 'I will sit with Leo and you must go back to the hotel.'

'I don't think Leo will be talking much,' she warned.

'He must sleep. But if he wakes, it will be good for him to see a face he knows. Now go. Get some sleep. And be sure to eat.'

She left Francisco arranging the chair in which she'd spent

the night, throwing her cushions onto the floor and spreading the day's newspaper across his lap. She would be back in a few hours, but in the meantime would do as she'd been told: wash, eat, sleep.

Before that, though, she would have to send the telegram to Archie. It was possible Leo would forget he'd asked her to contact his assistant—he'd been half asleep when he'd spoken to her in the night—but Nancy couldn't risk it. Her husband needed cosseting, his every wish taken care of. And this was a small thing to do. Whether or not his assistant would get on a plane, she had no idea. Knowing Archie, he would most likely think the telegram a joke or that the heat of Brazil had sent her crazy.

Once back in the hotel, her first action was to rummage through her suitcase to find the diary she'd packed. Soon after Archie had left Cavendish Street, she'd seen his new address on a scrap of paper on Leo's desk, and squirrelled it away.. Hiding it from herself, she'd thought at the time, and from anyone else who might think it important to her.

The telegram she drafted was brief: LEO IN HOSPITAL. STOP. WANTS YOU HERE. STOP. NANCY. STOP. Even those few words seemed to use up whatever energy she had and, foregoing breakfast, she walked wearily into the lift and within minutes had locked her door, fallen on the bed and was fast asleep.

It was the cleaner's vacuum that woke her a few hours later, and she made haste to return to the hospital to relieve Francisco of his watch.

In the interim, her husband had been x-rayed and the results, according to the doctor, had come back satisfactory. Leo, though, continued to relapse into a coma-like state, only occasionally able to speak, and this was worrying the medical team. It was worrying Nancy, too, and she decided that until her husband was anything like his old self, she would only leave the hospital to change her clothes and take a short nap.

By lunchtime the following day, she was utterly exhausted. Catching sight of her reflection in the mirror, she thought how little food and even less sleep had turned her into something resembling a scarecrow. Gradually, though, Leo was regaining full consciousness, and for most of the time now was alert enough to talk, if only sparingly.

Francisco Silva reappeared as the nursing assistant was clearing their lunch plates, Leo having poked and prodded at the food with little appetite.

'Leo, how are you?' he asked, his boundless energy seeming to fill the room and make it an entirely different place. 'And Nancy? I am so sorry I did not come back yesterday. That was my plan, but then things happen. I have interviews with the police to tell them of Leo and this terrible business— not with the policeman who investigates at the hotel—but another. This man is at a higher level. There is no news of our poor chambermaid, by the way. Her sister came to the hotel, looking for her, did you know?'

'I didn't, but did you see Es… the sister yourself?' Nancy corrected herself quickly.

'It was Diego who met her and he would be very kind, I am sure.'

He should be, Nancy thought savagely. She had convinced herself that Ramos was the man Inspector Alvarez should be arresting.

'The hotel has paid this lady the wages that were owing to Senhora Dias, and a little more—to help. The family is very poor, I understand.'

And that was probably that, as far as Francisco was concerned. Condolences spoken, a little money paid, a human life dismissed. Nancy knew she was being unfair, but the injustice had her seethe with frustration.

'How did the interview go with this new policeman?' Leo asked, seeming keen to get back to the assault on the beach. It was, after all, what mattered most to him.

Their host was happy to oblige. Clearly, Vitoria Dias and her murder was not something he wished to talk about. 'I tell this man of the way a visitor to Rio has been attacked and why I think it happens. He has promised to make an investigation and the cartel will be at the top of his list.'

'The policeman you spoke to—will he be questioning Senhor Monaro?' Nancy asked. 'As well as the cartel?'

'That man!' Silva was tight-lipped. 'He has much to answer for, but I cannot believe he ordered the attack. He is only just elected. It would not be good to have his name in the mud, as you say. But he is busy behind the scenes, of that I am sure. He plays the one off against the other—you understand? And no doubt he has accepted bribes to favour this business or that. I do not bribe,' he finished indignantly.

'I'm sure he is a guilty man.'

Nancy glanced at her husband. Their conversation must be unintelligible to him and, sure enough, she saw worry in Leo's eyes and his face furrowed in concentration as he tried to fathom what was being said.

'Enough of Monaro.' Francisco clapped his hands. 'Nancy, have you eaten?'

'I shared Leo's lunch with him.'

'It will do, though we must feed you both properly when you are back at the Tivoli. Now it is time for you to rest. I will be with Leo for as long as he wishes me to stay.'

'You can start with an explanation,' Leo put in. 'What on earth were the two of you talking about just now?'

'Certainly, my friend, I will explain. Now, go, Nancy!'

This time, her return to the hotel felt a good deal happier.

The x-ray had shown no permanent damage and Leo was now awake and able to talk. She asked the receptionist for an alarm call at four o'clock that afternoon and ordered a pot of tea to be delivered. It proved an excellent idea, the tea reviving her from a heavy sleep and the shower she took afterwards waking her fully. Looking through the dresses she'd brought from London, she chose a blue and white cotton print. The button-through tea dress was Leo's current favourite.

She had twisted the long strands of her hair into a knot and was ready to go, when there was a knock at the door. Good timing, she thought—that would be the maid come to collect the tea tray. But when she opened up, there was no maid to be seen. Instead, it was a man who stood on the threshold.

'You!'

Chapter Ten

London, March, 1957.

Archie covered his typewriter and, standing up to stretch, reached towards the ceiling, trying to release the tightness in his shoulders. He'd spent hours working his way through the wad of notes for Leo's forthcoming lectures at his old university. When his boss had passed them to Archie, he'd seemed unusually fussed about the commitment, though it wasn't like Leo to flap. Why would he? He had an encyclopaedic knowledge of his subject and was hugely respected in every part of the world that bought and sold Renaissance art. But for some reason, the lectures had troubled him.

Maybe his illness was to blame—these days Leo sometimes looked a shadow of himself—but, whatever it was, Archie had been left to sort out as best he could the rough collection of notes, references and slides that his boss had left. He'd been at it for the last three days, going through material on Renaissance and Baroque women painters—and if he'd ever wanted to know more about *Artemisia Gentileschi*, he certainly didn't now.

He'd go for a pint, he thought. A pint and a pie at the local would do him fine. He'd been out for breakfast today, and *Charlie's* full English meant he'd eaten enough for a fortnight. But the pub would be convivial, and he could do with some company. Right now, it was a strange life he was leading. Normally, by this time in the winter, he'd have made several overseas trips, but with Leo laid up with bronchitis, that hadn't happened. Tethered to London and living alone, Archie had found it isolating. He'd almost begun to hanker for Mrs Brindley, Leo's housekeeper. Almost, but not quite.

He was changing his shirt—he liked to look tidy, even for the *Hand and Flower*—when his bell rang. People were always ringing it by mistake when they actually wanted one of the flats downstairs. Or it was the little tykes of the neighbourhood, their idea of fun. They'd ring every bell on the board, then run away laughing. The caller wouldn't be for him and he ignored it. But when the bell rang a second and a third time, he swore softly and ran down the stairs to a front entrance that was shared by all the residents.

A telegram boy stood on the threshold, his bicycle thrown carelessly across a bed of stunted snowdrops.

'You Archie Jago?' the boy asked, tipping his uniform cap to a more acute angle. It made him look even cheekier and didn't improve Archie's temper.

'Yes,' he said shortly.

'This is for you.' The boy handed him a small brown envelope. 'All the way from Brazil, Annie said. She's the one what transcribed it.'

'Then tell Annie to mind her own business. Telegrams are private or should be.'

'Cor, yer a right old misery, ain't yer?'

'And you're a cheeky little sod. Now bugger off before you feel my boot on your backside.'

Seriously rattled, Archie slammed the door in the boy's face. The mention of Brazil had caught him on the raw. What the hell was wrong now? He tore open the envelope. Leo, he read, was in hospital again. Archie had known that Brazil was a stupid idea. Why couldn't the bloke have made do with Bournemouth? And Nancy—how was she coping? The telegram told him next to nothing.

He wondered if he should put through a call to the hotel, but it would be hours before he could book it and the situation must be urgent, else why would she have sent a telegram? Leo wanted him, Nancy had written. Did *she* want him, too? Even if she didn't, he would go. She was in trouble thousands of miles from home with a sick man on her hands. And if Nancy was in trouble, he wanted to be beside her.

Picking up the telephone, he called BOAC. There was a flight leaving London later that evening and if he arrived at the airport in good time, they would sell him a ticket. He would have to use Leo's business account to pay for it. The ticket cost more than he'd possessed in his entire life. But he had a cheque book and the authorisation to use it, and some petty cash in the neat little safe he'd installed in his wardrobe. When Leo was travelling, Archie had often to draw large amounts of currency to be available at short notice, and he'd needed somewhere secure. The East End was a friendly place, but sometimes too friendly.

When he consulted the map, the journey ahead looked horrendous. Long distances and refuelling stops at Lisbon and Las Palmas, and then ten or more hours from there to Rio de Janeiro. He'd get through it—he'd done plenty of difficult journeys in the past—but it wasn't something to be welcomed. Crossing to his wardrobe, he pulled out the bag that went with him everywhere and began to pack. London was four hours ahead of Brazil. He should get to her by teatime tomorrow, he reckoned.

*

'You! Archie!'

Nancy looked a shadow of herself, thin and pale and fragile. He felt the pain in her and his heart hurt.

'The very same. I believe you called, madam?' He gave a mock grin, trying not to betray his feelings.

'Leo… ' she began

'I know. I got the story downstairs when I arrived. How are you coping?'

'I… I… '

He could see the tears ready to spill and, without thinking, he held out his arms. For long minutes, he stood nestling her close until simultaneously they broke from each other, as though they'd been scorched.

'I wasn't sure you'd come.' Her voice was shaky. 'Leo wanted you here, but it seemed such an odd request. I thought you might ignore it.'

'He must have had his reason. Let's hope it's a good one. I've been travelling for so many hours, I don't know what day it is.'

A shadow passed across her face. 'You must be exhausted. You need to rest, but the hotel is full—I'm pretty sure that's what Francisco said.'

'It is. My arrival sent them into a minor panic at Reception until they telephoned Silva at the hospital. He's given me a room in the owner's suite no less.'

'You have gone up in the world.'

She was trying to smile, he saw, but it emerged a little crooked at the corners. It made him want to pull her close again, but instead he said lightly, 'Literally up in the world. I shall be snoring on the roof terrace. Talking of which, I better collect my key from the desk. I need a wash and a change of clothes, then I'll make my way to the hospital.' He looked her up and down, taking in the smart dress. 'You're off there now?'

She nodded. 'Francisco is with Leo, but he'll be eager to get back to work. To be honest, Leo doesn't need someone with him all the time. Not any longer. He's fully awake and apparently there's no injury to his brain. So don't rush. Perhaps you should sleep a while.'

'I can sleep later—I dozed on the plane. I'll get the receptionist to order a taxi. I'll be no longer than an hour.'

*

He was shocked when he walked into Leo's hospital room. Nancy had sounded optimistic when she spoke of her husband's condition, but seeing his boss's white face, his hair even more silver and the deep creases in his skin, Archie wondered what on earth he'd been like immediately after the attack. No wonder Nancy had fallen into his arms. It was relief, he told himself, that she had someone with whom to share the burden. But he knew that wasn't the full truth. As always, it was hard to be together and, as always, they would just have to keep pretending.

Nancy jumped up as soon as she saw him in the doorway and waved him into the vacant chair. 'Come and sit down. I'm going to look for the doctor. I want to find out if they've any idea when Leo can come back to the hotel.'

'Alright?' Archie asked, after she'd closed the door behind her. It was a typical Cornish greeting. 'How are you, boss?'

'Bloodied but unbowed, I think the phrase is.' Leo paused. 'Thanks for making the journey.'

'That's okay. I'm sorry to see you in this state, though.'

'I'm much better now, would you believe?' Leo gave a throaty laugh. 'We were walking on the beach and some ne'er-do-well decided he didn't much like me.'

'So I heard. Did no one help you? Was there no one to intervene?'

'It was dark and the beach was empty.'

'The two of you were walking on the beach alone and after dark?' Archie shook his head.

'I know—it was a foolish thing to do. But Rio seemed pretty safe... ' He trailed off, appearing lost in his thoughts.

'Have the police nabbed anyone yet?'

'Not as far as I know. Francisco has asked a chap he knows to investigate. Someone senior in the force, but I don't hold out much hope.' Leo sighed. 'I'm just grateful to be alive. And very grateful you came. I wasn't sure you would.'

Archie looked at him hard. 'I was surprised to get Nancy's telegram, for sure. Was there a particular reason you wanted me here?'

Leo nodded and, with some difficulty, heaved himself into a sitting position. 'This attack has taken the stuffing out of me. Nancy doesn't want to accept it, but you can see for yourself. I guess I wasn't too strong to start with, not after the winter I've had. That first night in hospital I was in and out of consciousness, worried I'd peg it, and she'd be left alone to cope.'

'You seem pretty far from pegging it now.' Archie spoke in what he hoped was a rousing voice.

'I'm very weak. I can't pretend otherwise. These last few months, my body has suffered an onslaught and I don't kid myself—I could take a turn for the worst at any moment. I wanted you here... in case.'

'Okay, I get it,' he said, thinking how wretched Leo must feel to be talking in this way.

'Archie... if anything should happen to me... ' Leo shifted his position again, his glance lowered, his eyes studying the counterpane. 'You'll be beside her, won't you?'

There was a wealth of meaning in that sentence, Archie was sure, but he said as easily as he could, 'Sure thing, boss.'

Chapter Eleven

When Nancy came back into the room, Archie could see immediately that she was aware of a difference in mood, an intensity that hadn't been there before, but she smiled at them both and crossed to the bedside.

'I'll stay a while,' she said, 'but, Archie, you need to go back and sleep.' She turned to Leo, smoothing his forehead. 'He's been given a room in the owner's suite, you know.'

'Honoured indeed!'

Archie got to his feet. 'I'll be off then. Let's hope the room is as good as it sounds.'

He could feel his eyes closing even as he waved a goodbye. The taxi ride to the hotel, the lift to the fifteenth floor, the key to his door—all a blur. The room *was* as comfortable as it sounded, the bed in particular, and throwing his clothes on the floor, he tumbled into its softness, knowing no more until the sun woke him the next morning, blazing hotly through the curtains.

*

He propped himself on his elbow and felt for his watch. The hands stood at eight. He'd slept the clock around. Stumbling out of bed, he made for the bathroom, wondering what he was to do with the day. There had been no chance yesterday to decide any kind of plan. Was he to alternate with Nancy at the sickbed, or would he be free to do as he wished? Explore Rio for himself? It seemed that his boss was on the mend, if only slowly, and surely he wouldn't want company all the time.

Nancy was likely to have time spare, too, and that was a temptation. Although he knew he shouldn't, he picked up the phone and dialled her room, catching her just as she was about to leave for breakfast.

He'd thought her subdued yesterday, happy to see him but the tears never far away. This morning, though, her voice had a new bounce to it.

'I thought I'd have breakfast in a café,' she said. 'The hotel restaurants are very good—the roof terrace is lovely—but I need to get out of the building. Saunter the streets, feel the buzz. It's Carnival, after all. Do you want to come? Or maybe you'd prefer to sleep on?'

'I haven't stopped sleeping since I got here! I'll meet you in the foyer. Be with you in a jif.'

It turned out to be a little more than a jif, but he shaved and showered in record time and within a quarter of an hour they were sauntering out of the hotel into a temperature that was already in the nineties. Carnival was in full swing and they had to ease their way through a street crowded with floats and along a pavement thronged with dancers and musicians.

Archie pushed back the floppy quiff of hair that would never lie flat. He'd given up a military haircut a year or so ago, but today he wished he hadn't. 'Don't let's walk too far. There isn't a breakfast worth the exhaustion.'

'It's hotter than ever,' Nancy said, fanning herself with her sunhat. 'There's a small place just around the corner from here—I saw it the day Leo and I joined the crowd. Shall we try there?'

'Your choice. I wouldn't know where to go, except the beach seems a definite no-no after what happened to Leo.'

'The beach is fine in daytime. It seems to be the city's playground. And to be fair, I think it's okay at night as well.'

'So Leo was just unlucky?'

'Francisco thinks Leo was attacked because he borrowed his jacket and was wearing it that evening—it's an unusual design, one that a lot of people know here. Francisco left it behind when he disappeared in a whirl to Minas Gerais.'

'You're saying it was a case of mistaken identity? So next question… who would want to club Francisco over the head?'

'Do you remember that business in Cornwall with Tomas Almeda and the cartel he was working for?'

He gave a slow nod as memory came flooding back. They had been an uncomfortable few weeks. Dead bodies everywhere.

'Francisco is convinced that the same cartel are after him again, this time wanting to put him out of action. I'm not sure he's right, though,' Nancy finished quietly.

'It sounds feasible to me. Other than a random mugger—and nothing was stolen, was it?—who else could it be?'

'There are other possibilities.'

Archie groaned. 'I knew there would be. Don't tell me.'

'I won't then.' He could see her lips tighten. Sick husband or not, Nancy was engaged in something she shouldn't be, he'd swear. 'Tell *me* something instead,' she went on. 'Have you had any news from Cornwall?'

It was so long since he'd spoken to Nancy, he realised, even seen her, that whole months of Cornish life had flown by without her knowing.

'I had a letter from Ma last week.'

'She's still well, I hope—no more problems with her heart?'

'She wouldn't tell me if there were, but she sounded fine.

She's given up the job—at last. It stuck in my throat, her working even part-time. Gutting fish at her age!'

Nancy made a sudden swerve to the left into a shadowed street, tall buildings lining either side. 'I think the café was down here,' she said. 'And your brothers? Are they well?'

'I don't know about Lowen or Steve. They're in Plymouth and if you're from Port Madron, that's a foreign land.' He gave a wry grin, dabbing a handkerchief at his forehead. His face and neck had already begun to burn from the sun's onslaught. 'Rich is doing more or less okay,' he went on. 'The fishing is never going to be great, but now that Grace is working, things are a lot better. Her job at Penleven has been a lifeline. Ned Tremayne is a crusty old bugger, but Gracie seems to know how to handle him.'

'She always did.' Nancy gave a sigh. 'I wish I had her knack.'

'It's not a knack, Nancy, and you know it. Prejudice, more like.'

'Leo's father will never accept I'm anything to do with his family.'

Her voice wasn't quite her own, and he stopped walking and looked at her in surprise. 'Does it bother you that much?'

The old man's hostility to the girl his youngest son had married—stupidly married, in Ned Tremayne's view—had been obvious from the start, but Nancy had never seemed unduly worried by it.

'If he could even acknowledge I exist, it would make staying at Penleven so much easier and I'm sure we'll end up there very soon. We haven't been back to Cornwall since…' She faltered and he knew she was thinking of her final visit and what had happened between them. 'But Leo has been so unwell these last few months and now this, he'll need to recuperate. I can't deny that Port Madron is the obvious place.'

'You don't want to go.' It was a flat statement.

'Would you?' she challenged. 'Perry is a dear but his father... there's my job, too. I'm almost through the apprenticeship and I need Connie to recommend me for a permanent post. If I'm miles away in Cornwall... it will be difficult.'

She looked frail and weary and he wanted to take her troubles from her.

'There's the café—opposite.' Nancy had started to cross the road, but then came to an abrupt halt. 'Well, look at that!'

She was pointing to a kiosk, each side decorated with bright rows of magazine covers, but it was the newspaper pinned to a billboard at one side that had caught Nancy's attention.

'Yeah, I can see. A newspaper. And?'

'I'm looking at what's on the front page.'

Archie squinted through the dazzle of sunshine. The page was almost entirely filled with a photograph. It looked as though a large building had caught fire and been destroyed, but for the life of him he couldn't see its attraction. Nancy, though, was already at the counter, leafing through a copy of the paper, bending to peer at the accompanying article.

'You read Portuguese now?' he asked, sardonically.

She turned to face him, her cheeks flushed bright pink. 'I can read the one word I was looking for—there. Monaro.'

Delving into her handbag, she bought out a few cruzeiros, and handed them to the news seller, then tucked the paper under her arm. 'Okay, let's go.'

The café had few customers and when they'd found a seat beneath a wide umbrella, Archie decided it was time to have it out with her. 'You're planning something, I know—so what is it?'

'What makes you think that?' She wore the falsely innocent

look that always meant trouble ahead.

'Cut the pretence. What is it?'

'I have to do something, Archie.' She leaned forward, her voice earnest. 'It's too important not to. A child's life is at stake.'

He stared at her. He was used to her sudden flights of fancy, the tenuous links she could make, the mad theories she could build. The fact that she was often right didn't mitigate the danger. But this was on a wholly different level. A child's life, for God's sake.'

'Is this one of the possibilities you aren't telling me about?' When she didn't answer, he said, 'If it is, enlighten me on how we got from Leo being attacked, to a burnt warehouse, to a child in danger.'

'I don't know for sure that any of it is connected. I've a strong sense, though, that it is.'

He couldn't stop a smirk. What Nancy found herself sensing had become an old joke.

'A child is missing,' she continued defiantly. 'That's a fact. Livia is the niece of the woman who was our chambermaid when we first arrived at the Tivoli. Vitoria Dias. And Vitoria is now dead. Murdered. That's another fact.'

He was temporarily stunned, but then fought back. 'Two facts don't make a whole.'

'No, they don't, and I admit it has me in a puzzle. But there's something there to be discovered, I'm sure of it. Vitoria quarrelled badly with that snake of an under-manager, Diego Ramos. I heard Monaro's name mentioned during their row—the Monaro who features in this article.' She tapped the newspaper. 'The next day Vitoria told me about Livia, how she wanted leave of absence from the hotel to look for the child, how distraught her sister was. Vitoria suspected Monaro of knowing something about the missing child even if he wasn't directly responsible. That was what she was saying to Ramos. The next day we found her dead in the hotel's cellar. She'd been drowned in a barrel of wine.'

'Jesus! But this child? Couldn't she just have gone walkabout?'

'She's eight years old, Archie, and she's been gone for nearly a week now.'

'So you're suggesting she was abducted? What for—a ransom?'

'She is a child of the favela. There have been others, too. Their families are poor, so there's no question of a ransom. But from what I've picked up so far, the children are groomed to become pickpockets. They're mainly girls. I was told they had the nimblest fingers and probably the most innocent faces. You can imagine what happens to them when they reach puberty.'

He pushed aside the plate of papaya the waiter had brought, his appetite blunted. 'How on earth did you get involved in this stuff?' He didn't really need to ask. It would have been enough for Nancy to have witnessed the quarrel and found the dead woman.

'It's horrible, I know, but it's not going to stop me. Vitoria was killed for fighting against it and someone has to fight for *her*.'

'But it doesn't have to be you.'

'If not me, who else? If Monaro is an example of Rio politicians, they have dubious reputations. That's if they're not completely corrupt. And I've no faith in the policeman who's investigating the murder. He seems determined to put it down to a random thief, or worse—an accomplice of Vitoria who fell out with her.'

Archie took a long draught of iced water, playing for time, trying to absorb just how deeply Nancy had ventured into this web of evil. Working out in his mind how quickly he could book tickets for their journey home. He needed to get her out of this, whatever it was.

She gave him a wistful smile. 'I'm not asking you to join me.' Then reached across the table and put her hand on his.

'You don't ask me to join you, yet somehow I do.'

'Maybe not this time? This is a particularly nasty business. Like I say, Livia isn't the only child to disappear. Before she died, Vitoria told me that others have been taken, but that the police have done nothing to find them and their mothers appear too scared to create trouble. This is actually happening. You can't accuse me of imagination this time.'

'You could still be making connections that don't exist. You don't speak Portuguese—how do you know what really went on in that quarrel? And you don't read it.' He pointed to the newspaper.

'I don't, but I know someone who does. Diego Ramos! If you spend the rest of the morning with Leo, I'll go back to the hotel and find the man. I'm as interested in how he'll react as in what the newspaper actually says.'

*

She found Senhor Ramos alone at the concierge's desk, filling in, it seemed, for his colleague. It was a perfect opportunity. After all, a concierge was there to fulfil every wish of the hotel's guests, and her wish this morning was to have the newspaper article translated.

With a bright smile, she pushed it across the desk to him.

He looked taken aback. 'We have English newspapers in this country, Senhora Tremayne. The hotel takes one every day. I will find it for you.'

'No, Mr Ramos. I'm keen to learn more about Rio, not events back home. It looks from the paper as though there has been a terrible fire. Where did that happen?'

'That!' He shrugged his shoulders dismissively. 'It was days ago. The fire is not news now.'

'Apparently it is. It's on the front page, so it must be. Why is that, do you think?'

'I have no idea. Carnival is a time when there is not much news,' he blustered. 'It is all fun and laughter, you know. Apart from pictures of the dancers and the floats, the papers have nothing to fill their pages but old stories.'

'I see.' Nancy tried to look as though she believed him.

Seemingly encouraged, he said with a simper, 'You have wasted your money, I fear.' When she said nothing, his tone became indulgent. 'The Tivoli always has newspapers for our guests, Senhora. All you must do is ask.'

'In future, I will,' she responded cheerfully. 'I bought the paper on impulse this morning—I saw a name. One I knew. Monaro. I met Senhor Monaro a few days ago. He was to take us to see the Corcovado—that was before my husband's accident.'

'Yes?' The man's smile had become rigid.

'We might still make the visit if my husband's health continues to improve, and I thought it sensible to know a little more about the gentleman. Before we meet again? He was incredibly kind in offering us the treat,' she gushed.

The man's smile had become so fixed, Nancy thought, he would need a chisel to remove it. She looked innocently up at him. 'Why is Senhor Monaro mentioned in the article?'

Ramos made a feint at scanning the paper and Nancy saw his fingers were sticky with perspiration.

'Ah, yes! I have it here. The warehouse is in the area for which Senhor Monaro is the mayor. The Senhor had a wonderful victory in recent elections, you know.' Nancy nodded, wondering just how badly Ramos was lying. 'Senhor

Monaro is worried by what has happened. It means that jobs have been lost and that is a great concern to him.'

'And that's it? That's all the article says?'

'Yes, Senhora Tremayne. Senhor Monaro is hardly mentioned.'

'How disappointing! It does look as though I've wasted my money.'

She took back the newspaper and walked to the lift, feeling her Portuguese dictionary bumping against her hip. The article would take hours to translate, but she would do it.

*

Lunch was being served when she arrived at the hospital. Leo looked up from the tray the nurse was arranging on his lap.

'Archie was just going and really there's no need for either of you to stay,' he said. 'Get out and about and enjoy the sun. Find a steak house. You haven't tried the *churrascaria* yet.'

'Would you prefer to be alone?' she asked anxiously. 'Are you feeling tired?'

'Or just bored with our company?' Archie put in.

'Neither. But I'm out of danger now and there's no need for babysitting. I've another x-ray coming up this afternoon, too, and heaven knows how long that will take.'

'Why a new x-ray?' she asked, worry again tinging her voice.

'No idea,' Leo said cheerfully. 'Just a formality, I expect. Now, go on—shoo! I've a meal to eat here.'

Chapter Twelve

'Do you fancy whatever it was that Leo mentioned?' Archie asked, as they walked through the hospital doors.

'I'd much rather have a drink than a heavy steak. Breakfast wasn't long ago.'

'Me, too. What's the local tipple?'

'Beer. Or there's a *caipirinha*. It's made with rum mixed with lime juice and sugar. I've had several—they're very good.'

'I think I'll stick to beer. My head is all over the place from that journey. And these pavements aren't helping either.' He pointed to the waving, undulating lines of black and white cobbles that patterned every street.

The bar they chose was down another narrow side road and a good distance from the noise and bustle of Carnival— little traffic made it through what was not much more than an alleyway. Several of the outside tables were quietly occupied, one patron having his shoes shone while he ate a leisurely lunch. Inside, the bar was even more peaceful and its floor of ceramic tiles blissfully cool. The dark wood counter was piled high on one side with fruit and on the other, with glasses and cocktail shakers, while several large ceiling fans toiled through the almost static air.

They chose a table immediately below one of the fans, and once their drinks arrived—a beer and a coconut water— Archie fixed her with a look that clearly told her she needed to start talking.

'What's been happening?' he asked, in case she was in any doubt. 'How did the interview with the snaky Ramos go?'

'It didn't, but I learned something.'

'How come?'

'He is definitely a liar. Mind you, I knew that already. And he's almost certainly in Monaro's pay. Ramos said the warehouse story was old news, even though it's on the front page. In a way he was right, I suppose. The warehouse burned down last week. But it's big news again because the fire department found things that suggested children had been there. I definitely got the word for children. The paper doesn't spell out what the firemen actually found—at least, I couldn't fathom it, I found the translation really difficult— but it's a warehouse and there should only have been what remained of the goods that were stored there. Something unusual must have been discovered, or it wouldn't be in the news. If children have been living there, that would certainly make the front page.'

'And conveniently fit your theory.'

Nancy ignored the comment. 'Ramos claimed that Monaro was mentioned in the article because the area for which he's mayor includes a chunk of land outside Rio—as well as a wealthy quarter like Leblon. He was at pains to stress how concerned Monaro was that livelihoods have been lost, now the warehouse has gone up in smoke.'

'Reasonable?'

'Perfectly, but what he failed to mention and what the article makes clear—even my translation skills managed that—is that Monaro is the owner of the warehouse.'

Archie took a long swallow of his beer. 'What next? Or perhaps I don't need to ask.'

'Perhaps you don't.' She felt her spirits lift. 'I'm going to find that warehouse. Find out what it was the fire department discovered.'

He took another large draught of his beer. 'Somehow, I've the feeling we're about to spend our afternoon getting very hot.'

'And no doubt very cross, but it has to be done. This is my first real clue as to where Livia might have been kept.'

Archie's fingers began a soft drum on the table. 'It's possible, Nancy...' He paused, before he tried again. 'You've got to take into account the possibility that this child, all the children, if they were there, could have perished in the fire.'

She shook her head. 'Not so. The fire department was clear about that. The paper reported there was no evidence to suggest that lives had been lost.'

'If the department are telling the truth, it's a relief.'

'Why wouldn't they tell the truth? They can't all be in Monaro's pay. It is a relief, but where are those children now? Where is Livia Barreto?'

The waiter stopped at their table on his way back to the counter.

'More?' He nodded to their empty glasses.

Nancy smiled up at him. 'Not right now, thanks.' She spread the newspaper across the table and pointed to the photograph. 'This warehouse—do you know where it is?'

The waiter shook his head. Suspecting it was the English that puzzled him, she flicked through her trusty dictionary. *'Onde, por favor?'*

The man looked surprised. He'd disentangled her dreadful accent and knew exactly what she was asking. But why should a pretty young woman, evidently on holiday, want to go to a burnt-out building in the middle of nowhere? She could see the question written across his face.

He rolled off a name but, lacking the language, she made no sense of it. She delved into her bag and found a pen.

'I'm sorry, but could you write it down?' She gestured to a blank space on the newspaper and thanked him with another smile.

'We must leave him a decent tip,' she whispered, as the waiter turned to go.

Archie grumpily delved into his pocket. 'I would if I could find something to tip him with. All these coins!'

Once outside the bar, he peered over her shoulder to read the name the waiter had written. 'Off on our travels then?' he asked.

'I think we are. It will have to be a taxi, though. I wouldn't have a clue how to get there otherwise.'

'What if the place turns out to be miles away? The photograph suggests it's way out in the countryside.'

'It won't be that far if it's in Monaro's fiefdom. It has to be part of the local district.'

When they showed the taxi driver the scribbled name, he looked as surprised as the waiter, but spread his hands wide, as though rejecting any responsibility for such a crazy act, and turned the car to head inland.

It was a bumpy journey, since once they'd left the city limits, the road gradually dwindled into a poorly maintained track through what seemed endless scrubland—friable sandy earth dotted by a scattering of stunted bushes. On either side, a featureless plain stretched for miles, the entire landscape encircled by a cluster of peaks, their serrated edges cutting into the sky. The further they travelled inland, the more stifling it became. Nancy wound down the cab window as far as it would go and, for her pains, was showered by a cloud of yellow dust.

At last, twenty minutes or so after joining the dilapidated road, she saw what she'd been looking for and grabbed Archie's arm. 'Look! That must be it.' The hulk of what had once been an immense building was just visible on their right hand side, some half a mile further on.

Archie nodded and tapped the driver on the shoulder. 'You can leave us here. *Aqui*,' he tried.

'*Aqui*?' the man echoed, looking around in amazement at the deserted scrubland.

'Yes. Here.'

Before Nancy could protest, they had been deposited by the side of the road and the taxi had turned on two tyres and was roaring off in the direction of the city.

'What was that about?' she demanded. 'The warehouse is at least half a mile away and now we have to walk. In this heat!'

'Exactly. Did you want to announce our arrival?'

She could see his point, but it didn't much help. Drops of sweat had begun to trickle down her neck and her sunhat had become so badly bent in the taxi, it hardly shaded her head. Had Archie been sitting on it? Resigned, she began to walk towards the building.

'Do we have to crawl between the bushes when we get nearer?' she asked a trifle acidly. 'Like the Special Forces?'

'Don't be snippy! No crawling, but it's sensible to keep to the shadows as much as we can. And best if we explore the perimeter first.'

'This place is giving you the creeps, isn't it?'

'It should give *you* them, too. If you're right, these people are child traffickers and no doubt part of an armed criminal gang who dabble in God knows what. So yes, it's giving me the creeps.'

There was very little shade to shelter them, but taking care to walk in whatever they could find, they cut across the rough land in a diagonal, aiming for the far corner of the perimeter fence. The fence turned out to be ten feet high and made of steel rather than wood, topped by cruel-looking spikes that made climbing impossible.

'We'll not get over that and we can't march through the front gates,' Archie said. 'We'll have to look for another way in.'

'You think there'll be one?'

'There must be, even if it's only a gap.' He moved off to the right. 'Like this one. There's a steel panel here that's slightly loose. If I push it to one side, can you squeeze through?'

'I haven't gained that much weight,' she said, a laugh in her voice.

'You haven't gained any. You're as skinny as a needle.'

'Thank you.'

'Don't worry, you still look beautiful.' He said it lightly but she knew he meant it.

Shimmying through the tiny gap, Nancy found herself looking at a scene of devastation. The inner structure had all but gone, with only charred columns and a few half-tumbled walls to suggest the rooms and passages that had once existed. The tiled floor, an azure and grey pattern, was all that had survived in any way intact.

'If we're going to investigate, we need to do it cautiously.' Archie had joined her from the other side of the fence.

'There doesn't seem to be anyone around.'

'It's a huge site and for all we know, they could have posted security guards anywhere. But even if we're alone here, we should be careful. Have a look up there.' Nancy raised her head, shading her eyes from a sun that pierced through the ruins. 'A part of the top floor is still hanging. Can you see it?

It could crash at any moment.'

'How comforting to know that.' She sounded peevish though she hadn't meant to.

Archie turned to face her, his expression severe. 'I could point out that you were the one determined to come here, though what there is to see, I can't imagine.'

'Nor me at the moment.' Nancy glanced around the huge space, feeling deflated. What had the fire crew found here that was so important the newspaper editor had made it his major story?

Side by side, they slowly picked their way forward, avoiding the dank puddles left by the fire hoses and navigating a path over lumps of burnt material, past tottering walls and through unstable doorways. A murky fog that made their eyes smart lingered in the atmosphere, the smell of smoke so strong that Nancy could feel her throat closing.

'Absolutely nothing,' she said, after they'd completed a tour along two sides of the building. 'And now I've got the creeps. I'm sure the floor above is going to land on us.' She gave a nervous glance upwards.

Archie followed her gaze. 'Definitely dodgy,' he commented, and then, 'What's that, do you think?'

She looked at where he was pointing. 'A bed? Is it a bed?'

He moved to one side. 'You can see better from this angle. It *is* a bed. Now what's a bed doing in a warehouse? If they were using the place for storing goods, any beds they had to sell wouldn't have covers on them, would they? And that bed definitely has covers, or what were covers before the fire got to them.'

Nancy manoeuvred her way round a small hill of burnt material to stand beside him. 'I think there maybe another one,' she said, glancing up again. 'I'm not tall enough to see properly.'

Archie walked forward and climbed on top of a heap of charred wood.

'You don't look safe,' she called out.

'I'm not, but it's given me a better view and what I see is a number of beds, all at crazy angles, all clinging for dear life to what's left of the floor.'

'People—children— were sleeping up there! Those small beds prove it. I wonder, were they sleeping down here, too?'

'The fire crew would likely have investigated the ground floor only. Anything else would be too dangerous. We should keep looking.'

Sure enough, when they penetrated to what had been rooms along the north-facing wall, the remains of a small narrow bed were easily distinguishable. Then another and another.

'This is what the fire brigade found,' Nancy said. 'A warehouse with dozens of small beds.'

'A front page story, if ever there was.'

She was eager to go on, eager to find more evidence, but suddenly Archie clutched her arm. 'Listen! '

The deep-throated sound of an engine came to them from close by.

'Someone is about to arrive, and we should be going,' he said.

Nancy's heart began to beat a little too fast. Archie had been right when he said that whoever was behind this operation were dangerous men. They would not be impressed to find intruders at the scene of a crime. At the scene of *their* crime. She swallowed hard, her mouth dry. She didn't need Archie's voice urging her to be quick.

Any caution they had shown on their way into the building was abandoned, Nancy almost breaking into a run as she weaved her way through the charred remains. She could hear

Archie's footsteps following swiftly behind.

They were out in the open and, for once, the hot sun felt a blessing. The dank of that desolate interior, the smell of rot, could be shaken off. Archie was beside her, taking her hand, pulling her towards the slit in the fence they'd passed through earlier.

But they had taken only a few steps when a line of men blocked their passage—black uniforms, black balaclavas. It was as though their figures had risen through the earth from whatever dark place they inhabited. Black weapons, too, lethal weapons that were slung across their chests—except for the leading figure. *His* gun was in his hand and it was levelled at them.

He shouted something in Portuguese.

'English,' Archie shouted back.

Nancy fumbled in her handbag for her dictionary, in the vain hope she might persuade the man they were here on a sightseeing trip, after finding the picture in the newspaper. Some people, she'd heard, derived pleasure from visiting this kind of disaster scene. But even as her hand touched her handbag, she heard the click of the gun as the safety catch was withdrawn.

'What the hell are you doing?' Archie hissed.

'I was looking for my dictionary.'

'For Christ's sake,' he exploded. 'We're not at a language seminar. Hold up your hands to show you're not carrying anything.'

Nancy held up her hands, and the man seemed to relax a little. If not relax, then at least engage the safety catch again.

'You,' the man said in English to Archie. 'Why you here?'

'Taxi.' Archie said. 'Mistake.'

'*Erro*,' Nancy put in. She'd heard the word earlier. Francisco talking to one of his staff about a mistake?

'Bad place here.' Archie went on painstakingly. 'We.' He waved his hand to include himself and Nancy. 'Rio hotel. Copacabana.'

He was playing the stupid tourist and doing it quite well, Nancy thought.

The man turned to speak to his colleagues. There seemed to be a heated argument going on, before the ringleader strode forward and pushed Nancy none too gently with the barrel of his gun towards the narrow gap in the fence. Stupid tourist seemed to have worked.

She caught sight of Archie's clenched fist. He was frightened for her, and she was frightened for him They were letting her go, but what would they do to Archie? She felt sick. Stranded miles from the city, how was she to get help in time? How save him from whatever horrible fate these men were contemplating?

One more rough shove of the gun butt had her toppling against the steel barrier. She scrambled to her feet and stepped through the fence. Looking back at the scene she'd left, her heart was in her mouth. What next?

The man with the gun raised his weapon and pointed it at Archie. Again, she heard the click of the safety catch being loosened.

'Okay. If you must,' Archie said, his voice strained in the effort to sound casual. 'But Senhor Monaro won't like it. Not one little bit.'

The name seemed to startle the gunman. Peering through the gap, Nancy saw him take a step back.

'Monaro, friend.' Archie nodded happily, as though such a friendship was all he had need of in the world.

There was more heated argument between the men, and then the gun was lowered, its butt banged into Archie's back, pushing him into the fence, too. He wasted no time in joining

Nancy.

'Let's get going before those goons change their mind,' he muttered.

Grabbing her hand, he ran with her across the scrub until they reached the dusty track they'd arrived by.

'Do you think he believed the story about Monaro?' Nancy panted.

'Who knows?' Archie was breathless, too. 'But I doubt it will be long before he realises a tourist who knows Monaro didn't arrive here by chance. We need to beat it back to Rio as fast as we can.'

'How?' she asked, looking along the deserted road.

'How indeed?' Archie uttered a heavy sigh. 'C'mon. It's going to be a long walk to civilisation and, when we get there, you're buying me at least half a dozen beers.

Chapter Thirteen

In the event, they had gone barely a mile before a horse and cart pulled up beside them. The driver, his skin a baked leather, gave them a friendly nod and pointed to what empty space he had in his cart. They didn't hesitate, scrambling to find a seat among the baskets of potatoes, beans, peppers and okra. He dropped them on the outskirts of the city and a ten minute taxi ride brought them back to the hotel.

Faced with an arduous walk, Archie had managed a joke, but when he finally opened the door to the owner's suite, he was far from feeling light-hearted. That gun had been pointing at his heart and the man behind it had quite definitely meant to shoot. If he hadn't had a sudden inspiration—panic-driven, he admitted—and remembered the name Nancy had mentioned a few hours earlier, he wouldn't be thinking of beer. He wouldn't be thinking of anything.

What the hell had she landed them in? Without any real thought, he'd gone along with her suggestion that they find the warehouse she'd seen in the newspaper. It had been an instinctive reaction. To please her? To be with her a few hours longer, knowing it wasn't to last? Soon enough, they'd be winging their way back to London. London and separation.

Being apart from her was difficult, but being with her was even more. Yet they inevitably gravitated towards each other. There had been nothing remotely romantic about this afternoon's trip to a burnt-out building, but that wasn't the point. They were good together, whatever they were doing. It was simply that they fitted.

He'd realised that particular truth when they'd been in Cornwall last year. Seeing her in Port Madron, in his family's harbour-side cottage, talking happily to his mother, he'd known that Nancy belonged. No matter how much he battled the feeling, no matter how many useless weapons he deployed—mockery, rudeness, tepid friendship—they belonged with each other. They shared the same restlessness, the same sense of incompleteness, that only came good when they were together.

He'd not even thought of refusing to go with her on the trip this afternoon. After all, what was it? An excursion into the hot hinterland, and a swift prowl around an empty building. He hadn't expected to find anything, though Nancy had believed otherwise. He should have believed it, too. She followed her deepest instincts and rarely got it wrong. What they'd found was devastating stuff: small beds for small children kept as prisoners, and seemingly forced to pickpocket under threat— either to themselves or their families, or both. It was gut-wrenching.

And to prove how serious it was, the goons in black, waving automatic rifles in their faces. Those blokes had meant business all right. They had been hired to protect the reputation of whoever was behind this sickening activity and that meant removing anything or anyone who threatened to reveal the truth. And Nancy was intent on doing just that. She had this talent for sniffing out the wickedness of the world, the Lord knew why. But once she discovered an injustice, she followed it through, come what may.

Had she always been this fighter for justice? Archie doubted it. He didn't doubt her determination or her courage. They must always have been part of her. She had certainly needed them in battling against parents who made the Borgias appear benign. The Nicholsons, it seemed, had undervalued their daughter from birth, crushing her with their disapproval, failing to support her youthful dreams. Worst of all, they had refused to come to her aid when she needed them most. It was the Nicholsons who had disbelieved Nancy, preferring to accept the word of her one-time fiancé, a man clearly out to destroy her. And the Nicholsons who'd eventually betrayed her, allowing Philip March to track down his prey. If Archie hadn't followed her to that cliff top…

The need to battle evil in the world was different, though. True, it demanded the same determination and courage, but a whole lot more. When had that fight become important to Nancy? When she found herself friendless, harried and pursued by a man who'd once professed to love her? She'd found out then what it felt like to be powerless, to be failed by parents, colleagues, even the police. To have no one on her side. Did the experience still resonate? It must do, despite the safety that marriage to Leo had brought. Only a kind of safety though, Archie mused. There was a yawning gap between husband and wife, no true meeting of their deepest feelings, and that was where real security lay.

*

Nancy stood beneath the shower for a good twenty minutes, desperate to wash off the afternoon's events. The rank smell of that forsaken building, the charred remains of those small beds, the black-helmeted men with guns, and the terror she had felt—for herself, but most of all for Archie. It had been far worse than anything she had ever encountered.

When she'd suggested to him that they go looking

for the warehouse, she had thought there was a chance, but only a chance, that she might find a clue to Livia Barreto's disappearance. If she were honest, she'd had no real expectation of discovering anything important. The photograph was blurred, but even so it was fairly clear that nothing had been left standing after the fire. It was only the fact that, following the fire brigade's report, the newspaper had chosen to make the conflagration its headline news, that had prompted Nancy to make the uncomfortable journey.

That and the opportunity to spend time with Archie. Leo had more or less given them permission to be together. *Shoo*, he'd said. *Go and have lunch*. It had puzzled her. Why after all these months, when she'd felt the low hum of her husband's suspicions, was he so willing for them to spend hours together? And why summon Archie to Brazil in the first place? She had never understood Leo's request, and neither he nor Archie had made any mention of the sheer oddity of bringing his assistant halfway round the world to sit at his bedside for a few hours and, for the rest, play escort to his wife.

Nancy sighed and reached for a towel. If there was a reason, she would find out in time, she supposed. It might simply be that in Leo's state of semi-consciousness that first night in the hospital, he'd instinctively wanted his closest colleague near him, and now Archie was here, unnecessarily as it turned out, he was making the best of it.

And Archie *was* still here, she remembered thankfully, her stomach twingeing at the thought that a few hours ago she might have lost him forever. That had been a truly terrifying moment, when the man in black had raised his weapon and aimed. Peering through the gap in the fence, she'd made out little of the man's face beneath the balaclava, except for his eyes, but she'd seen them all right. He had meant to kill

Archie, she was sure. Ironically, it was Monaro's name that had saved him. If Archie had died, it would have been her fault, her guilt. She had dragged him into danger, as she'd so often done before, and it was desperately unfair. He loved her, she knew, and he would risk his life for her. He'd done so in the past—but he wasn't going to again, she vowed. From now on she would walk her own lonely path.

A massively daunting one, too. Today, she had come face to face with a violent gang who could be hired to maim or to kill as long as the price was right. The same men who had attacked Leo and were threatening Francisco. Had they been responsible for the killing of Vitoria Dias, too? Her suspicions around Diego Ramos were strong but today's events had made her think again. There was another force at work.

The gang that had confronted them this afternoon was surely led by the man Francisco had mentioned, Leandro Sousa. A man whom the law appeared to find untouchable, who was connected to the great and good of Rio, funding his lavish lifestyle by, amongst other things, kidnapping small children and forcing them into criminality. How was she, a lone foreigner, to battle that?

Nancy took the child's photograph from her handbag and studied it. Livia was a prisoner somewhere. Her mother was grieving and her aunt dead. She had to be rescued and this evil trade stopped. Those in power seemed happy to dismiss "favella children" as unworthy of their concern—it was up to her to do what little she could. For Vitoria, who had died fighting. For Livia, wherever she was.

Chapter Fourteen

Nancy was still feeling tense when Francisco Silva appeared at her bedroom door around seven that evening. The shower and clean clothes had helped, but she ached with tiredness and her nerves were on edge. She had been hoping for a few quiet hours spent with Leo and then a retreat to bed. Their host, though, had come to suggest that she and Archie stroll with him to the hospital to join Leo after his supper.

Francisco seemed eager that they see the city at night and, not wanting to disappoint him, she agreed to meet in the foyer within half an hour. Archie was already there when she arrived, looking as unenthusiastic as she felt, but neither of them had been able to refuse Francisco's request without confessing what lay behind their weariness.

'I could have done without this jolly little party,' Archie grumbled, when Francisco left them to speak to the duty receptionist.

'Me, too, but did you get your beers?'

'They're on hold. I'm waiting for you to cough up. What's with this walk to the hospital anyway?'

'I think Francisco wants to show us Rio by night. Carnival is sure to be even more outrageous once the sun goes down, so be prepared.'

Returning from whatever matter he'd raised at the Reception desk, Silva guided them towards the swing doors of the hotel. 'We will walk along the beach, I think.'

Nancy held back. After what had happened to Leo, the Copacabana at night had little appeal, but once outside the hotel, she was forced to change her mind. The noise of Carnival was raucous. Traffic had more or less stopped and the street outside the Tivoli was jam-packed with gaudy floats and half-naked revellers. Yet another samba band began to play a few feet away, the beat of the snare drums thudding in her ears. It would be difficult to walk in this crush and impossible to hear each other speak.

'The beach will be better,' Francisco urged in a loud voice. 'Tranquil.' He rolled the word on his tongue, seeming to enjoy its sound.

It took them time to force a pathway through the dense crowd to the other side of the Avenida Atlantica, arriving on the promenade hot and sticky. The spread of cool sand ahead began to look more pleasurable.

'I wanted you to see Copacabana as it really is,' Silva said. 'Safe as houses—that is what you say, no?' He was trying hard to reassure her.

'Safe unless you're wearing a particular jacket,' Archie commented, and she saw Francisco's face fall a little.

The beach was not completely empty. A few stray couples were strolling the sands, but the hard core of revellers had stayed on the main thoroughfare. The Avenida Atlantica, being broad and long, was a perfect venue for a party. True, in fact, for most roads in the city's centre—wide green avenues reminiscent of Parisian boulevards, the legacy of a past mayor determined to demolish narrow streets and unhealthy tenements.

The sounds of samba drifted faintly towards them

through the air, but were soon overpowered by the clamour of Atlantic rollers. How romantic that phrase was, Nancy thought. And they were rollers, powering towards the beach, great magnificent peaks growing higher and higher until they outgrew their strength and toppled, crashing downwards and gouging a fierce path through the sand.

'We will walk parallel to the road,' Francisco said. 'Then four blocks along, we must turn back to the city. I will start counting now,' he joked.

For a while, the three of them walked in silence, the peace of the evening falling softly, even as the noise of the sea became too loud to speak easily between themselves. The small offerings that Nancy had seen the night she'd walked here with Leo were still in evidence. It gave her a strange feeling, like living the whole episode again, and made her eager to leave the beach behind and get to the hospital. The mention of a second x-ray had been chipping away at her mind since Leo had spoken of it. Did it mean the medical staff weren't entirely happy with his progress?

'We turn here,' Francisco Silva mouthed, smiling across at them, his teeth startlingly bright in the wash of moonlight.

The two men veered towards the promenade, but Nancy came to an abrupt halt. Her eyes searched the darkness, trying to pinpoint the movement she'd sensed. It *was* like reliving a past scene. Several boats had been drawn up onto the beach, pleasure craft rather than working vessels, and within the shadows they cast, there were figures, she was sure. Huddled figures that made her spine prickle with unease.

'Is anything wrong, Nancy?' Francisco had turned back to her.

'Those men,' she said. 'It gave me a start to realise someone was there.'

Her voice must have carried because at that moment the

figures moved, and for a fleeting second before they hurried away, one of their faces was just visible. A pale, pudgy face that, without the benefit of anything resembling a neck, seemed glued to the man's meaty shoulders.

Francisco's lips closed hard, disdain written large on his face, even in the muted light.

'You know them?' Nancy asked.

'I know them,' he said grimly. 'That one, I know very well.' He nodded at the retreating back of the man with no neck. 'But you did not recognise Senhor Monaro?'

'Monaro?'

Francisco nodded.

Nancy gave a little gasp. 'And the man with him? The one you know well?'

'Leandro Sousa.'

'The criminal?'

Francisco put a finger to his lips. 'This is what we do not say.'

'But he is,' Nancy insisted. 'You told me yourself that he heads a violent gang.'

'He is a free man, Nancy. Not accused, not sentenced, not in prison.'

'But still a criminal.'

She felt the pressure of Archie's hand on her arm. He wanted her to keep quiet. He was as convinced as she that it was Sousa's gang that had almost murdered him this afternoon.

'Come,' Francisco said 'We must walk this way.'

It seemed to close the conversation, but when they had recrossed the Avenida Atlantica, and turned inland towards the hospital, he said, 'You have to understand what Brazil is like. How life has been here.'

'It will make for interesting listening,' Archie said. 'If that bloke back there is the one who ordered the attack on Leo.'

'On me, my friend. And more than likely, he *is* the one. He serves whoever pays him and in this case, it is the cartel. But we have no proof.'

'So he's free to continue to maim and kill for money?' Nancy sounded bitter. And she was, remembering how ill Leo had been, how close Archie had come to death only a few hours ago.

'We have no proof,' Francisco repeated.

They were just then passing a cinema, images from *The King and I* pasted on every available space. A long queue of patrons had spilled out over the pavement, forcing them to fall back into single file. Hollywood films appeared to be as popular here as at home.

'Brazil is a difficult country,' Francisco resumed, when they were once more walking together. 'People do wicked things and are not always punished. This land has a bad past. For many years, it did not belong to us. And though the children born between slave and owner were raised free, there was always judgement. How black? How brown? And always shame. Things are different now.' He waved his hand towards the cinema behind them. 'Since the end of the war, this city has... has...'

'Blossomed?' she suggested.

'Like a flower, you mean? Yes, a good word. There is much optimism now. Okay, we have foreign customs, Hollywood films like you see, but in ourselves we are comfortable. In the past, we think the mix of races—we are Blacks, Whites, Indians, Asians—is something bad. Now we think it good. Being Brazilian is something to celebrate. On the beach, you see the mixing, how good it is. Everyone is equal there. And so much energy elsewhere, so much that is new.'

In the street light, Francisco's face glowed with pride. 'We have wonderful design. Hotels that are the most modern and luxurious. New films, new music.' he went on. 'Before you come, there is a concert here that makes big news. The *bossa nova*, that is the name of the new music. Samba with jazz. Very original and only from Brazil. Rio is my home for many years but now the rich and famous come to my city. It is a time of gold.'

'And that explains why Sousa's criminality is allowed to flourish?' Her question sounded sharp.

'Where you have money and energy and new beginnings, you also have bad things—people who make fortunes from evil deeds.'

'I imagine that includes paying criminals to ensure you're elected mayor?' Nancy's distaste for Monaro had grown by the day.

'Money talks,' Archie said, with weary cynicism. 'In every walk of life. In every country of the world.'

*

They were emerging from the lift opposite Leo's room, when a doctor Nancy knew by sight tapped her on the shoulder.

'Can we speak, Mrs Tremayne?'

'Yes, of course. ' Nancy frowned, uneasiness taking hold. 'You go on,' she said to her companions, 'I'll join you shortly.'

'Is there something wrong?' she asked, as the doctor led her into the cubby hole he called his office.

He didn't answer her question, but instead asked his own. 'Is your husband often breathless?'

'Yes,' she said in a quiet voice. 'Quite often. But he's had bronchitis this winter—twice. That would explain it?'

'And before the bronchitis?'

Nancy considered, remembering their stay in Cornwall last year when several times Leo had found hills difficult to climb.

'There have been a few occasions when he's found breathing difficult,' she admitted.

'He is more tired these days?'

'He would be, wouldn't he? After so much illness.'

The doctor nodded. 'Also, it fits with our diagnosis.'

'Diagnosis? But I thought his wound was healing well and the x-ray showed no permanent damage to his brain.'

'It is not his brain I am talking of,' the man said gently. 'We have a done a second x-ray, a chest x-ray this time. I presume that Professor Tremayne has not had one recently.'

'No, at least I'm not aware he has.' She floundered. 'His doctor listened to his lungs after we came back from holiday last year—and his verdict was that they were a bit crackly, but nothing too bad. Nothing to worry over.'

'A bit crackly.' The doctor nodded again. 'They are now very crackly, which is why we ordered another x-ray. Perhaps they have become more so in the months since your holiday. Pulmonary fibrosis is a progressive disease.'

Nancy was now seriously frightened. 'What is pulmonary fibrosis?' she asked, unsure that she really wanted to know.

'It is a scarring of the lungs and limits the amount of oxygen that gets into the blood. Which is why it causes people to feel tired and, of course, the lungs are not working as they should so breathlessness will happen, particularly when climbing the stairs—or climbing hills.'

'But how has Leo contracted such a disease?'

The doctor steepled his fingers. 'Most usually the cause is not known.'

Nancy sat forward in her chair. 'Could it possibly be inherited?'

She'd had a sudden ghastly thought. Leo's mother, Rachel Tremayne, had died prematurely. Nancy had assumed it had been her heart at fault, but then if the lungs weren't working properly to pump oxygenated blood through the body, wouldn't that lead to heart problems?

'It is not frequent for it to be an inherited disease, but it can happen, I believe.'

'There is a cure, though?' she asked, a trifle desperately.

'There are drugs, certainly. They can stabilise or slow down the rate of scarring in the lungs.'

'And if they don't?'

'We must not think of that, Mrs Tremayne.'

Nancy walked out of the doctor's office with a mind in turmoil. Finding it impossible to go immediately to Leo's room, she wandered up and down the corridor for several minutes before feeling able to put on a smile brave enough to fool at least two of the people in the room. Archie, she knew, would sense instinctively that something was wrong.

Leo was sitting in a chair by the window while his visitors were bunched together on one side of the bed. A loud peal of laughter greeted her as she came through the door. Her gaze rested on her husband: Leo looked so much better that it was difficult to believe he had any serious illness.

'Good news, darling,' he greeted her. 'I'm to be discharged at the end of the week.'

She went over to him and kissed him on the cheek. 'That *is* good news.'

'And when Leo is back, you are all welcome to stay at the Tivoli as long as you wish,' Francisco said grandly.

'That's very decent of you, old chap,' Leo responded, 'but I've a feeling we should be on our way back to London. What do you think, Nancy? It would mean shortening our holiday, but would you mind too much?'

Her mind had gone blank. She felt bewildered, distraught even. All she could be sure of was that she must get Leo home as soon as possible. When she managed to put words together, she was surprised at how calm she sounded.

'By the time we get a flight booked, we'll have been here almost as long as we planned. I think it might help you to be back in a cooler climate.'

'Cooler, for sure,' Archie put in, looking searchingly at her. 'It was below freezing the night I left London. I'll find a travel agents in the morning and see what they can do for us.'

'Splendid.' Leo looked sideways at his assistant. 'There is one more thing, Archie—'

'Nothing to do with work. That's banned!'

'This is entirely play, I promise.' When Leo grinned, he looked at least ten years younger, Nancy thought. 'I had a message waiting for me when I got back from x-ray. From Senhor Monaro. Somehow he's learned I'm in hospital, but he's still intent on going to the Corcovado and is very keen to take you, Nancy. I don't imagine, though, that you'd want to be on your own with the chap. I thought that maybe Archie could go with you—if that's okay?'

Archie's expression was hard to read. 'Okay, with me, boss. But what the Dickens is the Corcovado?'

'It's only the very large statue of Jesus that you saw when your plane was circling.'

Nancy attempted a smile. She was making light of the visit, but deeply grateful she wouldn't have to cope with Monaro alone, particularly after the news she'd just been given.

Chapter Fifteen

Archie woke from a deep sleep and scrabbled for his watch. Seven in the morning, he saw blearily. He still felt like death so why was he awake? The sound of loud voices on the other side of his bedroom door told him the answer. Francisco was talking animatedly to a woman—a chambermaid?—and she was talking back almost as loudly. Archie groaned and turned over, burying his head in the pillow. Didn't the bloke ever sleep? But he couldn't complain, not when Francisco had been good enough to share his own quarters.

A few minutes later, the deafening noise of a powerful vacuum cleaner penetrated the walls—the maid had begun to clean the sitting room. Relinquishing any thought of sleeping on, Archie groped his way to the bathroom. Breakfast could wait, he decided. He would go out early and find the travel agents he'd promised last night. Arranging their journey home couldn't come soon enough. Yesterday had been hairy, and today could turn out just as bad.

He was uneasy, unsure of which way Nancy would jump. There were so many loose ends, any of which might land her in deep trouble. When she'd come into Leo's room after seeing the doctor last night, there had been something different about her. He'd sensed it straightaway. Her smile wasn't convincing, her voice wasn't true. It was after she'd seen Monaro skulking on the beach with his best pal, the nastiest crook in Rio. Had that been responsible for the change in her? Had sighting those villains decided her on some wild course of action? It was only too likely. It wouldn't be enough for Nancy to be threatened by men with guns, he thought acidly. She'd have to go one further. This afternoon was tailor-made for disaster—a visit to the Corcovado with the venomous Monaro.

As Archie left the hotel, people were already thronging the street—dancing and making music, eating and drinking. Perhaps they had never gone to bed. It took a while for him to thread his way through the crowd and walk for several blocks before turning left and climbing to a road that ran parallel to the Avenida Atlantica. The receptionist at the Tivoli had recommended an agent with offices just off this second major thoroughfare.

At the top of the hill, he spotted the square the receptionist had mentioned and had started to cross to it when a shrill claxon sounded in his ear, forcing him to jump back onto the pavement. A crowded tram swept past, horn still sounding, and filled to overflowing with people on their way to work. Every seat was taken, and along the tram's exterior men, dressed for the city, hung from a line of steel handholds, their feet glued to the running board.

The world was already on the march, it seemed, but not the travel agent. He was only just raising his shutters when Archie arrived, and his expression suggested that he wasn't too pleased to entertain a customer so early in the morning. Grudgingly, he ushered Archie inside.

'I need to book our return journey to London,' Archie began, pulling airline tickets from his pocket.

The man took a sharp intake of breath and rapped his

desk with the pencil he was holding.

'Not easy, Senhor,' he said, giving a sad shake of his head. 'Only a few flights each week and London'—he spread his hands in despair—'it is popular.' He wore the air of a man astonished by London's appeal.

Archie felt himself bristle. The man's attitude rankled and he was too tired for any confected difficulty. There would be space somewhere, he was certain.

'Easy or not,' he said, 'we intend to fly home at the end of this week.'

Several minutes of flicking through index cards followed, accompanied by a good deal of head scratching. Finally, with a muttered curse, the agent grabbed his telephone and, once connected, directed a torrent of Portuguese at the unfortunate recipient.

He stopped his harangue to turn to Archie, switching into English. 'Maybe not until next week. At the moment, I cannot tell. Booking is very heavy.'

Archie shook his head. 'The end of *this* week,' he said implacably.

More angry exchanges down the telephone had Archie jump to his feet and slam the palm of his hand down on the desk. 'We have a sick man to get back to London. You need to organise those flights. I'll be back.'

Considerably ruffled and resurrecting a few choice army curses he'd almost forgotten, he stormed back down the hill towards the Avenida, deciding he'd find breakfast on the way back to the hotel. A full stomach would make him feel better. He'd go to the same café he'd visited with Nancy. The food was good and he could understand at least some of the menu. He had only a vague idea of its direction, but once back on the seafront road, he was sure to find it.

It wasn't that easy and, after trying numerous side streets

without success, he admitted defeat and turned back towards the Tivoli. It was then that he spotted a figure at the top of the side street he'd just walked down, a figure that seemed strangely familiar. Two, in fact. Diego, the hotel's under-manager, the chap about whom Nancy had a bee in her bonnet—Archie was sure it was him—and another man, dressed outlandishly in the costume of a Japanese geisha girl... he seemed to know him, too. Archie inched back along the street towards the two men, from doorway to doorway, keeping to the shadows where he could. He had a strong sense that it was important not to be recognised.

Ducking into the entrance of a shop a few feet away from the men, he heard a stream of muttered Portuguese. He cursed himself that he didn't know the language. He had a good understanding of Italian—he'd been there in the war and since then had made many trips back with Leo, Italy being the spiritual home of a Renaissance art expert—and because of Italian, he could make out a little Spanish. But Portuguese was too much of a stretch.

Not understanding the words, though, gave him time to concentrate on the men themselves. There was some kind of argument going on. Diego Ramos, and it *was* him, appeared reluctant to go along with whatever his companion was saying and the geisha was growing more irate as Archie watched, his hands flying everywhere, his voice rising until he was almost shouting. He was pointing to something now—one of the hills behind the city?—and to do that, he had to half turn. For the first time, Archie saw the man's face properly. Saw his eyes beneath the make-up and knew them. Well, that was a surprise—although perhaps it wasn't. His would-be killer of yesterday! So Nancy was right to suspect Ramos of bad dealings. He should have known it, Archie thought wryly.

He needed to be gone and quickly. But trying to slip away as quietly as he could, his foot hit an empty beer bottle left by some inebriate the night before. The heads of both men turned immediately in his direction and for a moment their eyes locked on him. Then the geisha started down the hill towards him. Archie didn't wait. He flew from the shop doorway and headed down the narrow side street to reach the main thoroughfare as swiftly as he could. His best hope was to mingle with the crowd, join one or other of the parties now in full swing along the Avenida.

He dared not look behind to see if the man was following, but attached himself to a group of men wearing polka dot bikinis, worming his way incongruously into their midst and staying with them until he reached the hotel entrance. The group partied on while he pushed through the glass doors and made for the lift. Undetected, he hoped.

Back in his room, he found himself sweating copiously and swearing aloud. He was angry. 'Jumping', he'd say back home, furious that he'd been forced to run from scoundrels. It was a new feeling. He'd felt sick, certainly, when Nancy had told him what she knew of the children, but not raging. Now he was. Pacing up and down the room, he made himself hotter by the minute.

It was a good while before he felt calm enough to think things through. What were those men plotting—what had happened or was to happen on that hill, for instance? And why had the geisha come after him? Because he'd recognised him from yesterday, realised that Archie wasn't the stupid tourist he'd taken him for, but someone who was on to him? Someone who could make trouble? What would the man have done if he'd caught up with him? What would he do if he ever caught up with him? It was at least three days before they could leave the city, if that churl at the agency got his finger out. Maybe more if he didn't. Would Archie be hunted during the whole of that time? Even worse, would Nancy?

Chapter Sixteen

The doctor's words had become a constant echo in Nancy's mind. Ever since their stay in Cornwall last year, she had been concerned for Leo's health, her worries exacerbated by the bronchitis he'd suffered during the winter. *The doc knows what he's doing and he says everything's fine,* her husband had said airily, dismissing her concerns. It seemed the doctor might have failed in his diagnosis, or Leo's illness had worsened so quickly that the problem was now acute. And just what did it mean for the future?

Nancy badly needed to share her fears, but last night there had been no opportunity to confide in Archie. After the hospital visit, Francisco had hailed a taxi and they'd returned to the hotel together, their host insisting they share a drink with him on the roof terrace before turning in. This afternoon, too, was unlikely to provide much opportunity for talking.

A visit to the iconic statue that rose high above the city had been top of Leo's plans for sightseeing. In London, they had talked excitedly about making the trip, but now under such different circumstances, it wasn't something Nancy could enjoy. Monaro had issued his invitation at *Buffet Bonito*—how long ago that seemed, though it could only be days—and she'd sensed then that the offer had been made on the spur of the moment, as part of the man's need to burnish his self-image at a party thrown in his honour. She had expected him to have forgotten the arrangement, and even if his assistant — Emilia, Leo had called her — had waved his diary at him, Monaro could surely have ignored the plan, knowing that Leo was now in hospital. But, annoyingly, he hadn't, and all Nancy could do was say a prayer of thanks that Archie would be by her side.

She spent the morning in her room, the balcony doors open to the noise of Carnival, now so much part of everyday life that the shouts and laughter of the crowds, the rhythm of the drums, the tooting of horns, hardly impinged on her. Francisco had sent up a large breakfast with a note to say how tired she had seemed last night and how she was to rest and enjoy her meal in peace. It was a kind thought and she was glad to follow the advice. She imagined that Archie would be keeping to his room as well. If she had looked tired last night, he had looked positively haggard.

When she met him in the foyer, though, just before two o'clock that afternoon, he surprised her by saying that he'd been out and about since early that morning.

'I called at the travel agents and then just wandered around,' he said, sounding, she thought, slightly furtive. 'Getting a feel for the place. Submerging myself in the culture.'

He was certainly dressed to fit in: a pair of khaki shorts, battered sandals and the brightest-coloured shirt Nancy had ever seen him wear. All that was missing was a cloud of glitter.

'Was there a purpose to the wandering? Did you discover anything interesting?'

'I might have done,' he said, pulling down his mouth in what Nancy considered an annoyingly mysterious manner.

She was about to demand he tell her exactly what he'd seen or heard, when a uniformed driver pushed his way through the glass doors of the Tivoli and clicked his heels at them.

The Germanic gesture surprised her. 'A lot of Nazis in South America,' Archie said in her ear. She hoped the man hadn't heard.

Senhor Monaro was waiting for them in a sleek limousine parked immediately outside the hotel. He gave her a benevolent nod as she clambered into the rear of the car, though his expression when he realised that Archie was riding with them wasn't quite so benevolent.

'Senhor Monaro, this is my husband's assistant, Archie Jago,' she introduced him. 'He's only just arrived in Rio and is very keen to see the city's amazing statue.'

'*Cristo Redentor*,' he murmured. 'It *is* amazing, you will see. You go by train.'

Unsure what exactly Monaro intended for them, Nancy wondered how they were ever to get through the afternoon. Limited language skills on both sides did nothing to mollify the rampant distaste she felt. They were simply an added problem. But when the saloon car pulled up at what looked like a station—*Cosme Velho,* she read—an unknown man appeared at the car door. He was young and smartly dressed and welcomed them with a bright smile.

His greeting for Monaro was effusive, and turning to them, he said cheerfully, 'I am Vito. I am your translator. I will tell you everything you would like to know. To begin, I have the tickets.' Opening the vehicle's rear door, he fluttered several flimsy pieces of paper in the air, then pointed to the small queue that was forming. 'We wait here. The trains are every half hour, but the journey is only twenty minutes.'

Their host had made no effort to leave his seat and Nancy looked back at him, a puzzled expression on her face.

'Senhor Monaro will travel by car,' Vito said quickly. 'It is a shorter journey, but the view is better from the train. And it is here!'

A bright red train had pulled in while they were speaking and Vito hastily shuffled them towards the station entrance.

'A cog train,' Archie observed, as they climbed aboard.

'It is interesting, no?' Vito beamed. 'It can become very hot, so I suggest we sit by the window. On the right—this is for the best views. You have to face backwards. Maybe you slip a little when it gets steep, but very good views.'

Within minutes, they were chugging their way slowly up the Corcovado mountain, surrounded on all sides by thick vegetation. A few minutes more, and they entered what appeared to be a luxuriant forest.

'Tijuca National Park,' Vito told them. 'It is the largest urban forest in the world. You will see it spread below when we reach *Cristo Redentor*. That is Christ the Redeemer, a wonderful religious symbol. Thirty metres tall, you know. It is the most famous Art Deco sculpture in the world.'

'I think we're going to get a lot of this,' Archie muttered peevishly, while Vito was busy pointing out the waterfall they were just then passing.

Nancy frowned at him and addressed herself to their companion. 'When was the statue unveiled?'

'1931, Mrs Tremayne,' Vito answered gladly. 'It is an extraordinary achievement. And you will love the beautiful views from the top—the forest and the city and Guanabara Bay.'

'I'm sure I will,' she replied amiably. 'I've seen very many pictures of the statue.'

'The reality is much, much better. Now we come to a stop. We are halfway up and must go to a siding to allow the return train to pass.'

Nancy looked out of the open window. Lush jungle was everywhere, a riot of tropical splendour. Lizards skittered into the bushes, a curious monkey, his head on one side, looked hard at her. She looked back at him and pulled a face.

The journey was as swift as Vito had promised and Senhor Monaro was waiting for them as the cog train pulled in. This time, he'd managed to climb from his car and, adjusting his sunglasses, walked over to meet them.

'You enjoy the ride?' he asked.

'Very much,' Nancy said, hoping she sounded enthusiastic enough, while Archie said nothing.

'Good, good,' he muttered. 'Now you can see...'

He pointed upwards and Nancy followed his direction. The statue was monumental, soaring high above Rio, a guardian keeping a watchful eye on the city.

Standing beside her, Archie shaded his eyes. 'All I can see is a giant block of concrete with outspread hands.'

He was determined to be unimpressed, Nancy thought. The statue fitted his description, but it was so much more. Close up, the figure emanated repose, a spiritual calm that offered sanctuary—its outstretched hands seemed to tender a blessing and the carved lines of its face a gentle beneficence.

'The statue protects us for very many years,' Vito put in. 'But there is more. You will see across the city to the mountains and the beaches.' He pointed to the viewing platform that jutted from the base of the statue.

'Are you not coming, Senhor Monaro?' Nancy turned to ask and, as she turned, caught for an instant a speck of black that whisked across her vision.

'I wait here,' their host said. 'Then we have tea.'

It seemed an odd arrangement. The man had issued them an invitation but then spent no more than a few minutes in their company. Perhaps tea was when he would begin to play the host. Perhaps tea might be when she confronted him with Livia's disappearance.

She didn't have long to ponder. Vito was ushering them

towards the platform and a view of Rio that unfolded into an endless stretch of forest and ocean: thick green mountainsides tumbled down into the deep blue of myriad bays and, couched between them, the bright white of the city.

'Certainly an experience,' Archie said, seeming at last to emerge from his tetchiness. 'I guess we're lucky to have good weather today.'

Vito nodded. 'The clouds can come down very quickly and then you see nothing. But this day is clear. Only a few clouds far away. When you have seen enough, we will rejoin Senhor Monaro, and after tea we will walk to the top of the statue.'

Once Vito was satisfied they had properly absorbed the astonishing view, he led them past the waiting crowds, guiding them to one side of the restaurants and along a path that led to a clearing, enclosed on three sides by low bushes. In their absence, the uniformed chauffeur had set up a picnic table and four chairs—at least, Nancy presumed it was the chauffeur and not Monaro who had been at work. A crisp linen cloth was spread with several platters of dainty sandwiches, dishes of fruit and a tiered stand of cakes.

Monaro gave a satisfied smile. 'I make an English tea for you,' he said.

Had she misjudged the man? Nancy doubted it, but he seemed to have gone to a lot of trouble to entertain them and, though the tea wasn't exactly English, it looked appetising. She had thought he must have an underhand motive in continuing this invitation, but it was possible that he simply wanted visitors to enjoy his city.

'How do you find being mayor?' she asked, after her third sandwich, conscious that she should make an attempt at conversation. Vito dutifully translated.

'It is very busy,' Monaro answered in English. 'Many

people to help.'

'I imagine so.' She helped herself to a slice of passion fruit. 'What are the main problems?'

'Crime?' Archie asked, unexpectedly.

Monaro understood and shook his head. 'Rio is a safe city. But...' He finished his sentence with a stream of Portuguese.

'Senhor Monaro says that sometimes people get drunk, get into trouble, don't go to work.'

'Is finding a job difficult?' Nancy asked, sensing an opportunity to point the conversation in the direction she wanted.

Monaro shrugged his shoulders and appeared uninterested.

'I hope those poor men who lost their jobs last week will soon find work.' She looked across at Vito to translate, but when he did, Monaro's expression was blank.

'I saw that a very large warehouse had burned down,' she said innocently. 'The workers there will be have lost their jobs, won't they?'

When Vito translated this time, a look of annoyance passed swiftly across their host's face.

'I know nothing of them.' His tone was severe.

'I'm sorry. I must be mistaken. I thought the warehouse belonged to you, Senhor Monaro.'

Vito gave her his employer's answer. 'Senhor Monaro owns many warehouses, but none have been destroyed.'

Nancy smiled sweetly. 'That is good news. May I?' she asked, indicating the cake stand. She could feel Archie's eyes on her. He was telling her to leave it at that, but perhaps she wouldn't.

'This is delicious. Try it,' she urged him.

'That is *nega maluca*,' Vito told her. 'Brazilian chocolate cake.'

'Very good.' Monaro nodded approval, the benevolent smile back once more.

Wiping her hands on a napkin, Nancy steeled herself for the fray. 'I know you help many people, Senhor. And I was wondering if you could help me?'

She felt Archie take a deep breath beside her.

'Naturally. Senhor Monaro will be pleased to help,' translated Vito.

'You see,' she continued, 'I have come across a very sad case. The lady who cleaned our hotel room—her name was Vitoria, Vitoria Dias—died the day after we arrived.' Monaro's face expressed a polite interest. 'I spoke to her before she... she passed away. She was very upset. Her niece, a little girl called Livia, had been taken from her home and could not be found.'

'Here.' She pulled out the photograph from her bag. 'This is Livia. She is a pretty child, isn't she?'

Monaro gave the photograph a brief glance and muttered a few words. 'All children are pretty, Mrs Tremayne,' Vito translated.

'Not all, alas, but Livia certainly. And a little girl, too. I understand girls are very much prized for their nimble fingers.'

Vito looked surprised but tried to translate, only for his employer to raise his hand in an exasperated gesture that bid him to silence. Nancy was not to be allowed to continue her plea.

'Another cup of tea?' the translator offered, trying to cover the awkward moment.

'Thank you, yes.' Nancy slipped the photograph back into her bag, satisfied that Monaro knew about the girl, or at least knew what happened to girls like Livia who suddenly went missing. His attitude was proof that he was embroiled in this crime in some form or other.

*

Tea over, Vito suggested they climb the steps that led to the statue's feet. 'The view is probably better from the platform,' he said, 'but the climb will give you a true feeling for the statue itself.'

There were over two hundred steps ahead of them and, though the clouds had begun to bank a trifle ominously, the afternoon was now well advanced and the day at its hottest. It wouldn't be an easy climb, but Nancy wanted to make it.

'What did that achieve?' Archie asked her under his breath, as they began the climb.

'It proved to me that he knows of the kidnapping, even if he isn't personally involved.'

'Because he didn't want to speak of it?'

'Exactly. Did you see his face when I showed him Livia's photograph? Anger first, then a studied indifference. He's the mayor of the quarter where she lives and it's his job to help people. He said so himself. Yet he didn't react. He made no promise to look into her disappearance. Didn't mention calling the police. Refused even to listen.'

'And that seals his guilt?'

'For me, it does.'

Vito was some way ahead and turned back to look for his charges. He seemed concerned he might lose sight of them, now the clouds were gradually lowering and a veil of new mist forming. The stairway had become a great deal more crowded, too, people climbing elbow to elbow and jostling each other to reach the feet of the statue.

Archie gave him a wave and picked up his pace to go several steps above Nancy. Then it happened.

She had been deep in thought, when a sudden fierce shove

138

to her back pushed her against the low retaining wall. She gave a cry as she lost her footing, the pressure of the crowd half-tipping her over the barrier. Dizzyingly aware of tree tops beneath her and of the sheer rock face spinning across her vision, she felt herself falling, falling.

Archie had heard the cry and, turning, saw through the lowering mist a hand grab at the retaining wall, a woman trying desperately to save herself. Nancy! He jumped—two, three, steps at a time, barging people out of his way, and managing to reach out and grasp the hem of her dress as she teetered in the air. Grimly, he hung on, then began to haul the garment in, fist over fist, expecting at any moment to hear the material rip. But he had stopped her headlong flight and, with a huge effort, Nancy managed to scramble herself upright and sink back onto the safety of the steps.

By the time Vito arrived, she was on her feet, Archie supporting her.

'Whatever happened?' the translator asked, his voice cracking with anxiety.

'I lost my balance—just for a moment.' She gave a ghostly smile.

'You trip?'

'Something like that. I'm not really sure. I wasn't paying attention. My fault.'

'I am so sorry.' Vito was almost wringing his hands.

'Don't be. As I said, it was my fault. I'm fine now, but I don't think I'll go any further. I'll meet you both at the base.'

'I'm coming with you,' Archie said. 'I can probably manage the day without a close-up of Jesus.'

When they were once more on the large flat area that provided the base of the statue, Vito went to escort them to Monaro's car, half-hidden in the thick mist that had descended.

'I think we'll go back by train,' Archie said abruptly. 'If that's okay with your boss.'

Nancy blinked.

'It was a great ride up, wasn't it?' He gave her a little pinch.

'Yes... beautiful... and I'd love to do the journey again. Now the weather's changed.' She felt herself floundering, trying to make sense of Archie's sudden decision. 'We must thank Senhor Monaro and say goodbye.'

'If you are sure... ' Vito was still worried. 'The train may be a while to come.'

'Then we'll wait,' Archie said firmly.

Monaro hardly looked at them as they murmured polite thanks for a delightful afternoon and, before they'd even joined the queue for the train, the limousine had turned a wide circle and was heading back to the city.

'Hey, we're lucky.' There was relief in Archie's voice when, within minutes, a train pulled in. Taking her hand, he found them seats at the end carriage, facing forwards. 'Might as well have a different view,' he said, 'though there might not be much to see this time.'

The sounds of music drifted towards them from the next carriage. A live samba band was apparently on board, the passengers singing and a few couples getting up to dance. Nancy looked at her companion and saw that his face was set.

Under cover of the music, she asked, 'Are you going to tell me why we're bumping our way back on this train instead of flying down the mountain in a luxurious saloon?'

'I don't want you anywhere near that man.'

'Because?'

'Your fall, your near fatal fall, wasn't an accident. Did you think it was?'

'I felt a shove in my back, but it was so crowded...'

'It was a deliberate shove, I'm pretty sure. When I grabbed

you, even through the mist I could see an ocean of heads, and all of them facing upwards—except for one. It was the head of someone making a hasty return down those steps.'

'A man? And you think he was the one who pushed me?'

'Don't you?'

'But if Monaro sent him… that's what you're suggesting? Why?'

'You ask too many questions, Nancy, that's why. And I don't necessarily think Monaro did send him, though someone he knows almost certainly did. This afternoon was a perfect opportunity to put you out of action. Permanently.'

She felt a hollow form inside, a disagreeable flip of her stomach. She had been threatened before. Others had wanted to be rid of her. This time, though, it felt different. More terrifying. It was the indifferent nature of the violence meted out that was so fearsome. The way human lives were disposed of with no more thought than you'd give to flicking away a fly.

She tried to still her pulse; her heart was beating far too rapidly. 'Did you make the man out in any detail?' she asked, finally.

'Unfortunately not. It happened too quickly. He was wearing black, though. I could see that. Unusual, wouldn't you say, when everyone in the crowd had chosen bright?'

'Yes,' she agreed. 'Unusual.'

Chapter Seventeen

Rather than taking a cab, they decided to walk back to the hotel from the *Cosme Velho* station. The temperature had cooled a little and there was an unspoken desire, Nancy felt, to be together, to prolong this afternoon as long as they could. Soon enough, she would be a wife again on her way to the hospital. The visit wouldn't be easy, though, trying to gauge how much the doctors had told Leo and deciding how best to tackle the subject.

'Leo's second x-ray,' she blurted out, when they had been walking in silence for several minutes, her thoughts flying ahead. 'The doctor told me some worrying news.'

Archie turned to her, lowering his sunglasses. 'How worrying is worrying?'

'They ordered another x-ray because of concerns over Leo's breathing. They've told me he has a disease of the lungs, pulmonary fibrosis.'

He said nothing for a moment. 'Is that why he's breathless climbing steep slopes?'

Nancy nodded. 'His lungs are scarred and that makes breathing more difficult. It also limits the amount of oxygen that gets into the blood, so he feels tireder than he should.'

'Right.' There was a pause before Archie said, 'And what's the treatment?'

'There are drugs, the doctor told me, but it's a progressive disease.' Nancy allowed her words to sink in before going on. 'It must have become a lot worse since last year. Leo's doctor examined him when we got back from Cornwall, but there was no mention of anything serious.'

'Didn't the bloke order an x-ray?'

'He may have done. I'm not sure. Leo can be tight-lipped about his health and if I ever ask, he accuses me of panicking or prying. I don't even know whether the doctors here have told him what they've found.'

'Then you're likely to have a problem when you see him next.'

'I know,' she said miserably. 'I'm going to the hospital this evening and I must try to talk honestly to him.'

'The sooner we get back to England, the better.' Archie dug his hands deep into his pockets. 'I'll get off to the travel agents again. Yesterday, they were faffing around—perhaps they could book a flight at the end of the week, perhaps they couldn't. They're bloody well going to now.'

Archie was upset, and it touched Nancy to see it. There was a strange bond between the two men that hadn't broken despite whatever jealousy or suspicion swirled beneath the surface. They had been boys in the same Cornish fishing village, but grown up to vastly different futures. Leo's family, owning the local tin mine on which most of the village depended for employment, lived a comfortable life in the 'big' house, while Archie's folk, crammed into tiny cottages by the harbour, scraped a living on their fishing boat. The social divide followed them inevitably into war, Archie enlisting as a private in the Duke of Cornwall's Light Infantry, while Leo, privately schooled and Cambridge-educated, had naturally become an officer in the same regiment. Their bond had formed there—they'd hardly known each other before—and it had endured.

'Good luck with the tickets,' she said lightly. Then, thinking back to their afternoon, she asked, 'Do you think Monaro continued with his invitation, even with Leo in hospital, so that someone could attack me? The Corcovado, that staircase, was a perfect place.' She stopped walking for a moment. 'Or maybe my fate wasn't sealed until I showed him Livia's photograph?'

Archie stopped, too. 'I reckon it must have been planned already. Leo got the call saying the visit was going ahead—when?'

'Last night.'

'Right, and that was after our exciting visit to the warehouse and meeting the men in black.'

'And today,' she said thoughtfully, 'I seem to have met another man in black.'

'Exactly. I reckon that if we hadn't gone to the warehouse, Monaro would have been happy to forget the invitation. Someone told him they'd had visitors and he needed to do something about it.'

'You reckon that someone is pulling his strings?'

'Undoubtedly. If his election was as crooked as it appears, he's up to his neck in corruption.'

'Was I supposed to die, do you think?' Her voice was a little shaky.

'To be honest, I don't think they cared one way or another, as long as they put you out of action. Stopped you from nosing around. To these men, one death more or less is nothing.'

'Vitoria was nosing around, as you call it. She was determined to find her niece and that would have meant exposing the whole terrible business. It could be one of those men, one of Leandro Sousa's gang, who killed Vitoria. A man in black and not Diego Ramos after all.'

'Hmm.' Archie pursed his lips.

'Why "hmm"?'

'My wanderings this morning,' he said. 'You asked about them earlier.'

'Yes, and you never told me.' For the moment, she'd forgotten that small mystery but she still wanted to know.

'I saw Diego Ramos, down a side street, talking to one of the men we met at gunpoint yesterday. One of the men in black, except that in this case he wasn't. He was dressed to fit in with Carnival. The chap who pushed you, another of the gang I think, made a bad mistake by not blending in.'

'Did you get close enough to hear what they were talking about?'

'I got close enough to hear a stream of Portuguese. '

Nancy felt deflated. It seemed that every small step they took forward was followed by one back.

'I might not have understood the words they were saying,' Archie said, as they walked on, 'but after this afternoon's drama, I'm pretty sure I know what was going on. It was a real ding-dong between them. The man who threatened us at the warehouse was gesturing towards the hill and the *Cristo Redentor*—he would know from Monaro that you'd be at the Corcovado this afternoon—but Ramos didn't seem too keen on what he was hearing.'

'You think he was being pressured into being part of the attack?'

'I wouldn't be surprised. It's cause and effect, isn't it? Our visit to the warehouse rings alarm bells, Monaro is told of it and ordered to do something to get rid of you, me, probably both of us. Someone has to stage the attack—who better than a man we know from the hotel, who could get close without causing suspicion?'

'Ramos couldn't have agreed to it. I didn't see him at the

Corcovado.'

'He wasn't there and I'm pretty sure the man I saw talking to him this morning wasn't either. He must have drafted in another member of the gang at short notice—hence the costume that stuck out like a sore thumb. It was a rush job.'

They had reached the Avenida Atlantica and the noise level had risen considerably. Buffeted by a stream of committed party goers, Nancy had almost to shout to make herself heard.

'You're saying it was planned in advance, but how do you know the man talking to Ramos was one of the gang who threatened us? You said he was in fancy dress. He could have been someone quite different.'

'Dressed as a geisha,' Archie said, his voice seeming to relish the fact. 'He was the bloke at the warehouse all right. The one who aimed his gun at me.'

'But how can you tell?' She sounded exasperated. 'He wore a balaclava. We could only see his eyes.'

Archie's grin was cocky. 'It was his eyes, Nancy, that gave him away.'

'They couldn't have.' She came to an abrupt halt and glared at her companion. 'It's simply not possible.'

'Believe me, when you're staring down the barrel of a gun, the eyes measuring you up for target practice are instantly memorable. *And* there was the little matter of a birthmark.'

'Stop playing games and tell me,' she said angrily.

'Tut, tut, Mrs Tremayne. Temper!' He flicked a strand of her hair back with his fingers. 'It was on one side of his neck, a spot where the balaclava didn't quite reach.' Archie pointed to the base of his neck. 'Today, he was wearing an open-necked kimono and the birthmark was clearly visible.'

Nancy forgot her annoyance. This was exciting after all. 'So Ramos *is* in contact with the gang. He knew I was to be attacked this afternoon. He could still be the one who killed

Vitoria—they could be pulling his strings as well as Monaro's.'

'They could. And behind them is their boss, Leandro Sousa. A very, very dangerous man.' He stopped and took her by the shoulders. 'Promise me that before I see you again you won't go haring after a clue you've just discovered or a blinding inspiration that's just struck. Sousa means business. He'll have no qualms in ridding the world of an English tourist and making it look an accident. This afternoon should tell you that.'

Nancy looked into a pair of deep blue eyes and knew Archie was right.

'Promise,' he urged again.

'I promise. I've got my hands full with this hospital visit anyway.'

'I'll leave you to it. The agency is at the top of this hill.' He indicated a tree-lined road to the right of them. 'Tell Leo I'll call in tomorrow, hopefully with news of the journey home. Good luck with this evening.'

She would need it, she thought. Failing that, a very delicate touch.

*

When she walked into the hotel, Nancy was immediately conscious of a buzz of excitement. The uniformed doorkeeper she passed was straining his head to peer through the glass doors, the bellboys behind the luggage counter were standing on tip-toe and even the staid receptionist had left her post and was idling at the front of her desk.

A small knot of men were gathered in the centre of the foyer, one of whom she recognised as the inspector assigned to investigating Vitoria's death, together with his sergeant or whatever was the Brazilian equivalent. Francisco Silva was the third man, though with his back to her, she hadn't at first recognised him.

She had a choice. Take the lift to her bedroom or walk over to the group and discover what progress the inspector had made. Or, she had a sinking feeling, more likely not made.

Francisco turned and saw her as she walked further into the foyer and the die was cast.

'Nancy! How are you? Today you have been on a trip... it was to the Corcovado?'

She walked up to him and gave his hand a warm shake. 'Yes, the Corcovado. It was magnificent! But how are you, Francisco?'

'As you see.' He spread his hands. 'The police have arrived again.'

'Is there a particular reason they've come back?'

'They have come to interview my staff. It makes difficulties for the hotel, but they tell me it is necessary.' He gave a heartfelt sigh.

'It might mean they are nearer to solving Vitoria's murder.' Nancy didn't believe it, but felt she should sound positive; Francisco's usual cheerfulness had deserted him. 'They wouldn't go to the trouble of a second round of interviews unless they had a new clue, would they?'

Francisco sighed again. 'It is really nothing,' he said despondently, 'but then I think they have nothing so...'

'What is it that's new?' She felt a prickling of excitement.

'It seems that one of our chambermaids, Isabella—she is very young and has only recently come to us—has told the housekeeper that poor Senhora Dias had a telephone call just before she went missing and that the call made her... what do you say... agitated? The housekeeper thought she must report it to me and in turn I report it to the police. I wish that I had not.'

'Don't wish it. If it means the murder is solved and the

killer caught, the hotel can start afresh. But I do wonder why Isabella didn't mention before what might be a crucial fact.' Had the girl been under some kind of duress, Nancy wondered privately.

'Her mother has been ill and the girl took a few days away to look after her. She left the hotel the evening that Senhora Dias went missing and returned only yesterday. It was the first time she knew of the dreadful event here.'

Inspector Alvarez had stopped talking to his assistant and edged closer to them. His suit, she noticed, sported even more wrinkles than the last time she'd seen him. He appeared to be listening to their conversation, though Nancy was unsure how much he'd understood.

'Inspector, good afternoon,' she greeted him. It was a chance to speak to him that she might not have again, and Francisco was here, able to translate if necessary. 'I understand from Senhor Silva that you are here to speak to the staff.' The inspector nodded and it gave Nancy confidence to plunge in.

'When you do, inspector, I think you should pay particular attention to the under-manager.'

Francisco by her side, turned a startled look on her. 'Diego? Diego Ramos?'

'Yes, Senhor Ramos,' she continued serenely. 'You see, I heard him quarrel with Vitoria Dias the evening she went missing. If I remember rightly, the last time you were here, Inspector, Ramos told you he knew of nothing that was upsetting Vitoria. It was a lie. She had a lot upsetting her—her niece had been abducted and Diego Ramos knew that very well. He wouldn't give her permission to leave the hotel to look for the girl and that's why they quarrelled so badly.'

'But a quarrel over free time is not a reason to murder, Nancy, if that is what you are suggesting,' Francisco protested gently.

'I'm not. Not necessarily. I don't know what happened between them after I left for your reception at *Buffet Bonito*. But I do know that Diego Ramos is involved in something bad, that he has contact with members of the gang you told us about.'

Inspector Alvarez had begun to look baffled and Francisco was forced to translate, though it was evident he did so with reluctance.

'Tell him,' Nancy continued, 'that Ramos has some very unsavoury friends. This morning he was talking to a man I believe is a criminal.'

'How can you possibly know such a thing?' Francisco spluttered.

'Because the person with whom Ramos was deep in conversation could be the man who tried to injure me this afternoon at the Corcovado. A criminal act, wouldn't you agree? And if not that man, then a member of the same gang who threatened me before.' It was an unguarded comment, but she had the presence of mind to say no more. The encounter at the warehouse must remain a secret.

'This is…this is…' Francisco's hands flailed in the air. 'All imagination, Nancy,' he produced at last.

Her lips tightened. 'No,' she said, her voice firm. 'It's not. You know the gang I'm talking of, Francisco. Last night you pointed out to me the gang's ringleader, consorting with Senhor Monaro on the beach. You suspect them both of underhand dealings that have hurt you and, even worse, dealings designed to harm you physically. I'm saying that your under-manager knows at least one member of this gang, so surely Inspector Alvarez should follow it up.'

Francisco spoke to the policeman in rapid Portuguese. Nancy had no idea whether he was passing on the information or telling the inspector that the heat had most probably got to this poor, deluded English tourist, and to ignore her. All she could hope was that it prompted the police to interrogate Ramos a little more stringently than they'd done before.

She touched Francisco on the shoulder. 'I must go—I have to get to the hospital soon, but please let me know if the inspector makes any progress.'

*

Nancy hadn't felt like eating and it was still early in the evening when she walked through the hospital entrance, her lack of appetite due in part to nerves at what lay ahead and in part to the bountiful tea still sitting heavily on her stomach. It *had* been bountiful and she could almost feel sorry for Senhor Monaro. He must have been bored to tears with yet another visit to Rio's iconic landmark, but he'd organised the treat, made sure it ran meticulously, and paid for a splendid repast. All of it to have his plans come to nothing. She was still here and very much alive. If the man was in debt to Leandro Sousa, as she suspected, would he be punished for his failure?

Leo had just finished his evening meal when she walked into his room.

'I think the food is getting worse,' he said, holding out a hand to her. 'Unless it's my appetite returning.'

'Probably the latter.' She bent to kiss his forehead. 'According to the doctor, you'll be fit to leave in a few days and Archie is at the travel agents trying to organise plane tickets for the end of the week. So don't despair—Mrs Brindley's cooking beckons.'

Leo sighed. 'I won't be sorry to get home. It's not been much of a holiday for either of us.'

'It's been an experience! And we could always think of doing something else, maybe in a few months' time. Spring will be here very soon and we could book a few days in a country hotel.'

He shook his head. 'Not possible, sweetheart. I've too much to do once we're back in London. This new lecture series, for one thing. Holidays will have to go by the board for now, I'm afraid.'

'You should think of taking it easy, Leo,' she said cautiously. 'You've had a difficult time.'

'"Had" is the operative word. I'm okay now. The cut in my head is mended and my brain is still intact. I don't know why they've kept me here for so long. Whenever I ask the doctors, they tell me I'm still under observation. Are they expecting me to run wild, do you think, with delayed shock?'

'I don't think it's the head injury that concerns them,' Nancy said meaningfully.

Leo stared at her, saying nothing for what seemed a very long time. 'The doctor told you then,' he muttered finally.

'Yes.' There was a rush of gratitude in her voice. Leo knew he had a problem. 'You have a serious condition. There are drugs available, the doctor said, but it would be good to wind down a little, don't you think?'

There was another long pause. 'I've thought about it, darling. Really, I have. But it's not in my nature. I can't just stop working. You've told me often enough how much your work means to you. I feel the same.'

'I'm not suggesting you stop work entirely,' she said mildly. 'Just cut down. Try to make sure the disease doesn't take a real grip.'

'I don't think I'll have much say in that.' He gave a mournful smile. 'But honestly, Nancy, how can I cut down? I have this long series of lectures that's happening in the next few weeks. I'm committed to it. Who else is going to step in? I can't let the university down.'

She felt like pointing out that he'd have to let them down

if he was taken badly ill, but contented herself with saying, 'When these lectures are over… will you try not to take on as much? At least, cut back on the trips abroad.'

'It won't be easy, but I'll try. I don't want you to have a permanently sick husband on your hands. You've had that for too long already.'

'And I don't want to know you're suffering. This last winter has been dreadful for you.'

'You've been an angel, and I'm sorry I've let you down. You deserve a younger, fitter man.'

She snatched up his hand. 'Don't say things like that. I married *you*, Leo, and I want you by my side, however you are. But in future you must take better care of yourself.'

Her face must have expressed deep worry because he raised her hand to his lips and kissed it. 'I will try, darling. Really, I will.'

'Promise?' she asked hopefully. A second promise being made today.

'Promise,' he replied.

Chapter Eighteen

Archie was hungry, very hungry. This morning, he'd finally shaken off the inertia that had bothered him since the long flight from London, and he wanted food. Monaro's tea had long since settled and apart from a street snack he'd picked up on his way back from the travel agents yesterday, he hadn't eaten.

He wanted to telephone Nancy's room, find out how she'd fared in her talk with Leo, but then decided it was better to leave her in peace. Leo could be funny about his health, and any suggestion he was under the weather was always refuted immediately. Maybe marrying a woman fifteen years younger had made his boss particularly sensitive. Or maybe he feared an early death. His father was still alive—crusty old sod—despite suffering a massive heart attack last year, but Leo's mother had died when he was still a boy. Something to do with the heart, or so Archie remembered his mother saying, and now Nancy had been told her husband suffered a similar problem.

For a while yesterday, he'd forgotten Leo and his troubles. Forgotten that the woman by his side had loyalties elsewhere. He'd simply enjoyed being with her, even though the trip had involved the objectionable Monaro and nearly ended in tragedy. The Corcovado site had been impressive, something to tell his children about, if he ever had any, which looked extremely unlikely. Even the attempt to injure Nancy hadn't marred his pleasure at being with her. And thank God he had been with her. She could have toppled over that flimsy barrier in seconds if he hadn't recognised her cry above the buzz of tourist chatter.

Worry joined forces with hunger, motivating him to shower and dress in record time. He needed to keep close to Nancy, he decided, in whatever way he could. Ensure that he kept her safe from falling victim to the men they had crossed. He would make that phone call after all. Maybe spend the day with her. Leo no longer needed constant attention—he was on the mend and would be discharged in a couple of days, and now they had tickets for a flight back to London, Nancy would be keen to know when they were leaving.

After they'd said their goodbyes yesterday, he'd hared up the hill to the travel agents, keeping a watchful eye for anyone following him. As soon as he'd got to the shop, its morose owner had begun on what seemed to be his usual routine— denying any aircraft were actually taking off from Rio—but Archie had sat himself down on the one visitor chair and announced that he was going nowhere until the chap booked their flights.

The sooner they were on that plane, the better. He'd had a vague hope that the danger Nancy had faced yesterday would make her think twice about continuing to probe, but it was wishful thinking. She was certain to keep looking for the child while she could, walking a road to extreme danger. The little girl's disappearance was sad—very sad, he had nieces of his own—but Nancy was a foreigner in an unfamiliar culture and she was tangling with people, not just deeply unpleasant as they'd been in Venice, in Malfuego, but thoroughly violent men, wholly indifferent to murder. The situation here was a different kettle of fish.

The phrase made him smile. Made him think of his family in Port Madron. Big brother, Rich, sailing in all weathers to catch enough to keep his family going, Ma in her sixties and only just stopped working shifts gutting fish. What they wouldn't give to be here, he thought. Yet, right now, he'd give everything he owned, which wasn't a great deal, to be home in Cornwall. Home, with Nancy by his side. He shook himself out of the daydream and picked up the telephone.

She answered it in a few rings.

'Fancy breakfast?' he asked.

'I'm starving,' she said, unexpectedly. 'Breakfast is just what I need. Where do you want to eat?'

'How about the roof terrace? The restaurant looks pretty good.'

'It is. Francisco put on a special meal for Leo and myself before… ' she faltered a little. 'Before that gang nearly killed him.'

'Meet you at the lift,' was all he said.

She looked fresh and pretty, emerging from the lift doors, her hair still damp from the shower. The pale cream sundress revealed a skin that had taken on the same golden tan he'd known in Malfuego.

Archie tried not to notice. 'The sun's already doing its worse, he said, 'but I've found a table tucked around the corner. There's an overhanging roof which gives a good bit of shade.'

When they'd made themselves comfortable and the waiter had brought them juice and fruit, Archie asked cautiously, 'How did it go with Leo last night?'

She bit her lip. 'Honestly, I'm not sure. He knows about the disease—the doctors have spoken to him. And he knows now that I know, so at least things are out in the open. Once we're back in London, he's promised to cut down on his commitments, although he's adamant he'll deliver this series of lectures at the university. How many sessions are there?'

Archie took a sip of mango juice. 'Twelve, last time I counted.'

'That's twelve weeks of teaching, preparing, marking, as well as fielding a hundred other calls on his time.'

'On the bright side, a good deal of the preparation has been done and I doubt he'll be marking student papers. That will be for their tutors. But you're right, I have a diary full of appointments once we're home, and a list of people I need to phone back.'

Dropping a forkful of papaya, she leaned across and grabbed Archie's hand so suddenly that she almost knocked the plate of sliced fruit to the floor. 'Don't make the calls,' she said urgently.

'I have to get back to these chaps,' he protested. 'It's Leo's business.'

'What about his life? Isn't that more important?'

He could have pointed out that it was Leo's business that kept her in comfort. If the work folded, so would the house in Cavendish Street, but he knew Nancy well enough to realise she'd be happy living much more modestly. Before all the trouble with Philip March, she'd been content enough in a shabby bedsitting room.

He decided on compromise. 'I'll try to put them off.'

She smiled across at him. 'Just so he gets the space to recover completely. The head injury seems to have mended well, but I can tell the doctors are concerned about his breathing.'

Archie didn't voice the obvious: that no matter how much work Leo turned down, a disease that was progressive wasn't going away.

'I've news for you.' He was keen to change the subject. 'I've managed to wring tickets from the worst travel agent in the world. We're on the Saturday flight. Assuming Leo is discharged at the end of the week, it should work well.'

She looked relieved. 'Leo needs to get home. So do I. I've loved being here but the city is exhausting. Maybe Carnival wasn't the best time to come. The drums were beating at six this morning! Up here, it's reasonably quiet, but I've had to shut my balcony doors. The noise is incredible.'

'How long does this shenanigan go on?'

'It ends today, I believe—Ash Wednesday. It's probably why it's even noisier than usual. Carnival's grand finale.'

'It *was* quiet up here,' Archie muttered under his breath.

He gestured with his head to a table they could only just glimpse from their corner. He'd noticed the couple earlier. An odd pairing, he'd thought—a young and very beautiful woman and a much older man, fleshy but pugnacious. There was certainly something pugnacious going on right now. Raised voices drifted across the open space and were growing louder by the second. A real blow-up of an argument.

Nancy pulled a face. 'Father and daughter,' she whispered.

'Do you think so?'

'Almost certainly.' Her smile was indulgent, but then he saw her expression arrested, the contours of her face suddenly frozen.

'That man,' she whispered. 'He's the same one as on the beach.'

'What beach? When?' Archie was confused.

'The night we walked to the hospital with Francisco. That man is Leandro Sousa and the woman...' Nancy leaned sideways, her eyes narrowing ...'the woman is Jessica.'

'The name should mean something to me?' he asked, as the waiter arrived with the next tranche of their breakfast.

'It won't, but I met her in Santa Cecilia. It's a favela. I met her at Ester Barreto's house. Jessica was supposedly there to be measured for a dress. Ester, that's Livia's mother, is a seamstress.' Nancy was silent for a moment. 'So,' she said thoughtfully, 'the boss of a criminal gang meets his daughter for breakfast.'

'And rows with her pretty comprehensively,' Archie said.

'It's a pity neither of us can speak Portuguese. I'd give a lot to know what the quarrel is about.'

'And if you found out?'

'It's a bit of a coincidence, isn't it? I meet someone at the house of a woman whose daughter has been kidnapped and she turns out to be related to one of the most violent men in Rio. A man who's embroiled in every kind of criminal racket.'

'What if she was there simply to order a dress? Even gangsters' molls need clothes.'

'She isn't a moll, she's his daughter. And look at the way she dresses. Designer clothes, definitely nothing made by a humble dressmaker, no matter how good Ester may be.'

'Jessica might be helping the poor. Doing her bit for charity.'

'Yes, I can imagine.' Nancy's tone was caustic. 'She's the kind of woman who would.'

'She's rich, she's beautiful. Why not?'

'Because she was in the favela for something else.'

'But what? If you're saying she was there to kidnap Ester's daughter, the child had already gone. It wouldn't be to demand a ransom either—the family are too poor to pay. You said so. Not that Sousa would send his daughter, in any case. One of his thugs would be ordered to collect any money.'

Nancy poured cups of coffee for them both. 'I don't know for sure why she was there. I couldn't work it out at the time, but when I walked down the hill to the main road, I saw a young man on the corner of the next street. He was hanging about, clearly waiting for someone. I think he was waiting for Jessica. And he's as beautiful as she,' she finished a trifle tartly.

'An assignation!' Archie was stupidly glad at the little spurt of jealousy he'd heard.

'Why not? I became more certain when I saw him again the next day. He was dancing with Jessica as part of a Carnival procession. And they looked very much like lovers.'

'There doesn't seem to be much love lost there,' Archie remarked mildly, as the young woman pushed her chair back with a screech and grabbed her handbag from the adjoining seat. Tossing her mane of shining dark hair over her shoulders, she stalked towards the lift, a thunderous look on her face.

'She seems to have had enough of disagreeing with Daddy.'

Nancy made no response. He could see that she was thinking, and that was always dangerous.

'Why don't we go for a swim?' he sprung on her. He was uneasy about leaving the hotel, knowing they were both on someone's to-do list, but it was the only way he could think to distract her from even deeper trouble. If he was watchful, it should be okay.

Nancy pondered the idea. 'It's true Leo won't expect us at the hospital until later. And I'd like to get my feet wet before I leave.' She held her head on one side, still considering the suggestion. 'As long as we're back by late afternoon.'

'How long does it take to walk across the road?'

She finished a slice of banana cake before she answered. 'I'd really like to go to a different beach. Leo was keen to visit Ipanema, but we never got there. It's the next bay along. It's a bit of a walk, but it might be quieter. I think today it's going to be difficult to find anywhere we can hear each other speak.'

'Ipanema it is then. I'll meet you in the foyer in ten minutes.' He patted his stomach. 'That was a good breakfast. Particularly the little cheese rolls. I'll have to get Charlie to put them on the menu.'

Chapter Nineteen

Ipanema was a good forty-five minute walk from the hotel and, by the time they arrived, Nancy was feeling extremely hot despite wearing nothing heavier than a sundress. Archie in shorts and shirt looked equally sticky. The sun might not yet be directly overhead, but even this early in the day, it was fiercely powerful.

Ipanema beach turned out to be not that different from its neighbour—the same tree-lined, black and white patterned promenade as Copacabana, the same mountain peaks guarding the bay, and the same white-gold sand and white-topped Atlantic rollers. A similar mix of sun oil and spice permeated the air, and there was yet another football game in progress, the players wearing the tiny red trunks that seemed ubiquitous on Brazilian beaches, their shouts mingling with those of the food sellers. Ipanema, though, was far less busy and far less noisy.

Padding through the sand, they looked for a spot that was relatively empty. A good part of the beach had been divided into sections, with young men stationed at different points hiring out their individual stacks of chairs and candy-striped umbrellas.

'We'll need one of those,' Archie said, pointing to the nearest pile of sunshades. 'I don't want to end up looking like a herring. How about chairs?'

'We could make do with a canga. I could take it home then as a souvenir.'

'Okay, in English this time.'

'It's a beach towel. They're quite cheap and they come in beautiful patterns.'

'A canga it is. Anything else madam requires?'

'You can do the drinks later,' she teased. 'I've only a few cruzeiros with me.'

He grimaced. 'The pickpockets are never going to make a living out of you.'

'Will stealing be a problem, do you think?' She glanced around.

'I'll ask the blokes hiring the umbrellas to keep an eye on our stuff when we swim. They won't want their customers' clothes stolen.'

Undressing on a crowded beach was not something Nancy had ever negotiated, but the presence of other women in the skimpiest beach wear—bikinis, they were called, she'd seen them advertised— appeared to attract little attention. It gave her greater confidence. Even so, she'd been sure to wear her swimsuit beneath the sundress and it took only a few minutes before they'd left cangas and clothes in a pile and were dipping their toes into what felt unusually cold water.

'I thought it would be warmer,' she complained.

'It's the Atlantic, not the Caribbean. Come on, don't be chicken.'

He held out his hand to her and she took it without thinking. Side by side, they waded out, taking only a few yards before they were chest-high in water.

'It shelves pretty deeply,' Archie said. 'Be careful not to swim out too far. I don't want to save you from drowning— grabbing you from the wall of death was quite sufficient.'

She ruffled his hair as he spoke and he splashed her with enough water to leave her gasping.

'You—'

But he was gone, swimming with a powerful stroke, parallel to the shore. Nancy followed suit, the cold fingers of the sea creeping insidiously over and around her body. It was a while before the water began to warm her bare limbs and slowly bewitch her with its movement.

Entranced by the feel of cool sea on hot skin, she was unaware of a particularly large wave rolling towards her, until it had picked her up and thrown her forwards, almost onto the beach. Archie had been engulfed, too. He stood treading water, shaking his head and trying to dislodge the torrent that had poured into his ears. The wave had almost swallowed him.

When he looked up, his face held a startled expression. 'Nancy!' he called to her urgently. 'Your swimsuit!'

'What?'

For a moment, she was confused. What was he talking about? Then she realised. The wave had been so strong, it had torn her swimsuit from her shoulders and her bare breasts were bobbing happily on the now much calmer sea. Frantically, she pulled the costume up. One of the shoulder straps had completely broken and she was left desperately grasping at the other, ducking back under the water as she did so.

Archie swam over to her and encircled her with his arms, supporting her while she frantically tried to adjust what was left of the top of her swimsuit.

'Don't laugh,' she instructed.

'Who's laughing?' he said, then both of them subsided into loud peals—for the absurdity of the situation, for the sheer joy of being alive together.

She leaned against him and felt his legs slowly entwine around hers. He was holding her so close, tangling his face in salt-soaked curls. Then finding her lips and kissing her, kissing her. Fulfilment, delight, longing. And guilt. Always the guilt.

They broke from each other as suddenly as they'd come together. 'A drink is what we need,' he said roughly. 'You'll have to hide in your canga till you're dry.'

By the time Archie returned with refreshments, she had recovered some of her composure.

'Iced tea,' he said, handing her a glass. 'They called it *maté* but I reckon it's iced tea.'

'And you found a beer.' She was trying to forget the kisses and knew he was, too.

'Yup. A Brahma beer, apparently. And to eat, if breakfast wasn't enough, there's'—he looked at the packet—'crackers. One bag is sweet flavour, the other salty. They really go for their finger food here.'

Nancy peered into the open bag and saw doughnut-shaped puffs. 'Interesting.'

'Indeed. And—I couldn't resist these—they're called *salgados*. Shredded chicken wrapped in some kind of dough and deep-fried. Here, wrap this napkin round one.'

She felt his eyes on her as she ate, waiting, watching for the moment to speak. Trying to find the right words. In the end, he simply drank his beer and Nancy was glad. Whatever they said couldn't mend this situation.

'The inspector was at the hotel again yesterday,' she told him, glad to have something to talk about. 'I managed to speak to him when you were collecting the tickets. I wanted to tell him how Vitoria had quarrelled with Diego Ramos just before she disappeared. And mention that Ramos has some very dubious friends. I was hoping I could persuade him to investigate the man seriously.'

'And did you?'

'Francisco had to translate most of it, so it's difficult to judge, but somehow I doubt it. Inspector Alvarez seems to prefer bumbling in the dark. I suspect he's waiting for the chance to wash his hands of the whole thing.'

'If he was at the Tivoli again, he can't be that keen to dump the investigation. Do you know why he came back?'

Nancy took a last drink of iced tea and mopped her forehead with the corner of the canga. 'It seems that one of the chambermaids returned to work the day before yesterday — she'd been away looking after her sick mother — so she knew nothing of what had happened to Vitoria. As soon as she did, it prompted her to mention to the housekeeper that, just before she went missing, Senhora Dias received a telephone call that made her very excited.'

Archie inclined his head, and she could see an immediate question forming. 'You think the call was from whoever murdered Vitoria?'

'It had to be. Or from their accomplice. This person telephones Vitoria, tells her something that agitates her — it can only have been information about her missing niece — and arranges to meet her in the cellar.'

'Why do that? I can see why the murderer would want to lure the poor woman down there, but why would Vitoria go? It can't be a place she'd normally visit.'

'It wasn't. Francisco made that point the morning we found her. But Vitoria wouldn't be thinking like that, would she? Here, possibly, was someone telling her they knew where to find Livia. Maybe saying that it was dangerous information and they needed to pass it on where they couldn't be seen or heard. The cellar then looks a reasonable meeting place.'

'Does this girl, the young chambermaid, have any idea

who was at the other end of the line?'

'Apparently not, but I'd love to talk to her. Francisco said her name is Isabella.'

'You've no need to talk to her. By the sound of it, the police are following it up.'

Nancy mumbled something inaudible, refusing to commit herself, and was glad that Archie didn't pursue it. She had every intention of speaking to Isabella, inspector or no inspector, and didn't want to deceive him.

'I don't think I can stay here much longer,' she said, fidgeting to find more shade for skin that had begun to prickle badly. 'The sunshade gives some cover, but I can feel myself very slowly roasting.'

'Me, too. And it's got a lot noisier. Time to leave?' When she nodded, he jumped to his feet and began to haul down the parasol.

'Where do you want to go?' she asked. 'Back to the hotel?'

'I guess, unless you've an alternative.'

'How about Leblon?'

'Who or what is that?'

She began to fold their towels. 'We'll take these with us. Leblon is a place. Rio's most expensive residential quarter.'

Archie stopped, the umbrella drooping in his hand. 'Oh, no!' He's worked it out, she thought. 'I remember now. It was where Francisco said Leandro Sousa lived, and we are definitely not looking for him.'

'Not him. His daughter. She lives in Leblon, too.'

'But in the same house, presumably.'

'I don't think so. Not the way she described it to me. Francisco said Sousa lived in something resembling a palace. The house Jessica told me about was beautiful but no palace.'

'Have you an address?'

'No,' she said a little defiantly. 'But I do have her

description. I'm sure I'd recognise it. The house faces a lake with a forest behind, and has a balcony that wraps around the entire building. There's also a spiral staircase leading to the front door—it's only just been built. Oh, and pink chimney pots.'

Archie looked sceptical. 'Was she having you on? It sounds more a fantasy than a house.'

'The design is fantastical all right, but the house is real enough.'

'There'll be dozens of streets to search,' he protested. 'Needle in the haystack time.'

Nancy gave a little shrug. 'Even if we don't find the house, it will be good to take a walk. I've eaten far too much. And Leblon is bound to have trees and where there are trees, there'll be shade. It will be cooler than the beach at least.'

'Why do my instincts tell me not to go?'

'Because they're wrong. Look, our swimsuits are almost dry. Perfect.'

'Perfect,' he agreed, but his tone was ironic.

Chapter Twenty

It took time to rid themselves of the sand that seemed to have infiltrated every crevice of their clothes, but when they finally made it back to the promenade, they continued to walk westward, following the line of the beach. Ahead, towering twin mountains, their peaks slicing through the cloudless sky, grew closer with every step, but it took another half an hour of clammy walking before they reached the channel that divided Ipanema from its neighbour, Leblon. Bordering the canal, was a thickly wooded park. Jardim de Alá, Nancy read. Was this Jessica's forest?

'Do we go on?'

Archie sounded wary. There had been no sign today of any man in black or even the odd geisha, but Nancy understood his concern. The further they wandered from the hotel, the more exposed they became.

She shaded her eyes, looking ahead. The promenade continued into the distance, unfurling itself beside a peaceful stretch of sand—fewer people here than on Ipanema beach, and certainly far fewer than Copacabana.

'It looks as though the city proper begins to merge into the suburbs,' she said. 'I think we should turn inland. Otherwise, we're likely to walk out of Leblon all together. If we follow the canal, it might bring us to the lake that Jessica spoke of.'

The street that bordered the canal turned out to be as leafy as Nancy had foretold, the dense shade of the trees a blessed relief from the midday heat and, as they ventured further into Leblon, it became clear why this area of Rio was the most affluent in the city. With its mix of elegant dress shops, smart bars and costly restaurants, it was easy to see why it had become a haven for the rich and famous.

They were passing an eaterie now, tiled tables spread wide across a tiled floor, the atmosphere cool and spacious. Along one wall, a bank of refrigerators displayed a mouth watering collection of seafood.

Archie looked longingly through the open door. 'I get why this is the most expensive quarter of Rio,' he said, echoing her thoughts. 'Probably the most expensive quarter in South America.'

'Come on.' She tugged at his arm. 'I'm fairly sure we couldn't afford even to sit there.'

A little further and the channel they had been following began to open out. If Nancy squinted hard, she could just make out a large lagoon taking shape ahead.

'This is where Jessica meant,' she said excitedly. 'I'm certain of it. The forest, or the park, or whatever you want to call it, with the mountains all around and this spread of water in front.'

'The Rodrigo de Freitas Lagon,' Archie announced, as they approached a large metal sign.

'There you are then.'

'Where are you exactly? I'm not clear. It's a huge lake, I grant you, and there are houses that border it. But where's the one you're looking for? It will take us forever to walk around that expanse of water on the off chance of finding this woman's house.'

In her heart, Nancy knew he was right, but she wasn't

giving up just yet. 'If we stay beneath the trees, we can manage part of the lake at least and you never know, the right house might swim into sight when we least expect it.'

For a moment, she stopped walking and turned in a circle, her gaze taking in the panorama. 'This place is fabulously beautiful, isn't it? No wonder Jessica was peeved when I asked her if she lived in the favella!'

'I could do without the fabulous beauty right now. A beer would be preferable.'

'Don't be a grump. We need to keep looking. By the sound of it, the house will be old. That should make it stand out.'

For some while, the buildings they'd passed had been blocks of apartments. Complexes that sat beneath the shade of large palm trees, their white elegance architecturally stunning. All of them boasted glass balconies and wrought iron entrance gates, firmly locked against intruders. Gradually, though, older houses had begun to take the place of this shining modernity.

'What makes you think the house is old?' Archie asked.

'One word, I guess. Chimney pots.'

He wrinkled his nose and flinched as he did so. 'Ouch. I've got burnt on that beach. What's with the chimney pots? Why would you have such things in a country where you never stop sweating?'

'It can't always be this hot, but in any case it's like you said, the house is a fantasy. The kind of thing someone might decide to build a hundred years ago, maybe after they'd travelled to Europe. A house that would be different, mark them out as somehow superior to their wealthy neighbours.'

'Where do you get this stuff?'

'I'll be proved right, you'll see.' Nancy said it with a confidence she was far from feeling.

By the time they had walked another fifteen minutes, they

were both close to giving up. The line of older houses was dwindling, unlike the path that circled the lake—that seemed to stretch into infinity.

Archie came to a halt, pulling a handkerchief from his pocket and wiping the back of his neck. 'We go to where these houses finish and the apartments start again, then we turn round.' His tone brooked no argument.

The modern blocks he'd mentioned were close, no more than three hundred yards ahead, and Nancy sent a prayer heavenwards that somehow they'd strike lucky. The prayer appeared to work. They had walked only a few steps more when she pointed wordlessly to the roof of the house a few doors on.

'Pink chimney pots,' Archie confirmed. 'And a spiral staircase. Okay, you've found it. But now what? If we're going to knock at that door, have you any kind of story ready?'

'I'll play it by ear.'

He gave a derisive snort. 'That should be fun.'

She ignored him and walked up the paved path to the glistening dark wood of the front door. Pink shutters enclosed each window and were closed tight. It looked as though there was no one at home but, trying to still what was now an erratic heartbeat, she took hold of the iron knocker and gave the door a sharp rap.

She had to knock twice before there was any response and was just about to retrace her steps, when the door opened a few inches. Jessica's curtain of dark hair appeared first, then her perfect heart-shaped face, wearing an expression that was decidedly cross. Was she still smarting from this morning's argument with her father?

'Hallo,' Nancy said brightly. 'I don't know if you remember, but we met a few days ago. At Ester Barreto's house in Santa Cecilia.'

If anything, the young woman's expression grew crosser. She seemed to be grappling with the sight of two virtual strangers on her doorstep.

'You told me about your house then. How beautiful it was. How beautiful Leblon was,' Nancy gushed. 'And I simply had to come and look for myself. We were walking around the lake—my friend and I,' she gestured towards Archie standing at her shoulder, 'on a small adventure. And then I saw it. Your house. I knew immediately it was the one you'd described to me. It's simply wonderful.'

'Yes, it is, isn't it?' Jessica's voice was without expression and she remained firmly wedged in her doorway, showing no inclination to invite them in.

'I wonder—I know it's an imposition—but my friend here,' she gestured to Archie again, 'is feeling a little under the weather. It's so very hot.' She heard him give a furious grunt, but carried on. 'Would it be possible to beg a glass of water?'

Jessica seemed taken aback by the request and wavered just long enough for Nancy to take a step forward. Suddenly both she and Archie were inside the house. The hall was wide, the ceiling tall, and a glorious coolness pervaded the space.

'This is wonderful,' Nancy said, shaking damp waves and allowing the fresh air to wash over her. That, at least, wasn't a lie.

'You better come through,' Jessica said crisply.

They followed their reluctant hostess along the hall, passing an array of dark wood doors, all firmly shut, to the rear of what, by Nancy's estimation, was a very large house.

The room they arrived in was filled with brilliant light. Tall glass doors had been flung open and led to a sun-soaked garden.

'I was sitting by the pool,' Jessica said indifferently, 'but I don't suppose that would be any good—for him.'

It was as though Archie was some unknown insect that had arrived in her house by mysterious means and somehow had to be accommodated.

Nancy caught a glimpse of the pool through the glass doors. It was at the bottom of a flight of wooden steps and surrounded by a veritable jungle of palms and ferns. Every kind of green. Dark wicker sun beds were positioned around the poolside, brightly coloured towels thrown negligently to one side.

A paved square lay directly above the pool, cotton-covered sofas lining each side. In the centre, a wicker table had been set with glasses and what looked to be a jug of iced juice. It was a tempting scene and Nancy would love to have sat herself down on one of those very comfortable sofas, but she had to maintain the fiction that Archie was suffering from dehydration and needed shade. And if there was anything to find at this address, it wouldn't be outside.

'The garden looks wonderful,' she said regretfully, 'but I think it's best we stay in the cool—if you don't mind.'

'We had better go into the drawing room then.' The young woman pointed to an archway on their left. 'Through there. I'll fetch some water.'

The room they'd been ushered into was in shadow and made dimmer by walls painted a dark green. Another set of cotton-covered sofas, this time in a matching green, was arranged around a low table, and they had barely found themselves a seat when a jug of water and two plastic glasses were dumped unceremoniously in front of them. Jessica had been swift to return. She doesn't trust us, Nancy thought. She needs to keep us in sight.

Having poured her unwelcome visitors their water, the young woman perched on the edge of the sofa opposite, as though ready to leap to her feet and show them out the minute their glasses were empty. They drank the water in a silence so intense that even the sound of her swallowing felt loud to Nancy. This wasn't getting them anywhere, she scolded herself. They had found the house, found Jessica, but now…

'Have you seen Ester recently?' she tried.

Jessica looked blank.

'Ester Barreto? We met at Ester's house,' she reminded her again. 'She was making clothes for you. I think it was a dress? You were there to be measured, you said.'

'Yes.' The woman sounded uncertain. 'Yes, that's right. I was measured, but in the end I decided not to go ahead. The material Ester showed me wasn't quite right.'

'What a shame. I imagine she would have welcomed your commission.'

'More than likely,' Jessica said in a voice dripping with boredom. 'There are plenty of dressmakers to choose from in the *favelas* and they are all poor. Any of them would be delighted to get my custom.'

Nancy felt her companion stiffen. The woman was arrogant and insensitive, too sure of her privileged position, qualities unlikely to endear her to Archie. He had never quite forgotten the chip he'd borne since childhood when his mother had sold fish to Leo's family. Penleven's back door was where she had to knock. Not good enough for the front entrance, he'd once remarked to Nancy, his tone bitter. For the Tremaynes, a village woman was too lowly to rate anything better.

'I've thought of Ester quite a bit since I met her,' Nancy tried again, shuffling a few inches along the sofa. It had seemed a comfortable seat but there was something decidedly uncomfortable digging into her back. She sensed Archie giving her a sideways glance as she moved closer.

Jessica made no comment and continued to look bored.

'I wondered if her little girl had been found,' Nancy ploughed on. 'Have you heard anything?'

'Why would I?' she asked blightingly.

Nancy shuffled again. There was definitely something very irritating poking into her. She nudged her companion in the hope that Archie might keep the conversation going. She had said she would play it by ear but the tune was getting decidedly monotone.

'How old is the house?' he asked, and Nancy blessed him.

'It was built over a hundred years ago.' The young woman positively glowed as she spoke. It seemed that Archie had hit a right note. 'It was built by the Murillos. They were a very wealthy family and very well travelled. They brought many ideas back with them from their journeys. Of course, you have older houses in England, but here my home is very admired. For its history as much as its beauty.'

'I can believe—' he began, when Nancy gave him a sudden, sharp poke in the ribs, knocking the glass from his hand. Water cascaded over his bare knees and down onto the polished wood floor.

'I'm so sorry,' she was quick to say, 'how clumsy of me. But I think I've been stung and…' She made a play of gingerly patting at her neck. 'Though maybe not. Perhaps it was only a fly. How silly! Mind you, I do find flies very annoying.' She had gone into full scatterbrained mode now, but Jessica wasn't listening. She was looking in fury at the splashes on her wooden floor.

'Can I—?' Nancy began.

'No, you can't. I will get a cloth,' the woman rapped out.

As soon as she'd left the room, Nancy drew something out from behind her back and slipped it into her handbag.

'What the—' Archie was bewildered.

'I'll explain later,' she muttered. 'She's coming back.'

Jessica appeared in the room wielding a large mop that she was unlikely ever to have touched before.

'So sorry,' Nancy murmured again, and got to her feet. Archie, taking his cue, rose alongside. 'You've been most kind and thank you, but I think it's probably time we left.'

'That would be a good idea.' Jessica glared at them, before switching her attention back to her ravaged floor.

'We can find our own way out,' Nancy said airily, leaving the woman mopping ineptly at the polished wood.

She walked quickly through the archway and back into the wide hall, pausing for a split second at the ironwork console table. A letter, she noticed—just the one—and scanned the address as quickly as she could. A small bubble of excitement burst deep within, sending a mind that was already whirling into a frantic spin. Could she have read the name on the envelope correctly?

Archie followed her out of the house and back onto the lakeside path, neither of them speaking a word. They had walked a good way back in the direction of the beach, before he said, 'Are you going to tell me some time what that was all about?'

In answer, Nancy delved into her handbag. 'This was down the back of the sofa. I felt something digging into me and when I realised what it was, I knew it was time to go.'

Archie took her hands and spread them wide. He looked astonished at the object she was cradling. 'A child's shoe?'

'Not just a child's shoe. It's red and has a tee-bar. A little girl's shoe.'

Chapter Twenty-One

'Okay, it's a girl's shoe, but it doesn't necessarily belong to the child you're looking for,' Archie warned. 'You can't jump to conclusions—though knowing you, you will.'

'What other explanation is there? Jessica has no children of her own, that's plain.'

'She doesn't have to. She could have a niece who visits. Or a neighbour's child.'

Nancy looked bemused. 'Do you honestly believe the woman we've just left would ever entertain a child in that house? The mess, the damage to her prized possessions! You saw how she reacted when you spilt water. Believe me, no child has ever voluntarily crossed that threshold.'

'A child has evidently been there in some form or other, so they must have.'

'But not voluntarily. Bundled out of a car, maybe, half-drugged, and deposited for a short while on that sofa before being locked up somewhere else.'

Archie ran a finger around his shirt collar and puffed. 'This heat is punishing. Can we make for those trees again?'

Several minutes' walking brought them to the shade he craved, prompting him, it seemed, to continue the argument. 'Bundled out of a car? Drugged? Imprisoned? It's that imagination of yours. It's on one of its wild rampages.'

'Not so wild this time,' she protested. 'Admit that some of what I've said must be true.'

'I won't admit it. All you've discovered is a girl's shoe. And that's after we've had a very hot walk and a very uncomfortable few minutes in a house where we were clearly unwelcome. The rest is pure speculation. Your own brand of storytelling, Nancy.'

'Individually, the clues don't mean much, I agree, but put them together—'

'And you have a crazy conjecture,' he finished.

Intent on their dispute, they were not looking where they were going, and Archie almost cannoned into an oncoming figure in a bright blue tee-shirt, only veering out of the way at the last minute.

'Sorry,' he said to the newcomer. He mopped his forehead again. 'My fault.'

'No worry,' the young man said. 'It very hot?'

Archie gave a limp nod and was about to move on when the man put out a detaining hand.

'I know you,' he said to Nancy. 'I see you at Santa Cecilia.'

Nancy looked at him properly. It was the man who had been waiting at the street corner when she'd visited Ester, the young man who had been dancing so passionately with Jessica.

'I am Mateus. Mateus Cariba,' he introduced himself.

'Nancy Tremayne.' She held out her hand to him, feeling that somehow this meeting had been destined. 'And this is Archie Jago.'

Archie's face wore a determined blank. He wasn't going to help join those clues together, she thought.

Mateus was as handsome close up as he had been from a distance—smooth, brown skin, soft dark eyes and, when he smiled, the whitest of teeth. He was charming, too. Nancy

179

could see the attraction he held for Jessica. But the other way round? The woman was beautiful and no doubt rich... perhaps that was sufficient?

'You come to Leblon,' he remarked. 'Different from Santa Cecilia.'

'We were hoping to discover a little more of Rio. Do you live in the favella?' She felt a trifle nervous asking the question. In the days since she'd arrived in Rio, she'd learned that sensitivities around the favellas went beyond their poverty.

'I live in Santa Cecilia,' he agreed. 'A beautiful place.'

The remark had Nancy widen her eyes. The contrast with this enclave of wealth was extreme.

'Not like Leblon,' he said, understanding her hesitation. 'Much money.' He waved his hand randomly at the grand apartments they had been passing. 'But here—it empty. No *alma*, no *espírito*.'

'And the favella has spirit, has a soul?'

'Yes,' he said eagerly. 'The people make it so. Much important history. The *favelas* very old.'

'So my husband told me. At one time the only place, he said, that people without money could make a home.'

Mateus nodded vigorously. 'Portuguese bring many slaves to Brazil, then slavery go and free people nowhere to live. No work, no home. So *favela* grow. People come from countryside, too. Gather wood. Build houses where no one want to live.'

'I didn't see that many wooden houses in Santa Cecilia.'

'Not now. Not much. The houses become tin, brick. They spread wide.' He stretched out both arms to indicate the expanse the favellas now covered.

'It was certainly a very busy place,' she said. 'Plenty of shops—everything you'd want.'

'Plenty everything.' He grinned. 'People, big people, say

favelas bad places. Dirty, stupid people there. Much crime, much sickness. But not true. They try destroy us.' He leaned forward pugnaciously. 'But people fight back. Fight for good water, for shops, for schools, for doctors. And they go work for big people in Leblon, in Copacabana. Who else clean, wash clothes, do garden?'

Nancy would have liked to ask him whether it was work that had brought him to Leblon today, but she guessed that might force him to lie. Instead, she returned to Santa Cecilia. 'I enjoyed talking to Ester Barreto,' she said. 'Do you know her?'

'My mama know Ester. Very good *roupas*,' he said, pulling at his tee-shirt.

'So I believe. But so sad that her little girl is still missing.'

She watched his face carefully, but it was without guile when he replied, 'Very sad. We help Ester look but no good. We know that.'

'How do you know?' Nancy's senses sharpened.

'Ester not alone. Many missing in *favela*. Mama, papa, not see them again.'

'What do you think happened to them?'

Mateus moved closer, looking over his shoulder, before he said very quietly, 'Bad men take.'

'Why?' She pretended ignorance.

'Make *crianças* work. Earn money.'

'And no one reports it to the police?'

Mateus looked grave. 'Much danger—police no good.'

'Do any of the children ever come back?'

'Sometime.' He moved even closer. 'If they free, they hide. Or mama hide. But some no mama,' he whispered. 'They very afraid. People want help them, but too dangerous.'

'If they come back, do they say where they've been? Where they were made to live?' She was hoping at last to fit together at least a few pieces of this puzzle.

Mateus was silent, shrugging his shoulders as though he had no further interest. Nancy imagined him feeling that he'd said too much and was regretting it.

'I go now,' he muttered awkwardly.

'It's been very good to meet you,' Nancy said.

'Yes, very good.' It was the first time Archie had spoken and there was a wry note in his voice.

'Well, the wonder boy gave you something,' he remarked, when they had walked on and were once more passing the restaurants and clothes shops they'd seen earlier. 'It confirms your theory that children have been kidnapped and kept prisoner somewhere.'

'In a warehouse owned by Senhor Monaro! I won't say I told you so—although perhaps I will.' She gave a soft laugh, but then grew serious.

'How dreadful for those children, even if they manage to escape. And they must have done when the warehouse burnt down. It was why the fire service decided that no one had perished in the blaze. Those little ones must have been terrified—the fire, the burning building, then trying to find their way back to the city. And even if or when they made it back to Santa Cecilia, they'd be terrified of being captured again. Of having to spend their young lives in hiding.' She thought for a moment. 'It doesn't explain, though, why Livia is still missing.'

'You think she would have made her way back to her mother?'

'If other children have, why not her? Ester would be sure to hide her.'

'Perhaps she has. She could have come back any time since your visit.'

Nancy shook her head. 'Mateus was certain the child was

still missing. So where on earth is she?'

'Perhaps there are other warehouses, not just the one we know of. Other prisons. They might have shipped the kids there after the fire.'

'There could be, I suppose. Unless the gang didn't have time to organise one. The fire must have been sudden—a huge blaze to have destroyed so much. It happened the day Leo and I arrived in Brazil. The first evening we were here, we met Monaro at *Buffet Bonito*, and I'm convinced that he didn't know then that his property had been levelled.'

'And that's important?'

'Well, yes,' she continued excitedly. 'Diego Ramos came to the restaurant at the end of the evening. He'd drawn Monaro to one side when I saw them talking. It looked as though it was urgent. Afterwards, I assumed it had been about Vitoria. Ramos had had a monumental row with her a few hours earlier and I thought he was warning Monaro that the woman meant trouble. But he could equally have been telling Monaro that his warehouse had gone up in flames.'

'A double dose of bad news perhaps, but it still doesn't prove Monaro knew what his warehouse was being used for.'

'It doesn't prove he didn't either. Be honest, Archie, if you were renting out a huge space to a known gang of criminals, you'd have a pretty good inkling of what was going on there.'

Archie made no response, and she went on, 'There's a pattern here. I can feel it. If only I could put the pieces together to make the whole picture. Leandro Sousa is running a racket exploiting poor children in Santa Cecilia and probably other favellas, too. He rents a huge warehouse from Monaro—who he's already in league with—a good way out of Rio and keeps the children there under threat of violence to them or to their families. Trains them to become pickpockets, or his gang members do. Diego Ramos is somehow involved, though at the moment I'm not sure exactly how, but when Vitoria makes threats to expose who she thinks is responsible, he has to act. He goes to Monaro at *Buffet Bonito* and tells him she poses a danger and/or the warehouse has burned down. Monaro tells him to get rid of the woman and alert Sousa—we mustn't forget that he's in hock to the man. Sousa's henchmen will be sent out to find the children who have escaped.'

'Or something like that.'

'I know it's guesswork but that's how the pieces are falling. Ramos returns to the hotel after speaking to Monaro, telephones the housekeeper's office and, using a disguised voice, asks to speak to Vitoria. Then he lures her down to the cellar with a promise of information on Livia, strangles her and puts her into a barrel of wine.'

Nancy shuddered inwardly at the image of a drowned Vitoria. It was still vivid in her mind. She had never been able to lose it.

'Any bar staff going to the cellar would be there for a purpose and too busy to investigate a barrel with a lid slightly open,' she went on. 'There'd be no trace of Vitoria. No sign of a struggle, no smell, and when she didn't turn up for work that evening, the housekeeper would think she had simply left the job without saying anything. People do. It was only the fact that Francisco took us on a tour of the hotel early the next morning, that we found her. She could have been there for days otherwise.'

'It sounds plausible,' Archie agreed, at last. 'But if these children have escaped as you think, it doesn't explain what's happened to her niece.'

Nancy fiddled with a strand of hair that had come loose. 'And that's the problem. Or one of them.'

'Do you think you can trust wonder boy? He could be lying about Livia being missing still. He may know where she is.'

'Stop calling him wonder boy. And why would he lie? I do trust him. He has such an open face.'

'And such an engaging smile.'

'There are plenty of attractive men in the world,' she teased, 'but there are few I would trust.'

'But why was the bloke here, in this super rich enclave? If he lives in the favela, like he says, what's he doing in this posh place? He's evidently not working. He had no tools with him, no means of transport.'

'That's simple. He's here to see Jessica.'

'What!'

'It's obvious. He was hanging around waiting for her when I left Ester's. I told you.'

'But that's where he lives. Why wouldn't he be hanging around?'

'He was also dancing with Jessica, ' she continued inexorably. 'In one of the Carnival processions. I told you that, too.'

'Yeah, but—'

'No but, Archie. He's here to see her. And there's something more.'

'I don't want to hear it.'

'Maybe not, but you're going to. There was a letter on the hall table as we left, addressed to Jessica, and I managed a quick glance. I've been irritated that I had to keep calling her Jessica, not knowing her last name. Guess what it is?'

'Go on, surprise me.'

'It will surprise you. It's Ramos. Jessica Ramos.'

He groaned. 'I'd wager that Ramos is one of the most popular surnames in Brazil.'

Nancy nodded. 'I wouldn't take your bet. It probably is, but if she's married to Diego Ramos, that fits beautifully with what we know so far. It begins to explain his involvement—

he's Sousa's son-in-law.'

'It fits what you want it to. I'm pretty certain an under-manager doesn't earn the kind of dosh that could possibly afford a house here, even with a boss as generous as Francisco.'

'No, of course he doesn't. He doesn't have to. He's married to the daughter of the richest criminal in Rio. She's no need to depend on what a hotel manager earns—they're a couple who will never be short of money.'

Archie looked thoughtful. 'I'd forgotten who her father is. That argument we saw this morning between her and her father—do you think Sousa knows about the boyfriend?'

Nancy's eyes widened. It wasn't something that had occurred to her. 'He could do. This is a Catholic country and an extra-marital affair wouldn't easily be tolerated, particularly if Daddy is funding their lifestyle in Leblon and depending on Diego to do his bidding and keep his mouth shut. A restive son-in-law wouldn't be an asset.'

'It's always possible they quarrelled about something else entirely,' Archie said in a tired voice.

'But it fits.'

'It fits,' he agreed.

By the time they'd regained the promenade, neither of them could bear the thought of walking back to the Tivoli. The sun was directly overhead and shade almost non-existent. The beach from which they'd swam was far busier now and the promenade itself crowded, even more so eastwards towards Copacabana.

'Taxi?' Archie queried.

'Absolutely.'

Ten minutes later, they pushed through the hotel's glass doors and breathed in the cool air with a sigh of pleasure.

'A shower, I think,' Archie said, making for the lift.

The concierge had slid from behind his desk as soon as he

saw them arrive, and now bounced across the foyer as Archie had his finger on the lift button.

'Senhor Jago? I have a message for you.'

Archie frowned but took the piece of paper he was offered and scanned it quickly.

'Is anything wrong.' Nancy felt her face tense. The day's discoveries had brought new anxieties.

'I don't think so,' Archie said slowly. 'It's from Leo. He wants me at the hospital later this afternoon.'

'Only you?'

'That's what it says. Don't worry, he's probably getting agitated over his schedule. He'll want me to start making those phone calls. The ones you don't want me to make.'

'Try to stall him,' she said, as they got into the lift together.

'I'll do what I can.'

'I'll be along later —if you're still at the hospital. This is my floor.' She touched his arm as a goodbye, trying not to want more. 'Thanks for the trip.'

He caught hold of her as the lift door opened. 'Nancy—' he began.

But she shook her head, disentangling herself, and walked into the corridor.

Chapter Twenty-Two

She knew what Archie had wanted to say, but she couldn't let him. It would only hurt to put into words what was impossible. Three years ago, she had wed in good faith, making clear to Leo that she didn't love him in the way he deserved, but determined to make the marriage work. Her honesty hadn't deterred him. He'd accepted what she could offer and been keen to put a ring on her finger. That had been a mistake — for both of them — yet how could they have known how colossal the mistake would turn out to be? But having erred so badly once, she wouldn't compound her fault by committing another. Leo needed her, now more than ever; beside him is where she must stay.

The trip to Ipanema had proved once more, if she needed proof, how deeply happy she could be if only... but "if only" was how it must stay. The day had been challenging in all kinds of ways and a slide show of images was filling her mind: the beach, Leblon, Mateus Cariba, Jessica Ramos. Rummaging in her handbag, she brought out the small shoe she had recovered, turning it in her hand, noticing the scuffs, the creases, the spots where the polish hadn't quite reached, and felt immense sadness. Where was it's small owner? Had the child even survived? It was clear to Nancy that she must go to Santa Cecilia again. Speak to Ester, take the shoe. It was the least she could do.

Attempting to lift her spirits, she showered and changed and settled into the easy chair, picking up the book she'd brought from England. Gerald Durrell was an intriguing writer and these last few days she had neglected him shamefully. But try as she might, she could not concentrate. In the end, she gave up, tossing the book to one side and clambering onto the bed. It was as though a switch had been pressed. The moment she laid down on the smooth white counterpane, stretched her limbs and closed her eyes, she was instantly asleep.

It was the sound of a floor polisher immediately outside her door that woke her. Groggily, Nancy roused herself onto her elbow and looked at her watch in disbelief. She had slept for two whole hours.

She swung her legs off the bed, gradually coming back to life. The sleep had done her good, cleared her mind. There was something she had promised herself she'd do, and now was a good time—before she joined Archie at the hospital.

Opening her door, she called out to the maid who was wielding the machine energetically across the wooden floor.

The woman switched off the cleaner and looked as if she was about to apologise for the disturbance when Nancy asked, 'Are you Isabella, by any chance?'

The chambermaid shook her head, pointing down the corridor to her companion, busily packing bedlinen into a tall cupboard.

'That is Isabella? Thank you. *Obrigada.*'

The maid she'd been directed to was very young, just as Francisco had said. A sweet, gentle face looked up at Nancy when she asked, 'Isabella?'

'My name is Nancy,' she introduced herself. 'My room is 405, just along there.'

The maid looked confused and Nancy hurried on. 'When I first came to the hotel, Vitoria Dias was our chambermaid.'

Isabella was plainly having difficulty in following the English, but at the sound of Vitoria's name she nodded, her young face suddenly grave.

'Vitoria had a phone call.' Nancy mimed holding a telephone receiver.

Again, Isabella nodded.

'Who?' she asked. '*Quem*?'

Isabella replied as best she could. 'Not know,' she said.

'It was a man? *Um homem*?' She'd been careful to check the word in her dictionary beforehand.

'Not know,' the girl said again.

'But Vitoria was happy? *Feliz*?'

'*Sim, sim, muito animado.*'

Nancy flicked through the trusty dictionary. 'Very excited,' she translated. 'Why? *Porque*?'

'Not know.'

She felt defeated, but only for a moment. The dictionary was once more raided. '*Onde de estava o telefonema*?' she asked, feeling proud of herself. Where was the telephone?

'Senhora Rapoza. Housekeeper,' the girl said slowly.

'*Obrigada. Muito obrigada. Onde é, Senhora Rapoza*?'

'*Duas.*' Smiling, Isabella held up two fingers, and turned back to the laundry.

'The second floor. Thank you again.'

The housekeeper's office was tucked away at the end of a very long corridor on the second floor and not the easiest place to find, but Nancy was fortunate that the door was open and Senhora Rapoza at her desk.

'Good afternoon, Senhora,' she said from the doorway.

The housekeeper looked up, evidently surprised to see a hotel guest standing there.

'I can help you?' the woman enquired.

Nancy murmured a silent thanks that the senhora spoke English. Her Portuguese was improving but far too slowly to be of much use.

'I hope so. My name is Nancy Tremayne. I'm in room 405. When my husband and I first arrived, our chambermaid was a lady called Vitoria Dias.'

A shadow passed across the woman's face. 'She is not here now.'

'I know. I was with Senhor Silva when we found the poor lady. I believe she had a telephone call the night she went missing?'

'She did, but this I tell to the Inspector.'

'Yes, he mentioned it to me.' If she suggested that in some way she was a confidante of the policeman, she might get further, Nancy reasoned, walking a few paces into the office. 'But maybe there were questions he didn't ask. For instance, was it usual for members of staff to take phone calls?'

Senhora Rapoza adjusted her spectacles and looked severe. 'Not usual. Not at all, and Vitoria knows it is not allowed. I tell her this is not good, that I am not happy.'

'But you fetched her to come to the phone?'

'I think that I must. The call is urgent, this is what they say.'

'Who said?' Nancy felt she was dancing on spikes. She was so close.

'I do not know, Senhora Tremayne.'

The senhora's forehead developed a deep frown. Nancy could see the questions had unsettled her. She would be unused to being quizzed by the hotel's guests and particularly guests who had witnessed the shocking aftermath of a murder.

Nancy, though, was undeterred. 'Can I ask, was it a man's

voice that you heard?'

'Yes, a man's voice, but I do not know this person. The line is bad.'

Had the line been bad or had someone deliberately disguised their voice?

'Do you know what this man wanted?' she asked.

The housekeeper shook her head, irritation displacing her earlier unease. 'I call Vitoria to the office and I leave her here. I have work to do. There is a problem with room service in the top suite. When I come back, Vitoria has gone.'

The woman compressed her lips, looking pointedly at the doorway. It was plain she wanted her visitor gone, and Nancy made haste to leave. For the second time that day, she had outstayed her welcome, but she had also gained a greater understanding of what had happened to Vitoria on that fateful evening. Now she must discover what had happened to Vitoria's niece.

*

Once outside the Tivoli, Archie had to push through several groups of revellers, one flaunting top hats, bow ties and very little else, and the other a group of young men dressed as babies, complete with nappies and milk from an oversized bottle. Negotiating his way through a horde of arms, legs, drinks and musical instruments, he cursed that he hadn't taken a cab to the hospital. The sooner this damn party was over, the better.

More negotiating lay ahead, persuading Leo to backpedal on the commitments he'd agreed for the next few months. It wouldn't be easy. And nor would this business with the child's shoe. Nancy would be fizzing now, eager to follow the trail wherever it led, uncaring of any danger. When she was on a rampage to find the truth, she was like the terrier he'd told her about, his old Jack Russell, hanging on for dear life to whatever he got his teeth into.

She had a profound sense of justice, that was the problem. It was what drove her and, with so much injustice in the world, it was no wonder she had a genius for nosing it out. But there was more to it than that, Archie was sure. A frustration with her life, a lack of fulfilment that she needed to assuage, even though the apprenticeship had gone a long way to filling the void—once Leo had stopped jibbing at her need to work. Nancy had a love for painting that went way beyond his own simple enjoyment. A deep, abiding love. She didn't talk of it much, but Archie guessed that when she was working on those delicate masterpieces, she lost herself, transported into a different world.

The doctors were with Leo when he arrived at the hospital and he was forced to spend time idling in the corridor.

'I've just been told I'm to be discharged tomorrow,' Leo called to him, when he saw his assistant hovering in the doorway. 'It won't be till late in the afternoon—after the docs have done one last check.'

'Great news. At least, you'll get one night's sleep in the hotel. We're due to leave on Saturday, if that suits—I picked up the plane tickets yesterday.'

'Good, good,' Leo said absently. 'It's time I was out of this place.' His face hardened. 'More than time. Nancy appears to be out of control.'

Archie looked at him, astonished.

'What! You don't think I hear anything in here? She's been creating havoc by all accounts, and you've let her.'

What the hell was this? He felt himself bristle, but tried to keep his voice even. 'I don't know what you've heard, Leo, but I haven't witnessed any havoc. And as for responsibility, I'm not Nancy's minder.'

'No, you're not her minder.' Leo paused on the word, giving it unnecessary emphasis. 'But I thought I could trust you to keep her in check until I got out of here.'

Archie tried to still a rising annoyance. Leo was speaking as though Nancy were a wayward child and he her jailer. He walked over to the chair and sat down by the bedside.

'Why don't you tell me what you've heard?' he asked, trying for a calm voice.

'I've had Francisco visit. He came to see me out of kindness, wanting to know how I was feeling, when I'd be discharged, but he had more to say than that. He told me how dismayed he'd been that Nancy is dabbling in something she shouldn't.' Leo paused, before adding sourly, 'Not for the first time. She makes a habit of it.'

'Dabbling sounds pretty vague.' Archie was still in control of his temper, but only just.

'Apparently, she's been interfering in the investigation into that chambermaid's death. Haranguing the inspector in charge. Trying to insinuate herself into something that has nothing to do with her and, incidentally, according to Francisco, putting herself in danger. But then doesn't she always do that?'

'I believe she spoke to Inspector Alvarez. I wasn't there, but I doubt she harangued him. Francisco is guilty of exaggeration. But then perhaps he's not used to women who have minds of their own.'

'So you condone what she's doing? And you're helping her? I've suspected it before—in Venice, in Malfuego.'

Archie jumped up and walked to the window and back, his limbs stiff with a hidden anger. 'And in Cornwall. Don't forget that,' he said tartly. 'If I remember rightly, it was the fact that I was there to "help" her, that saved Nancy's life.'

Leo fidgeted irritably with his pillows. 'You wouldn't

have had to save her life, if she hadn't been poking around in something that was nothing to do with her.'

'Surely, you can't believe that? When both your father and your brother nearly died. Nancy got to the bottom of the business. If it wasn't for her, you'd have little of your family left. You've a short memory, Leo.'

'For some things, I've a long memory, believe me.' His boss's mouth tightened ominously. 'I'm not as strong as I once was, I'm very aware of it, but I can still pick up what's been going on. Realise the trouble she's getting into. And put a stop to it.'

'Then I wish you good luck,' Archie said, annoyingly casual.

Leo struggled to sit upright, his face flushed and his mouth now a thin line. 'Nancy has no boundaries,' he said furiously. 'She throws herself into danger without thought for anyone else. That's bad enough, but you, my assistant, someone supposedly working for me—you've been her partner.'

All the anger, the hurt, the sheer unhappiness of their mutual situation, was contained in that last phrase.

'I shouldn't even be here,' Archie replied quietly. 'I should be in London. It was you who insisted I come to Brazil.'

'Only because I thought I might die in this place.'

'Fortunately you didn't and, as it turned out, my journey was wasted.'

Leo turned his head away, refusing to speak. They sat in silence, until Archie looked at his watch and decided he'd had enough. 'I think it's time I left,' he said. 'Unless there's something you wanted to talk to me about. Other than Nancy, that is. Work, for instance.'

'I'm tired.' Leo laid back against the pillows, the face that was flushed a minute ago now drained of all colour.

For a moment, compassion overcame Archie's anger.

'Then get some sleep and I'll see you tomorrow—back at the hotel.' This would be his last visit to the hospital, he vowed. Let Nancy come and be the dutiful wife.

Leo raised a weary hand in goodbye and closed his eyes.

Outside on the pavement, Archie was nearly swept off his feet by a cavalcade of long-limbed girls dressed as Chinese peasants, except that Chinese peasants had never in their lives worn anything as skimpy. He pushed through their singing and dancing and headed towards the hotel. As he walked, the anger he'd managed to suppress erupted in full, shaking him with its ferocity. How dare the man accuse him of not looking after Nancy? It was the one thing he'd tried to do from the moment he'd become enmeshed with her in Venice. He'd been there for her every step of the way. And why should he have been? She wasn't his wife. She was simply the woman he loved. And couldn't have. Ever.

He would leave this job. He had to. He'd thought about it after Cornwall, after that evening with her on the beach, and then chickened out. Getting another job that paid half as well and was half as interesting was impossible and he'd settled instead for moving out of Cavendish Street, finding his own place. It had worked okay. Nancy had been busy at the studio and he'd hardly ever seen her when he went to the house. On the few occasions they'd met, their conversation had been trivial, both trying, he supposed, to forget what had happened. Some hope. Those kisses a few hours ago showed how forlorn that hope was. They were both still living a lie.

He gave a heavy sigh, inaudible amid the din of surrounding music. Was there ever a rhythm so at odds with his present mood? It wasn't enough to change where he lived. He knew that now. He'd have to change his life completely. Find another job, accept he'd be paid less, or if there was nothing in London, go back to Cornwall. He could always take Ma's old job gutting fish, he thought wryly. Anything had to be better than this. His feelings for Nancy were killing him. And killing Leo, too, by the look of it.

In a mad moment, Archie had once asked her to leave, to throw her future to the winds and be with him. She couldn't do it. Not that she was scared of penury—she'd known plenty—but that she owed her husband too much. That was how she thought. And now Leo was a sick man, she would stay by his side. In any case, what could he offer her? He had no money, would soon be unemployed and most likely homeless.

He was half way back to the Tivoli when he met her in the street, weaving her way round a man dressed in a polka dot tutu. She looked up suddenly and noticed him. Her smile made his heart tighten.

'I thought I'd find you still with Leo,' she said, arriving breathless at his side.

'My visit was short and sharp.'

'Did you fall out?' she asked anxiously. 'Did he insist you make those telephone calls?'

'We didn't get round to talking about work.'

Nancy's face shadowed. 'What happened? Something has.'

'Francisco has been telling tales apparently. Telling Leo you've been interesting yourself too much in the Vitoria investigation and putting yourself in danger. As for me, I've been lacking in my duty. I was supposed to have stopped you, but instead I've encouraged your foolhardiness.'

'How unfair!'

'Of course, it's unfair, but the bloke's angry. At you, at me, at the fact that he's a sick man.'

Nancy looked at the ground, shuffling her open-toed sandals in the sand that had found its way up from the beach. 'Did you tell him we're going home on Saturday?'

'I told him,' Archie said wearily. He gazed into the distance, unseeing of the crowds, the floats, the rolling seas beyond, thinking of the life that lay ahead of him.

There was a long silence, both of them standing motionless and buffeted by the constantly moiling crowd.

'I can't do this any longer,' he said at last.

'What do you mean?'

'You know what I mean. This situation… this torture. I can't do it.'

She said nothing for a while, but he saw her face pale beneath the tan. He wouldn't weaken, though. He'd made the decision and, once back in London, he'd see it through.

'Leo is being discharged late tomorrow,' he told her. 'You better be around when he gets back.' He knew he sounded surly, but he couldn't help it. It was how he felt.

'Don't worry, I'll go to the hospital and collect him,' she responded, her chin raised. She had been hurt by his words, Archie knew.

'First, though,' she continued, 'I'm going back to Santa Cecilia.'

'You can't.' He put out his hand as if to stop her. 'It's too dangerous. And I'm supposed to be your keeper.'

'You're not. No one is. And I have to go. I have to take that shoe and give it to Ester.'

'How is she going to feel if it is her daughter's? Have you thought of that?'

'Of course I have. It will cause her great pain, I know. But if it is Livia's, I can tell Inspector Alvarez where I found it and get him to search Jessica's house. That's something I can't do, and the police won't—unless I take them irrefutable evidence that the child has been there. The shoe is that evidence.'

'And what if Sousa and his merry men turn up while you're at the favella?'

'If it happens, I'll have to deal with it.' She paused and took hold of his hand. 'Archie, I have to do it. I owe it to Ester. Whether you come with me or not is your choice.'

Chapter Twenty-Three

Nancy woke the next day, her limbs heavy and ungainly and her stomach tight with tension. Yesterday, when she'd left Archie in the street, she'd braced herself for an uncomfortable hour at the hospital. Her inability to steer clear of trouble infuriated Leo and always had done, and whether he believed Francisco's version of events or not, her husband must be angry that once more she had put herself in danger. But her visit had passed off without incident, Leo saying nothing of his conversation with his assistant, nor taking her to task himself.

Later no doubt there would be a reckoning, but this morning it was Archie causing her distress. His sudden outburst was lodged deep in Nancy's mind. He was leaving, that's what it amounted to. Leaving—the phrase drummed in her head, its noise louder by the minute. He'd already left the house in Cavendish Street and now, when they returned to London, he'd relinquish the job with Leo, the only link that remained between them. He hadn't said it in so many words, but it was evident that's what he intended. It was a final severance.

In her heart, she knew he was right—the situation *was* torture. They had tried to pretend, to keep their distance, to fudge feelings, but it hadn't worked and it never would.

Nancy had no idea how she had come to love this man so deeply. Nothing could have prepared her for it at their first meeting. Archie had been hostile, bristling, confrontational. And yet... there had been something in that very first handshake, though she'd been too naïve to recognise it. He had been the sensible one. He'd known from the start that she was danger.

It was desperately unfair on him. Any time these last few years, he could have met and married someone who could have made him happy. He was a single man and free to love, but she wasn't. Yet she had a choice—there were always choices. She could leave this marriage or she could forget the one man she'd ever truly loved. Or try to. But really there wasn't a choice, was there?

Leo had been her saviour, rescuing her from Philip March's persecution, providing a safe harbour in a sea of increasing violence. And since their marriage, he had been a good husband. Irascible at times, demanding, too, but always honest and generous. And most always loving, she reminded herself, feeling guilt consume her as it so often did.

She wished she could have talked things over with Rose. Her friend had no idea of the maelstrom of feelings Nancy had learnt to suppress. Whenever Archie's name had come up in conversation, it had been as Leo's assistant and nothing more. She would go to see Rose, she decided, when they returned to England. Her friend had spoken of moving house—out of the city to a quieter life by the sea. Dorset, perhaps. It would be good to visit, to talk, to share a little of this pain. Rose would listen to her without offering advice. Advice was something Nancy didn't need—she knew very well what she had to do. Now Leo was ill, he needed her more than ever.

She could go the favella, though. It was early still and, if she left before breakfast, she'd be back well in time to bring

Leo home from the hospital. He need never know of this last adventure. It felt scary to be going to Santa Cecilia alone, knowing what she did now, but still not knowing what had happened to the missing children. What might still be happening. Mateus Cariba had sounded nervous even talking of them. He'd been vague about the abductions, speaking about "bad men" when he must have known who those men were and who was their boss. How did the young man square his passion for Jessica Ramos, Nancy wondered, knowing how much blood was on her father's hands? But then passion was inexplicable.

Scared or not, she would take the shoe to Ester this morning and if, as she believed, it belonged to the little girl, she would seek out Inspector Alvarez and insist he search the Leblon house. It made for a packed few hours before she was due at the hospital, but she dressed in record time, arriving in the foyer just as the doorman was donning his top hat for the day.

'Carnival over, madam,' he said.

She smiled at him. 'Then I should be able to hear myself think again!'

Walking out of the hotel into a steaming city, she stood on the front steps and glanced along the street, looking for a cab.

'Taxi, madam?'

Archie was at the bottom of the steps, pointing to a vehicle at the kerbside a little way along the Avenida Atlantica.

'You're coming with me?' She felt a lightness in her chest.

'I'm your keeper, remember.'

'Stop using that horrible word! But thank you.' She clung briefly to his arm before he hurried her to the waiting taxi.

'We need to be to be careful,' he said in a low voice, as the car wound through the Copacabana streets on their way to Santa Cecilia.

'You think Sousa's men will be at the favella?'

'I think it's highly likely. Don't forget, that some of the children who escaped from the warehouse could have returned to Santa Cecilia. The gang will be looking for them, and we've no idea if or how many they've found.'

'Looking for them so they can drag them back into captivity,' she said bitterly.

Archie's face became expressionless. 'What?' she asked.

'Children can tell tales,' he said abruptly. 'They're witnesses if ever the police decide to investigate. The gang might think it safer to silence them.'

Nancy's hands flew to her face, pressing her palms into her cheeks. 'You can't think...'

'Not for certain, but these blokes are ruthless.'

'But the children could tell tales at any time, couldn't they?' she asked, seeking what reassurance she could. 'If they were recaptured and sent out to steal, they could speak of it years later. Tell the authorities what had happened to them and who was responsible. It must be a risk that the gang has always taken.'

'They could also be silenced at any time during those years. In any case, how likely are they to squeal as time goes by? If the gang rounds them up and keeps them imprisoned, every one of them will grow up a criminal. The boys, if there are any, will become gang members for certain and the girls prostitutes. The longer the children are allowed to live, the less likely they are to tell anyone in authority—if there is anyone interested in justice. It's at the age they are now, I reckon, that they're most dangerous for Sousa and his goons if they've manage to free themselves. An age when they could talk without realising what they're saying.'

Nancy felt her fists curl at the thought that, after all these children had suffered, their lives could still be forfeit, and forced herself to concentrate on what she must do once they reached Santa Cecilia.

As soon as she stepped out of the cab, though, at the spot she'd been dropped before, she was filled with foreboding. Turning her head, she saw the vehicle speed away and had to take a deep breath. Whether it was Archie's words or whether the atmosphere in the favella had changed since her last visit, she wasn't sure. The sun burnt down as brightly as ever, but there seemed a darker feel to the place. Imagination perhaps, but as they made their way uphill along the main street, she saw the shops that had once been busy now had their doors closed and the few people they saw looked away as she and Archie passed. The usual cheerful Carioca greeting was horribly absent. Even the dogs had gone to ground.

They climbed a good way up the main street before branching off into one of the alleyways that Nancy remembered she had taken previously.

'I think if we go this way—' she began to say, when Archie dragged her back into the shadow of one of the few two storey buildings. He gave her arm a sharp squeeze and she knew she must keep quiet. The sound of boots on gravel rang out clearly and in a matter of seconds two men, balaclavas covering their faces and guns slung across their chests, sauntered casually past, along the lane they'd been following.

She stood beside Archie, knees locked and her elbows pressing into her sides, making her body as small as possible. It was several minutes before either of them spoke.

'Our men in black,' he said very quietly. 'On patrol. Is there any way of getting to the house other than along this lane?'

'There must be, but the place is a maze. I got thoroughly lost the first time I came and I can barely remember the way I took. Anything else will be beyond me. Perhaps if we choose another alleyway but keep climbing, I'll recognise Ester's turning. Or even her house. It's painted bright yellow.'

'So are a fair number.'

'We'll find it,' she said with determination, 'but those men—'

'Looking for children who managed to escape?'

She had known that in her heart, but it was too painful to believe. 'How dreadful!' There was a break in her voice. 'It's like a… like a horror film.'

'Horror film or not, I reckon that's what they're here for. It's possible they might be on the look out for other children, new recruits, but the kids that have been in Monaro's warehouse are dynamite.'

Nancy's frown was deep. 'I understand why you think the children are a danger to the gang, but there must have been others who have escaped before. I can't believe that no child ever found their way out of that place. So do those men always come here, always hunt them down?'

'Probably not. An individual child wouldn't be too much of a problem. Say one girl goes missing and eventually finds her way home—though it wouldn't be easy for a small child when you think how far from the city that warehouse is. But let's just assume she reaches home and relates what's happened to her. Her mother will believe her, one or two neighbours will, particularly if they've lost a child themselves or know someone who has. But what will the authorities say if any of them report what the child has told them? I can tell you. The girl is delirious. She's been naughty, run away, and this is her excuse for bad behaviour. Such things don't happen in real life. And so on. You have only to think of the inspector's attitude to Livia Barreto to know what the official response would be.'

'But if a whole group of them return home…' Nancy said slowly.

'Exactly. The authorities couldn't ignore that number, all of them relating the same story. I reckon there must have been at least twenty beds in that wretched place. If only half those girls reach home and tell the same tale, the police would have to take notice.'

'I can't hear their boots any more.' She leant cautiously out of the shadow. 'Shall we go?'

Heart in mouth, she walked back into the lane, with Archie following. Their progress was creeping, all the time needing to check behind, ahead, to the side, in case the men had circled round and were once again close. She was aiming for what she thought must be Ester's general direction, passing from one small alley to another, but always walking uphill and to the left of where the taxi had dropped them. It took them several wrong turnings and various cul-de-sacs, before Nancy thought she recognised the lane she had walked along before.

She took a few tentative steps and, in the distance, saw with relief walls of bright yellow.

'It's down here,' she said over her shoulder, thankful to have found the house. Her body was still stiff with fear. The men with guns were nowhere in sight, but she had a strong sense they were being watched from behind curtained windows.

'We'd better get inside quickly,' Archie said, catching her up.

When the front door opened, though, and Ester stood on the threshold, there was no welcoming smile, the woman holding up her hand as though to bar them from entering.

'You go,' she ordered.

'We will, but first I need to speak to you,' Nancy said.

'No. You go,' Ester insisted. 'Much danger.'

'We won't stay, I promise. Here, I have something to

show you.'

Highly agitated, the woman caught hold of Nancy's arm and pulled her bodily into the house. Archie was only just able to follow before the front door was slammed behind him.

'Bad men?' Nancy queried, since this was the phrase that for most people seemed to sum up the gang.

Ester nodded. 'Vitoria...' she mumbled, and looked away.

'Your poor sister.' Nancy took her hand and held it tight. 'I am so sorry.'

'Now children come home and men search. But you sit, please.'

The small, shabby room looked exactly the same as on Nancy's previous visit, the sewing machine still in use and the table piled high with a heap of braiding and lace and rolls of material. The macaw was still there, cocking his head on one side and piercing her with his eye, then banging his beak against the cage. What was different then? There was a difference, Nancy could feel it—a deeper sadness perhaps, if that was possible.

'Did the men search here?'

Ester nodded.

'But Livia hasn't come back?'

'No Livia.' Ester brushed her hand against her eyes. 'No Livia,' she repeated.

'I need to ask you a question. I'm sorry but...'

The woman looked bewildered and Archie muttered, 'You can't sugar coat it even if you could speak Portuguese.'

Nancy delved into her handbag once more and drew out the shoe. At the sight of it, Ester gasped and, snatching it from Nancy's hands, held it to her heart. It was plain that it was Livia's.

Their hostess began rocking herself backwards and forwards, clutching the shoe and murmuring broken words beneath her breath. Nancy waited until the storm had passed, allowing Ester to speak first.

'How you get it?' their hostess stuttered.

'I found it—'

'*Onde*? Where?' Ester interrupted.

'In Leblon. In Jessica's house.'

The woman's face was a picture of confusion. 'Jessica?' she asked, her voice faint. 'Jessica?' She sank down into one of the battered chairs.

'She *is* the daughter of Leandro Sousa,' Nancy reminded her. 'You must know what kind of man he is.'

It was unclear whether Ester had understood any of Nancy's words. Shaking her head and muttering, she was talking to herself. 'But she good girl. She good girl.'

'Maybe she is.' Nancy had the dictionary in her hand. *Jessica não sabe?* Maybe she doesn't know about Livia being taken by the gang.'

Ester was silent for a while, obviously trying absorb what she'd been told. Then she asked, 'Monaro? Where he?'

'I don't know what his connection is, but I think he is a guilty man. *Culpado*.'

Ester nodded. 'Money,' she said succinctly, rubbing her thumb and forefinger together.

'I'm sure you're right. Just one question before we go. Is Jessica married to Diego Ramos?'

'*Sim*. Big man in hotel.'

Nancy tried not to feel triumphant. It was hardly the place or time to celebrate being right. 'I found Livia's shoe and now I will find Livia, I promise.' She got to her feet, holding out her hand again

She had been hoping to take the shoe back with her—it would certainly have helped her case with Alvarez—but she could see it would hurt this poor woman too much to have it wrested away. All Nancy could do was tell her tale to the inspector and hope he would check for himself.

How much Ester understood still wasn't clear, but she grasped Nancy's hand and shook it firmly. 'You go now. Not safe.'

'Definitely not safe,' Archie remarked, as they walked from the house and turned back down the hill.

They had taken only a few steps along the road, when they heard footsteps behind. Fearing the worst, Nancy turned to face what was coming. But it was Ester who had followed them.

'You take.' She pushed the shoe into Nancy's hand. 'You make trouble. And Monaro, Sousa. You no worry... I make sure they go.' And then she was gone herself, hurrying back to the small yellow house.

They stood for a while, too surprised to begin walking.

'How is she going to make them go?' Archie asked at last. He sounded incredulous.

'I'm not sure,' she said slowly. 'I noticed what looked like a small shrine in Ester's sitting room—a candle that had been snuffed out and a posy of flowers. She must follow one of the native religions. I wonder... did she mean she'd get rid of them with a prayer? Or a curse?'

'Are curses part of the ritual? If so, let's believe they work.'

'Leo told me about Umbunda. He didn't mention curses, though. But I guess stranger things have happened.'

Chapter Twenty-Four

It was only when they became aware of several pairs of eyes watching them from behind the curtained windows that they started back on the downhill journey.

'We'd better follow the same route back.' Archie's voice was uneasy. 'It winds about and will take longer but it should save us from meeting any of Sousa's goons.'

'And if it doesn't?'

'Then we're in very big trouble. I told you this trip would be dangerous.'

'Maybe, but it's been worth the risk. I know for sure now that the shoe belongs to Livia. It means Alvarez will have to investigate. He might even find her.'

'Always assuming that we get out of this place alive! And assuming you can run your awkward policeman to ground and convince him it's worth his while to search the Leblon house.'

'I can be very persuasive.' There was a sparkle in Nancy's eyes.

Halfway down the hill, she stopped to take her bearings, unsure which of the intersecting alleyways they should take. In that split second of indecision, she sensed rather than saw a movement to the left of her. Peering down a passage that was so narrow it was hardly a foot wide and ended in a wall of brick, all she could see was a collection of rusty iron drums.

'There's somebody there,' she said to Archie. 'I saw a movement.'

'A rat most likely.'

'I don't think so.' She walked cautiously into the passage, her heartbeat banging in her ears. Stopping at the jumble of empty barrels, she looked down and saw a terrified pair of eyes.

'Hello,' she said. 'I'm sorry we scared you.'

The eyes continued to stare. 'Are you playing a game?' Nancy delved into her handbag for the well-thumbed dictionary. '*Um jogo?*'

The child shook her head.

'But you're hiding from someone?' she said gently. '*Se escondendo?*'

This time the little girl nodded.

'My name is Nancy. What is yours?'

'Tristessa,' the child answered, coming to her feet. She must have learned a little English at school.

'Do you know Livia Barreto?'

At the mention of Livia's name, the girl looked even more scared and bobbed back into her hiding place.

'I know Livia's mama,' Nancy said soothingly. 'Here—I have a photograph .' This time she pulled from her handbag the photo that Ester had given her days ago. 'You know her?' she asked.

Tristessa nodded.

'Do you know where she is? Her mama is very sad. *Mama muito triste.*'

There was no answer and Nancy tried again. 'I think she may have been in a fire. *Em um incêndio?*' At that, the child shook her head.

'But you were?' Nancy asked softly. 'You were locked up.

Um prisioneiro?'

The girl's eyes began to fill with tears.

'You poor child,' Nancy said. 'For how long?' She flicked through the phrases at the back of her dictionary. '*Quanto tempo?*'

'*Muito tempo mas então um fogo ruim.*'

'Try that one,' Archie muttered.

'Bad fire,' the girl said slowly.

'You were there until the fire. *Muito assustador*. Very frightening. Livia was in the fire?'

Tristessa shook her head again.

'*Certa?* You're certain?'

'*Sim, sim.*'

Nancy stroked the little girl's head. 'You should go home. Home to mama.'

Tristessa half closed her eyes. '*Morta,*' she said. 'Dead.'

The child bore a fitting name, Nancy thought, wanting to scoop the poor mite up in her arms. Then felt Archie gripping her hand none too gently.

'We need to go,' he said. 'The longer we stand here, the more danger there is for the child.'

'Thank you, Tristessa. I hope… ' But what Nancy hoped she was never able to say. The child had disappeared from sight.

A crunch of gravel had them both turn their heads. A figure was filling the square of light at the end of the passage, essentially blocking any escape. Nancy peered at what seemed to be the figure of a man. It was difficult to make out details with bright light immediately behind him and deep shadow in front. For a moment, she assumed it was one of the men with guns, attracted here by the murmur of voices and waited for the worst to happen. But when her vision cleared and her eyes focussed, she saw exactly who it was. Alvar Monaro.

'Senhora Tremayne?' he said, his voice expressing a false surprise. 'You here? But why?'

Archie still had hold of her hand and she squeezed it for courage. 'How nice to see you, Senhor. I'm here as a tourist, plain and simple. I wanted very much to see a different face to the city and I'd read about the favellas. Nobody seems to visit, though, so I thought I'd be different. But how about you, Senhor Monaro,' she asked, walking towards him. 'I'm fairly sure that Santa Cecilia is not your home.'

She saw a smirk grow on his face. 'I am mayor, Senhora Tremayne. These are my people and I must come. But this not a good place.' He cast a pained glance at the rows of shacks marching downhill in crazy companionship, one on top of the other. 'Not good for you,' he added in a different voice.

It was plainly a threat. Those armed men must be very near, around the corner even, waiting to do this man's bidding.

'I'd forgotten that you are mayor for this district as well as for more affluent areas,' she said sweetly. 'How good that you take such an interest.'

She was hoping to keep him talking, distract him from summoning the black-clothed men to his side. Once they arrived, there was no hope of escape. She felt Archie give her a sharp nudge and knew he was planning to make a bolt for it. But Monaro's stocky figure filled the entire width of the passage and there was no way they'd break free without a scuffle. And any sudden noise could bring terror to them.

Monaro gave a tight little smile. 'I do good things for people here, yes, but now I must go. You come, too, and your... your bodyguard.' He meant Archie, she realised. 'Santa Cecilia not safe and I have my car below.'

'We need to get away from this bloke,' Archie said in her ear. 'And quick.'

Nancy sidled towards their gaoler, flattening herself against the passage wall, trying to become as thin as she could. She had a mad idea that she might just be able to ease her way past Monaro, and when he turned to grab her, Archie would have the chance to escape. 'That's very kind,' she said. 'But we also have a car waiting. Senhor Silva is meeting us at the bottom of the hill.'

It was a pretty good lie on the spur of the moment, she thought, and saw Monaro hesitate. Just as she'd decided to seize the moment, though, the chinking of boots came clearly on the air. Monaro's eyes narrowed, as though he were weighing up his options. Kidnap them and dispose of them later or kill them right here and now. Whatever his intention, it wasn't good.

They had to act. She could feel Archie close behind and somehow, reading each other's minds, they threw themselves simultaneously at Monaro's squat figure, toppling him off balance and squirming through the small space that had opened up. Running at full tilt down the hill, zigzagging their way from alley to alley, they arrived back at their starting point, bent almost double and hardly able to breathe.

'We can't stay here,' Archie panted. 'That louse could follow us and his nasty friends with him. We need to make for the city centre. Cross your fingers that a taxi comes by.'

A few minutes later, they were in luck. With huge relief, they hailed the cab and fell onto its rear seat, still holding hands.

'I could kill you, Nancy,' Archie said, releasing her at last.

'Don't! We escaped, didn't we? And we've gained important proof. Of Monaro's guilt, for one thing. He couldn't have been in Santa Cecilia for any other reason than to help those dreadful men in their search. *And* we have a clue now to Livia's whereabouts.'

'We do? How exactly?'

'If that little girl, Tristessa, is right, Livia Barreto wasn't kept at the warehouse with the other children.'

'She said not, I grant you, but she was very scared. She could be confused.'

'It's the timing that makes me think the girl was right. Tristessa seemed to think she'd been a prisoner for a long time. She said *muito tempo*. I know a child's understanding of time is different, but Livia was taken—how long before the warehouse burnt down? A few days at most? It would explain why Tristessa never saw Livia at the warehouse. What if when children are first taken, they're hidden somewhere before being driven out of the city? What if it's Diego Ramos who hides them? Houses them until the gang pick them up for the warehouse. That house in Leblon would be a perfect choice. It's an expensive area and the neighbours would be unlikely to suspect anything wrong. We mustn't forget the house Ramos lives in is paid for by his father-in-law—a man who is up to his neck in this business. *And*—I've just had a thought—it helps to explain even more why you saw Ramos talking to one of the gang in the street. They had business to transact.'

'Great theory, but don't get too excited. Why wouldn't the gang drive any children they nabbed directly to the warehouse? It would be much simpler.'

'Because realistically they could only grab one child at a time, and to drive children out to that warehouse one by one would be a waste of time. Think of all the journeys it would take. This is a business. Time is money and they could be extorting it in some other horrible way. I'd bet anything that the house in Leblon is a collection point. When there are sufficient children to make the trip to the warehouse worth the money, the gang pick them up from Leblon. Livia never made it to the warehouse—it caught fire before they could take her there. You know what that means?'

'She could still be in the house,' Archie said heavily. 'And you could still be wrong.'

The taxi swerved to a stop outside the Tivoli, but Nancy hardly noticed. She was thinking hard and her thoughts were not pleasant. 'Imagine if Livia was in that house when we knocked on the door. We actually sat in the drawing room, drank water and talked about nothing, while she was there all the time. We didn't rescue her!'

'*If* she was there. Did you see any sign of a child because I didn't? All you have to suggest that Livia was ever under that roof is a shoe.'

'The cellar,' Nancy announced elatedly. 'There's bound to be a cellar. She could be there.'

'Or an attic? Or a bunker in the garden?'

'Don't be facetious. This is a child's life we're discussing.'

He looked suddenly serious. 'Or a child's death, Nancy. You need to think that the worst might happen. These blokes mean business.'

She glanced at him, sick with fear. 'We have to go to Leblon. Break into that house.'

'*We* don't have to go anywhere. Get the concierge to ring the police station and ask for Alvarez to call on you—show him the shoe, then send him off to storm the barricades.'

Chapter Twenty-Five

'Alvarez won't be storming anything if I can't find him.' She sounded downbeat. 'He's been drifting in and out of the hotel, but where does he hide most of the time?'

'I told you, ask the concierge. He'll know where the man is based. Ask him to phone for you.'

'You think the inspector will take notice of a concierge?'

'Then speak to him yourself. Sound urgent. Say you have crucial evidence.'

'If I do, it will probably ensure I never see him again.' Her voice held a note of dejection. 'From what Francisco said, it's plain Alvarez considers me a busybody he'll do anything to avoid.'

'You can only try.'

'I'll have to do more than try.'

Holding the door of the taxi open for her, Archie tried not to sigh too loudly. He knew the look on Nancy's face. It meant that nothing was going to stop her, even if she had to raid the Leblon house single-handedly.

The minute they stepped into the foyer, though, the immediate problem faded from his mind. It was plain that something unusual, even desperate, had happened. The concierge had deserted his post, the receptionist had three telephones ringing simultaneously and there were people everywhere, most of them talking at the tops of their voices. Clustered around the flight of stairs that led to the basement was a group of uniformed police.

Archie caught the sleeve of a passing waiter. 'What's going on?'

'Bad trouble, sir. You must leave please. You must go to your room.'

Nancy caught at his words. 'What trouble and why are the police here?' she asked him.

The waiter looked at her sorrowfully. 'There has been a death, Senhora. All guests must go to their rooms. The inspector will speak with you later if he needs.'

'Inspector Alvarez?'

'Yes, Senhora.'

'Excellent. He's just the man I want to see. Thank you.' Nancy beamed at the man.

'But Senhora—,' the waiter began.

'Leave it,' Archie advised. 'I'll make sure she gets to her room.'

Nancy turned to him, looking amused. 'Really?'

'No, not really. I refuse to be your minder. I was simply getting him off your back.'

'The trouble seems to be down there.' She pointed to the stairs. 'The cellars again.'

'Another drowning in a barrel of malmsey? Whatever that was.'

Before Nancy could reply, she was pushed aside by another guest, talking angrily to her husband. 'It's a disgrace, Hank. Tonight's gonna be ruined if we can't get to pick up our car. Why is this guy keeping us? We weren't even in the hotel when it happened, let alone the car park'

Archie's eyebrows rose. 'Not the cellars then,' he said quietly. 'The car park.'

'The stairs must lead to the car park as well as down to the cellars. And we can't get there.' She glanced across at the gathering of policemen. 'How annoying.'

'You could be wrong there.' It was Archie's turn to feel triumphant. 'You might not know, but you can get to the car park from the back of the building. I took a wrong turning the first day I arrived and walked right past it.'

Her face broke into a wide smile. 'So what are we waiting for? We could take a look at least.'

Together, they slid out of the glass doors, careful to avoid the several waiters who were busy shepherding guests into the lifts.

'We need to turn right, and then right again.' Archie said, walking ahead. 'Two minutes max.'

The entrance to the car park was cordoned off, with policemen on guard either side of the yellow tape. It didn't surprise him, though he knew Nancy would be disappointed. Looking over the barrier, he spotted the inspector in a huddle with several colleagues. Something or somebody was lying prostrate on the gravel. It seemed that Nancy had seen it, too. Without a moment's hesitation, she walked up to one of the policemen.

'I need to speak to the inspector,' she said in English.

The policeman shook his head, not understanding.

'Alvarez,' she said, pointing to the inspector, then to herself.

The policeman again shook his head.

Out came the dictionary. '*Urgente.*'

The policeman averted his eyes and gazed over her head. He was immovable, Archie could see, and the lack of language meant there was no possibility of explaining just how *urgente* it was.

He glanced at Nancy and saw that impatience had turned

to despair. She was thinking of the little girl, he knew, and it was eating away at her. There was no help for it—he would have to try his luck. Going up to the police officer who had refused to listen to her, he gave him a mild push in the chest. The man glared angrily at him. Archie pushed him again, this time harder. His adversary looked as if he was about to swing a punch and Archie readied himself to duck, but the man did not respond.

Okay, he thought, let's go for broke. This time he went right up to the policeman so that he was almost breathing up his nostrils and waved a fist in his face. That brought the man's colleague running. Seemingly alarmed by this sudden show of violence from a stray tourist, he'd abandoned his post to help his fellow restrain the madman who had appeared out of nowhere.

Out of the corner of his eye, Archie saw Nancy slip beneath the yellow tape. Job done.

*

Nancy walked as quietly as she could towards the group of men gathered in the centre of the car park. There were three of them in all, dressed in plain clothes. She stood a little behind the inspector, while he spoke rapidly to his colleagues— his subordinates, she presumed—his hand tugging at his moustache. From where Nancy stood, it appeared to droop more than ever.

She shuffled forward a little, but the men were deep in conversation and she stayed unnoticed. Peering around the substantial figure of Alvarez, she saw the crumpled body spread-eagled on the gravel. A ghastly red stain seeped from the man's blue tee-shirt, and dribbled down on to the car park's grey surface.

As she watched, the two younger men bent down on either

side of the body, looking closely at the injury and talking to Alvarez all the while. One of them produced a notebook and from what Nancy could make out, was sketching the victim's position, while the other outlined the body in chalk. Alvarez himself bent down and gingerly withdrew a wallet from the victim's pocket.

For a good minute, Nancy stood there, taking in the scene but refusing to look at the face of the man lying sprawled on his back. She had seen a bright blue tee-shirt very lately and she was filled with a dreadful premonition. When she finally allowed her eyes to travel up the man's body to his once handsome face, she felt a sickness grip her stomach. Her foreboding had been right.

It was Mateus Cariba, the man they had spoken to no more than a day ago, a young man full of life, of enthusiasm, of love. Love for Jessica. Was this why the poor boy had met his end in this miserable space? What exactly had happened between the time they'd said goodbye to Cariba in Leblon and his murder here in the Tivoli car park? Images shuttled through Nancy's mind as she looked with sadness on the dead man—Mateus waiting for Jessica in the favella, dancing with her in Carnival, walking to meet her in Leblon and finally, Jessica's argument with her father. She was a married woman, but she was also the daughter of a man with a host of deadly secrets and a reputation to match. Is that why Mateus had died, because he knew too much, because he'd got too close to Sousa's daughter?

It was then that Inspector Alvarez turned from issuing orders to his henchmen and saw her.

'Senhora Tremayne! You must not be here!'

'But I am, inspector, and I need to talk to you.'

'No, no.'

He went to hustle her out of the car park, calling to the

policemen at the entrance to come to his aid. She saw them duck beneath the yellow tape and begin walking towards her. Archie must have got away from any scuffle—with little damage, she hoped.

Swiftly, she pulled the shoe from her handbag and thrust it at Alvarez. 'I found this child's shoe at a house in Leblon. The house belongs to Jessica Ramos.' Then in case the inspector hadn't understood the significance, she added, 'Jessica has no children but she is Leandro Sousa's daughter.'

'What is this?' He spluttered, clearly uninterested, and angry that she had dared to accost him. 'What do you want with me?'

'I'm trying to tell you,' she said, impatient that the man did not appear to be listening. 'The shoe belongs to Livia Barreto. The missing child.'

'How can you know that?'

'Her mother, Ester Barreto, confirmed to me a few hours ago that this shoe belonged to her daughter. The little girl is in that house, inspector. You need to go there. You need to search.'

'This is *absurdo*. A shoe, a child?'

'A child missing for days, along with many other children. A child who is the niece of another of your murder victims,' she reminded him. 'Can't you see that it all hangs together?'

'This shoe you give me. You find it in the house of Senhora Ramos?'

Nancy nodded.

'But there could be good reason.'

'Tell me one,' she challenged. 'What possible reason would a small child have to go to a house in Leblon, without her mother and without telling anyone where she was going? Livia didn't go there voluntarily. She was taken by force, abducted for criminal purposes. And you must rescue her.'

How much Alvarez understood of this speech, Nancy was unsure. He seemed to have understood as much as he needed. 'I do not think you are right, Senhora Tremayne. The shoe is one many children wear and Senhora Barreto makes a mistake. She is upset and thinks it must be from her daughter.'

'Ester recognised the shoe,' Nancy said mulishly. 'It had damage on the toes, a heel that had worn down.' She was making it up as she went along, but she had to convince this man. 'You must go to that house now.'

'If the child is missing, she can be anywhere. This I have told you. The shoe maybe is in the house for months.'

'So that makes it not worth investigating? In any case, it wasn't there for months and Livia is nowhere else. She would have been taken to a warehouse to join other children, if that warehouse had not burnt down. The fire was huge. It was in the newspaper, front page news—you must have seen it. The building belonged to Senhor Monaro who, it turns out, is a close friend of Leandro Sousa. It all fits together,' she repeated loudly.

The inspector's brows twitched. Nancy was uncertain what this meant, but he held up his hand to her, as though wishing to push her away. 'I hear no more. I am busy. I have a body, two bodies. Please—' He nodded to the uniformed policemen who, all this time, had been waiting patiently by his side.

It was useless. If she struggled to stay, they would simply manhandle her out of the way. If she continued to harangue the inspector, as Francisco had called it, he would continue to deny there was any truth to her claims. He might, she thought, even be in the pay of the criminals. In the pay of Monaro or Sousa or both. It was hopeless and Nancy could have cried with frustration.

Allowing herself to be marched to the entrance, she was

pushed roughly beneath the yellow tape, and saw Archie in the distance, idling on the street corner.

'Well, intrepid one?' he greeted her.

'Useless,' she said bitterly. 'Utterly useless. He won't listen, let alone do anything. He's too busy to bother with a missing child when he has two murders on his hands. At least, that's what he claims.'

'He has a point. The Tivoli should come with a health warning. I couldn't see properly, but was it another chambermaid who's been despatched?'

'You're so callous, Archie.' She looked away from him, her lips compressed. 'It's not another maid,' she said, 'it's Mateus Cariba.'

Archie whistled between his teeth. 'That was swift. We only saw him when? Yesterday?'

'And when we met him, he was headed for Jessica's house which means—'

'That Daddy found out he was visiting and sent one of his clowns to put an end to the irritation—if the quarrel we witnessed on the roof terrace really was about the boyfriend.'

Nancy nodded slowly. 'I'm sure it was, in some way or other. That must have been what happened. But why dump the poor man here? He lived in the favella—why not kill him there? Or in Leblon itself?'

'Maybe they lured him here, then shot him when he arrived. I'm presuming he was shot.'

'I think so. I saw a stray bullet on the ground. But why here? It makes no sense.'

'It's neutral territory. The place has no obvious link to the killers, or who we reckon are the killers. And most of the time the car park is empty of people. No witnesses.'

'But what made Mateus come here? What could have lured him?'

'Maybe he wasn't lured. Maybe he was picked up in Santa Cecilia or Leblon, bundled into a car and bobs your uncle. Yes, I know — I'm callous. But it seems to me that death is part of everyday life in this city.'

'I suppose he could have come to the hotel on his own account, for a reason we don't know, and they tracked him here. Maybe he suspected what was going on in that house and came here to tackle Ramos.' Nancy felt tears well and brushed her face with the back of her hand. 'So much waste. So much sadness. Why can't the police arrest Leandro Sousa? They must know he's behind all this.'

'I guess because he pays the kind of protection money that keeps him safe from arrest. Come on, I'll buy you one of those cocktails — a *caipirinha*, wasn't it? It will make you feel better.'

'Nothing will make me feel better. I'm certain that Livia Barreto is in that house, but she won't be there much longer. They'll find somewhere else to keep her — and any other children they get their hands on. They may already have found somewhere. And we're powerless to stop them.'

Archie reached out for her hand, and she felt his warmth, his strength, flood through her. For the first time, she looked at him properly. There was a bruise on his cheek, red at the moment but growing ominously dark. She reached up and touched it gently. 'They got you,' she said sympathetically.

'In the end, but I landed one first.'

'You were lucky not to be arrested.'

'They were jangling the handcuffs but I pulled free and ran for it. Melted into the crowd, then walked back into the hotel. It's quietened down considerably now. The concierge was behind his desk, the receptionist was off the phone, and there was no sign of Ramos. I buzzed around the foyer so all of them could see me, just in case the police came looking. If they thought to charge me for assaulting an officer, I was never anywhere near that car park.'

'And the bruise?'

'Walked into the wardrobe this morning. Careless of me.'

She gave a weak smile. 'Thank you for trying.'

'We've done all we can, Nancy,' he said, hugging her briefly. 'You've done all you can. You'll have to let it go.'

She took a deep breath. 'Maybe I'll feel better after that *caipirinha* you're buying me, though somehow I doubt it.'

'On the other hand,' Archie glanced down at his watch, 'weren't you supposed to be at the hospital collecting Leo around this time?'

She grabbed his wrist and checked the time for herself. 'Oh God,' she groaned. 'You're right. I must find a cab.'

They had reached the Avenida Atlantica and she looked frantically up and down the tree-lined street. A little way ahead of them, a taxi was pulling in at the hotel entrance.

'There's one,' she said. 'I'll grab him before he drives off.'

When she got to the vehicle, the driver was opening the rear door and it was Leo who was climbing out.

'Nancy,' he said, his lips stretched to a tight smile. 'A little late, but I'm glad you managed to turn up at last.'

Chapter Twenty-Six

'I'm so sorry,' Nancy stammered. 'I lost count of the time. '

'So I imagine.' Leo looked over her head at Archie standing awkwardly to one side. Her husband's face lacked all expression.

'There's been a tremendous kerfuffle in the hotel,' she said, trying to bridge the chasm that had suddenly opened between them all. 'Another murder, Leo.' When he said nothing, she added desperately, 'Everything's been at sixes or sevens.'

'And you're investigating this one, too, are you?' Leo's voice was smooth, but threaded with a splinter of ice.

'No, of course not. But the young man—' Nancy broke off. She had been about to say that she knew Mateus Cariba, but then thought better of it. That would be opening a whole new can of worms and what good would it do? Whether she knew the murder victim or not, it didn't excuse the fact that she'd left her husband to make the journey back from the hospital alone.

'Shall we go up to the room?' she asked. 'Or perhaps a drink on the roof terrace? We could have tea and those lovely chocolate fudge balls.'

'I'd like to rest,' he said shortly, stooping to collect his bag.

Archie was before him. 'I'll drop it off at your door,' he

said, and disappeared into the hotel, bag in hand.

Nancy thought him wise. It was sensible that Archie play least-in-sight. The fact that she'd been with him, while Leo had been forced to travel alone, had soured her husband's homecoming. Thinking it best not to take his arm, she walked beside him as he made his way across the foyer, adapting her step to fit his slower pace. He was walking like an elderly man, she realised, and they had only just reached the lift when Francisco came bouncing up to them.

'Leo! I did not know the hospital wave you goodbye. I telephone at twelve and a nurse say you will come back tomorrow.'

'She was wrong, Francisco, I'm glad to say. It's good to be back, though. We fly home tomorrow evening, but I have tonight to rest.'

'So sorry to see you go, my friend. Such a bad holiday for you. No holiday at all! You must come again—when you are stronger. You and Nancy. But next time, not at Carnival.'

'Thank you, old chap. That's kind. I'll be sure to remember the invitation.'

'But come, we will have a drink together to celebrate your return!'

'Perhaps later? I'm feeling a little tired. It's the first time I've been properly dressed in days.'

'Of course, my friend. We will make it later.' Francisco gave him a tremendous hug, worrying Nancy that her husband might buckle beneath the onslaught. 'I will telephone in a few hours,' he said joyfully.

Leo's bag was waiting for them outside room 405 and, as soon as Nancy had coaxed her husband into a chair by the window, she unpacked the few items he'd brought back with him. She saw his eyes fixed on the world below. Traffic still poured down the Avenida Atlantica—Romi-Isettas jousting for space with Fords and brand new Volkswagens — the beach was still full of swimmers and walkers and tennis players, and the sea still thundered its way to shore. But a kind of peace had descended.

'It's a good deal quieter, now that Carnival is over,' she remarked.

Leo did not respond immediately and, after a while, said, 'Will you sit down, Nancy. I want to speak to you.'

'Let's talk later. For now, you should relax. I can get iced tea sent up if you'd like.'

'I am relaxed,' he snapped. 'And I've had enough iced tea to last me for the next twenty years.'

She darted a glance at him. His face was cold and hard. What on earth was coming? Surely he couldn't be that angry that she had let the time slip?

'I'm sorry I didn't get to the hospital on time,' she apologised again, her voice uncertain. 'Inspector Alvarez was here, asking questions.' It was a white lie, but she couldn't feel too bad about it if it helped soften his anger.

'It really doesn't matter,' he said, sounding weary and defeated. 'At least, it does, but it's only a small part of the problem.'

'The problem?' she echoed.

'You, Nancy. And me. And this so-called marriage we're in.'

'You're tired, Leo, and I've been at fault this afternoon. Why don't you leave what you want to say until you're feeling more rested?'

'I'm not so tired to say what I need to. I've hours ahead of me to rest.'

Nancy resigned herself to what she couldn't stop, but crossed her arms as though they were a barrier to ward off what she'd no wish to hear. Her chest felt unbelievably tight.

'I know you didn't love me when we married,' Leo began, his voice cracking a little. 'You made that clear. You were perfectly honest with me and I accepted it. I loved you dearly, I wanted to protect you from that madman, March, and I wanted to have you by my side for the rest of my life. I was prepared to accept less than love—respect, affection, mutual interest. In time, I hoped, I believed, that you'd come to feel as deeply about me as I did about you. But that hasn't happened.'

She went to speak but he held up his hand. 'I don't blame you for it. You can't manufacture a feeling that doesn't exist. I'm the one at fault. I should never have asked—never hoped—for sentiments that aren't there. The most I should have expected was that we'd walk through life together in reasonable amity. And that's the problem. We haven't.'

'You think we are enemies?' Nancy felt her face fold into unhappiness. How could he think that?

'Not enemies. No, not enemies. But our life together has been a rollercoaster. A series of stops and starts. There have been patches where we've rubbed along together tolerably well, even patches, dare I say, when I've thought you genuinely loved me.'

'I have loved you, Leo,' she said quietly. 'I do love you.'

'Yes, I believe you do, but not in the way I want to be loved.'

'So you do blame me for it?'

He shook his head. 'That would be unfair. Only look at the ruin I've made of your life and to a lesser extent, of mine. I've said it already—I take full responsibility. I pressured you into this marriage when you were at your most vulnerable and I shouldn't have done it. Since then I've tried to be there for you, tried to give you everything I can. But it's never been enough, has it?'

Nancy had no answer. There was a huge void in her that Leo couldn't fill, but this was something she would never confess.

'I've provided a beautiful home,' he went on, 'allowed you to do the apprenticeship you were set on, though I wished you wouldn't, accepted that we'll never have a child. That was a bitter blow to me, but somehow I overcame it. I really can't see what more I could have done.'

Nancy swallowed hard. She wanted to take him to task. The beautiful home wasn't truly hers, she had a right to pursue a career as much as he had, and why think himself magnanimous over her inability to bear a living child. The miscarriage had hurt her badly and its echoes still resonated — this whole business with Livia Barreto. She wanted to take him to task, but she couldn't. He was suffering and she was the cause.

'You've done all those things and I'm eternally grateful,' she said.

'I don't want your damn gratitude.' He almost growled the words.

At that, she jumped up and walked to the window, looking down on the lively scene below. 'What you want from me is what I can't ever give,' she said at last. She knew the words would hurt, but she had to be honest. This might be the most important moment of their marriage.

'I know that now.' A sardonic smile lit his face. 'It's taken me a few years to see it, though deep down I think I've known it right from the start. From the moment I carried you over the threshold and Archie Jago held out his hand to you.'

'It's not like that, Leo,' she said, desperate and appalled at the same time. To think that Leo had guessed her deepest secret from the very beginning. She could hardly bear it.

Again, he held up his hand. 'I don't want to know what

it's like. What I want to know is how do we negotiate the rest of our lives?'

'We don't. We don't negotiate our lives, we live them. We have years ahead of us, Leo, and they can be good years. You'll regain your strength and, once you do, things will look brighter. We'll spend more time together. We've said it before, but this time we'll do it. You've promised not to work as hard as you've been doing, and I finish my apprenticeship this summer.'

She saw his face lighten and was quick to say, 'I can't give up work entirely. I know you'd like that, but I can't. What I can do, though, is speak to Connie at the studio. If she's happy to give me a job, she might agree to my working on a part-time basis. It would give us more hours together and maybe, then, we'd realise how much we do share.'

'And what is it that we share?'

Nancy could see he was unconvinced. 'Exactly what you said: affection, respect, mutual interest. It might not be the life you hoped for at the outset, but these things are precious and we should value them.'

'Will it be good enough for you, though?' The question was posed lightly, but Leo's voice betrayed his anxiety.

'Why wouldn't it be?' Nancy asked, making her smile as bright as she could. It would have to be good enough, she thought, though her heart told her differently.

'Perhaps because you're talking to a sick man? Because you feel sorry for me?'

He was asking her if she was staying with him out of sympathy and she was swift to discount the notion. 'At the moment, I feel sorry for you certainly. You're still bruised and battered from the attack. But you'll regain your strength, be back on your feet, and I'll have the old Leo with me very soon.'

There was a long silence while Leo looked down into his lap, his face taut. 'You really believe we can make this marriage work?'

She walked back from the window and took both his hands in hers. 'I hope we can,' she said. 'You have been the best friend I've ever had.'

His face twisted at this.

'Sometimes friendship matters most,' she said gently.

*

Leo was asleep that night in minutes. The painful conversation had taken its toll as much as the effort to dress for the first time in days. Nancy curled up close, glad to have him by her side, but feeling wretched. In the few years of their marriage, they had weathered many upsets, but this evening, for the first time, they'd come close to saying a final goodbye, and the thought festered. She had married for security — and that's what Leo had given her. Unstintingly. He had fulfilled his side of the promise and she must fulfil hers, the promise she had made in the Fitzrovia Chapel. The news that he had a debilitating illness, one that could only get worse as the years passed, was an added reason if she needed one. But she didn't.

While he snored gently beside her, she lay watching the ceiling, its smooth surface patterned by flashes of light that strobed upwards from the street. Carnival may have finished but Copacabana didn't sleep. And neither did Nancy. It was unsurprising — she had lived through a tumultuous day. The constant sense of impending threat in the favela, the vile Monaro blocking their escape, and the little girl, terrified and hiding. And Ester, poor Ester, seizing her daughter's shoe and holding it to her heart. And if that were not sufficient emotion for one day, the haunting sight of that handsome young man, lying broken on the floor of a car park, his life blood staining the gravel. Then, finally, the reckoning with Leo. No wonder she couldn't sleep.

It was Ester's distress, though, that remained most vivid. Nancy shuffled to one side of the bed and reached down into her handbag, fumbling for the child's photograph. Holding it to one side so that it caught a shaft of brightness from the street below, she made out the contours of the young face, traced the wide smile of a child who loved and knew herself loved. A child now lost to the mother who adored her.

It was no good Archie saying she had done all she could and must leave it now. There was no way she could stand by and allow this little girl to be shipped to whatever prison was chosen by Sousa or Monaro, or whoever else was behind this most dreadful crime. Could not allow her to be trained as a criminal, groomed as a prostitute. If Livia was still in the house in Leblon, Nancy was going to rescue her.

For the rest of that night, the child's name beat a loud refrain in her mind, and she could do little more than doze, but once the first thin strand of sunlight pierced its way through the folds of the curtains, she checked her watch— it was six o'clock. Sliding from the bed without disturbing her sleeping husband, she crossed to the chair where she'd draped her clothes the night before, wriggling into a sundress and fishing a pair of sandals from under the bed.

In a quarter of an hour, she was knocking on Archie's door.

Chapter Twenty-Seven

A rchie appeared in the doorway, his eyes half-closed, his hair standing in small upright sprouts. It was evident he had stumbled out of bed and grabbed the nearest covering — the hotel's counterpane was draped loosely around his naked figure.

'Am I supposed to be somewhere?' He squinted at her.

'No, but I can't sleep. I can't stop thinking of the child.'

He looked behind him at a closed door. 'Francisco is still sleeping. I don't want to disturb him. You better come in.'

Nancy glanced around the apartment as he led her through the palatial sitting room and into one of the bedrooms leading from it.

'Quite a place,' she said.

'Particularly,' he picked up his watch from the bedside table, 'at six o'clock in the morning.'

'Don't be bad tempered. You've obviously slept well.'

'Not that obviously. I was drinking until two.'

'That's why your bad tempered,' she said sagely.

'I am *not* bad tempered,' he almost yelled, then appeared to remember his host was sleeping in the adjoining room. 'I'm probably still drunk,' he said more quietly.

'Why were you out so late?'

'Oh, you know, this and that.' He sounded

deliberately vague.

'Were you concerned about Livia?'

'Amongst other things. How did it go with Leo after I left you?'

'Oh, you know,' she mimicked. 'This and that.'

'Is it why you're here so early?'

'I'm here because we need to do something. I know that Livia is in that house, I can feel it. Right now, the inspector should be searching the place, but he won't lift a finger. It's up to us to do it—there's no one else. We need to find Livia before *they* find another place to keep her.'

'It could be a fool's errand.' Archie gave a deep yawn. 'The girl could have been shipped out already—if she was there in the first place.'

It had been Nancy's great fear for some time that if they ever discovered where Livia was being held, they'd arrive too late. But it wasn't going to stop her going.

'If they have already spirited her away, there might still be evidence that she's been kept a prisoner there. More than just a shoe in the drawing room. If we can come back with more, Alvarez can have no excuse not to raid the place. No excuse not to question Ramos.'

'So how exactly do we search the house? Knock politely and ask to see the cellar?'

'Don't be annoying—of course not. We won't go near the front door.'

'I could point out that *we* won't be going anywhere. *We* haven't agreed to go to Leblon.'

Nancy ignored him. 'There is a way in. I've been thinking about it. The room Jessica first took us into looked out over the garden. I glimpsed a gate at the very bottom. It was half-hidden by trees, but I'm sure it was there. If we can find a way round to the rear of the building, we could go through that gate, walk past the swimming pool and up to the house.'

Archie stood blinking, still only half awake, a pained expression on his face.

'There are those glass doors, though...' she said slowly, in a moment of misgiving. Then a second thought cheered her. 'I'm pretty sure they're never shut—not at this time of the year.'

'Hold on a minute. Why do you say that? They could well be shut.' Archie's counterpane was in serious danger of slipping to the floor and he hastily rearranged it. 'Jessica is Sousa's daughter and he'll have made sure she's protected. The whole place is probably alarmed. She won't be leaving any doors open. It's crazy to think so.'

'We'll just have to see,' Nancy said calmly, refusing to be daunted. 'We need to go now, before it gets light. Jessica—and her husband, probably—will be out of the way, upstairs, sleeping. If we can get into the house, we can find the staircase that leads to the basement.'

'Or the attic.'

'Just get dressed, Archie. Please!'

'I need a wash,' he protested.

'Then be quick.'

He looked at her for a long minute and she thought he was going to refuse, but then he turned and shambled off to the bathroom.

'Don't bother shaving,' she called after him. 'It won't be a courtesy call.'

While she waited, she walked back into the sitting room and began a wander around its walls, enjoying the way their host had decorated his private apartment.

'I must say Francisco has done himself proud,' she remarked over splashing sounds from the bathroom. 'There are paintings here that would go for a great deal at auction.'

She went over to the far wall to examine more closely a pair of abstract works that had caught her attention. 'I love the way the artist has fused colours here—modernist and native together. The effect is stunning.' She turned in a circle. 'And the sculpture there, in the corner—it's a bronze angel, I think.' She walked over to it. '*The Soul of Gratitude*,' she read aloud. 'It's quite beautiful. I wish we'd had time to see something of Brazilian art. Leo mentioned the São Paulo Biennial when we first arrived. I think he might have been planning a dash down there. I doubt we'll ever see it now, though.'

'I doubt either of us will ever see very much if we get banged up in a Brazilian jail for breaking and entering. '

Archie was back. He had been as swift as she'd asked and, though he was unshaven and still looked a trifle rough around the edges, he wore a bright blue shirt, freshly laundered, and his shorts were newly pressed. He would never match Leo's tall elegance, he was too solidly built—the Cornish were a short race, he'd told her once, something to do with the Armada and Spanish sailors swimming to shore from their wrecked ships—but in Nancy's eyes, he always looked good.

'I think we should leave the hotel singly,' she said, as they travelled down in the lift, refusing to catch his eye. 'I'll walk out first.'

'Is this your sleuth mode or is there an actual reason?'

She considered offering him a trivial response. It was a problem she'd prefer not to put into words, any more than she wanted to recount her conversation with Leo, the hurt and recriminations her husband had voiced. But Archie deserved better.

'I don't want the staff to see us together,' she confessed. 'If Leo should wake early and wander down to look for me, I don't want him to be told that I left the hotel with you.'

Archie pulled a wry grimace. 'What on earth went on

between you two last night? No, don't tell me. I don't want to know. You best walk up the road then and look for a cab. I'll keep to the lift for a few minutes until you get clear.'

The taxi was easy to find. This early in the morning, there was a stream of cabs looking for a fare, and they were soon speeding towards Leblon.

Turning off the Avenida Atlantica and into the road that ran beside the canal, Archie said, 'We should get the driver to drop us away from the house.' His tone was serious. 'Maybe at the point where the apartments finish and the old houses begin. That way our interest in pink chimney pots won't be so noticeable.'

'Yes, that's sensible. Walking from there, we might discover there's a gap between the houses. A lane or some kind of passageway running behind them. Last time, we were too concerned looking out for the house itself to take much notice.'

The cab driver dropped them, as they'd asked, where the apartments petered out and the historic part of Leblon made an appearance. Walking towards the Ramos house for a second time, they peered into any likely gap that presented itself. It took a few trespasses into private gardens before they found what they were looking for: a narrow path leading from the street and running between a colonial style house and a mock-Hollywood extravagance. It was a short track but, at its end, made a sharp right hand turn into a wider path that skirted what was a dense jungle of bushes, the forest just behind. As far as Nancy could see, this new pathway continued along the rear of all the older properties. If she remembered rightly, the house belonging to Jessica Ramos was the second from the end.

Archie had walked ahead, but turned to give a thumbs up. 'Bingo!' he mouthed. He had found what they were looking for.

The gate that Nancy had spied from the living room was locked. She hadn't truly expected anything else, but her hope had been that it wouldn't prove insuperable. In fact, the gate was a mere ten feet high and lacked anything that might seriously deter intruders.

'No spikes, no barbed wire,' Archie commented.

The property was strangely unprotected for a house belonging to the daughter of one of the most feared men in Rio and Nancy crossed her fingers that, even now, somewhere in the house, a burglar alarm wasn't shrilling out a warning.

Archie jumped for the top of the gate and swung himself easily up and over, sliding back the bolts to let Nancy through. He hadn't been a soldier for years but retained a fitness that had proved more than fortunate on several occasions. They stood for a while, taking in the garden. It was a vast affair but with little interest, consisting mainly of a spread of gravel with pots of half-hearted flowers scattered here and there.

'Jessica certainly isn't a gardener! The gravel could be a problem, though,' Nancy whispered.

Archie looked down at his soft shoes, then at hers. 'Not if we walk carefully.'

She could see the flight of wooden steps ahead, leading down to the swimming pool with its dark wicker sunbeds and colourful umbrellas. Creeping quietly forwards, she ignored the pool and pushed past a border of giant ferns to weave her way around the square of sofas she'd coveted on her previous visit. Archie followed suit and together they reached the tall glass doors that led into the house. A few days ago, Nancy had stood on the other side of them. They'd been unlocked then, and they had to be unlocked now. She sent up a silent prayer.

Very gently, she grasped a handle and pulled. The door

slid easily back along its groove and she was inside the house, Archie only a breath behind. With infinite care, they walked through the room and out into the hall. The door of the drawing room where they'd been begrudgingly entertained was open and they peered inside.

'Lucky she doesn't keep a dog,' Archie whispered in her ear.

'Can you imagine? The hair, the mess, the destruction!'

Flitting in and out of the remaining ground floor rooms, they found nothing, while all the time the house slept peacefully, and Jessica with it. Maybe, Diego Ramos, too. He'd not been on duty when they left the hotel this morning and Archie hadn't see him the previous evening.

'Well?' Archie asked. 'We've explored at least five rooms, but found nothing.'

'Five rooms, yet no kitchen. There must be a kitchen—it has to be on a lower floor. A basement. There's going to be a way down to it somewhere, and any staircase that leads to the basement will lead to the cellar as well.'

'Where is it then? I didn't see a staircase the last time we were here, and I can't see one now.'

'There are stairs going up, there must be stairs going down,' she said stubbornly. 'And we have to find them.'

He raised his eyebrows. 'Good luck with that. If they are around, they're very well hidden.'

'Think, Archie. Where could there be a concealed staircase?'

'The drawing room? Maybe worth trying there again. I'm pretty sure there was a hefty door on the far wall when we walked through. It might only lead to a cupboard or it's possible there might be stairs—to this mythical basement.'

They glided silently back to the drawing room. Archie had been right about a substantial door and she was about to open it when she heard him give a muttered curse.

'What the—!'

Nancy turned swiftly to hush him and then saw what looked like blood splashed across his blue shirt.

'You're bleeding.' Bewildered, she rushed over to him.

'Not me, but somebody is.'

Their eyes went immediately to the ceiling. A dark red stain had spread amoeba-like across the plaster work, a few globules of blood gathering in the centre and falling, one at a time, very slowly to the floor. A small puddle had begun to form on the elegant wood tiles.

'Upstairs,' Archie said urgently. 'I'll go.'

'If you go, so do I. Archie—' she caught at his sleeve '—do you think… do you think it could be Livia?' There was a pain in her chest and her throat was constricted.

'There's only one way to find out. Come on.'

Chapter Twenty-Eight

A rchie led the way up the stairs to the first floor, his feet padding softly on the wooden treads. Following in his wake, Nancy tried to still the terror of what they might find, her pulse thudding so loudly she thought it must warn anyone lurking above. At the head of the stairs, a bathroom door stood ajar. Archie gave a quick glance inside and shook his head. The adjoining room, though, had its door firmly shut and, very slowly, he turned the handle and allowed it to swing open. There was a loud creak, freezing them both to the spot, as though the White Witch had cast her spell. But when Archie pushed the door further ajar, it was to give another shake of his head.

With one accord, they crept along the landing, passing several more closed doors, until they reached the room at its very end. From Nancy's reckoning, this one must lie directly above the drawing room. It was another open door, so another empty room? Huddled together in the doorway, they saw nothing at first and Archie was about to turn round and usher her out, when he paused and walked forward a few paces. Following him, Nancy stood stunned and appalled at what she saw: a body, limbs flung wide, bloodstained and unmoving.

Creeping closer, she peered down at the face of the woman

sprawled across the cowhide rug. Jessica Ramos!

Archie crouched beside the body and placed his fingers at the side of the woman's neck. He shook his head, signalling death.

'Shot,' he said quietly. 'At point blank range, it looks. I'd say she's been dead for hours. The blood that's seeping through the floor is old blood.'

Nancy stared blindly down at the dead woman. A huge wave of relief had rolled through her when she'd realised the body was not that of a child's. Now, though, confusion had taken its place.

'I don't understand. Who could have done this?' She glanced distractedly around the room. 'There's no obvious sign of a struggle. There's not a thing out of place—it doesn't look like the scene of a burglary gone wrong.'

Archie got to his feet and followed her gaze. 'Not a burglary,' he agreed. 'A deliberate killing, I'd say.'

'But why? And who would dare, knowing her father, knowing he'd seek instant revenge? Unless... she found out what's been happening here and had to be silenced immediately. It's likely she never once visited the cellar— why would she? But yesterday, perhaps, she did.'

'If there is a cellar,' Archie interrupted.

'There has to be. Yesterday, maybe, she went there for whatever reason—we'll never know—and discovered for the first time how her home was being used. What her husband had been doing.'

'Ramos has been absent from the hotel for at least twenty-four hours,' Archie said thoughtfully. 'He wasn't there when all the fuss over Cariba was going on and he wasn't there this morning. Legged it, do you think?'

Nancy nodded. 'It looks pretty suspicious, doesn't it? Jessica must have confronted him with what he'd done, and he decided to silence her.'

'You think my wife *inocente*?'

The voice cut through the air. Startled, they swung around to see Diego Ramos filling the doorway. There was a gun in his hand, a gun that was pointing directly at them.

'I am the *inocente*,' he said. His voice was harsh and grating, yet little more than a whisper. 'I am the stupid one. *Um idiota*.' He began to walk towards them.

'You killed her!' Nancy exclaimed, unable to stop herself. She felt Archie's hand on her arm, warning her to say no more. The man was evidently unstable, wielding a weapon he had already used, and just feet away.

Diego's face was ravaged, his eyes raw, and his skin bereft of colour. His hand was trembling so badly that the gun almost jumped in his grip. 'I have to kill her.' He bowed his head and when he raised it again, Nancy saw the tears trickling down his cheeks. He brushed them angrily aside. 'Jessica is a wicked woman. She took my heart and walked over it.'

Nancy was scared—Ramos could kill them both without a second thought—but attempting to still her panic, she put her mind to work, trying to piece together the different strands of the puzzle. Ramos must have discovered his wife had been unfaithful, she reasoned, then lashed out with dreadful consequences. Had he done worse, though?

'Did you kill Mateus Cariba as well?' she asked.

'That *merda*. What else is there to do with a dog who steals your wife?'

There was a long, tense silence before Archie spoke, his voice friendly and conversational. 'We were in the car park yesterday and saw the body. We thought Leandro Sousa had killed the chap.'

Archie was trying to distract the man, she realised,

encourage him to talk, hoping he might forget he was holding a gun.

'Sousa?' Diego spat on the wooden floor. 'He is the one who told me the truth.'

It was clear that Ramos had only just learned of his wife's affair, though it must have flourished for many months. He'd had his suspicions, though—Nancy remembered him searching the Carnival crowd and the look on his face—but it was Jessica's father who had plunged the knife to a depth that proved fatal.

'You know what Sousa said?' Diego gave a crazed laugh. 'He said that he has spoken to his daughter, and now it is me who must stop it. Spoken to her? What use is that? He must punish her. Beat her hard. But for Sousa, his daughter is his light.' He paused, giving a loud swallow. 'Was his light,' he corrected himself.

There was another long silence, while Nancy watched with horrible fascination the way in which Ramos was twirling the gun in his hand, muttering inaudibly to himself. Round and round in dizzying circles, but always returning the weapon to point at them.

'His light,' he repeated. 'She is shut from the light now. Sousa, also. They deserve it.'

'That was her crime? That she was unfaithful?' Archie asked, still intent, it seemed, on softening up the man.

Nancy feared it wasn't going to work. Diego's form was rigid, so tightly compressed that one small movement could hurl him into manic action, like an over-wound mechanical figure ready to fly at the push of a button.

He jabbed the gun towards Archie. 'Why not?' he demanded loudly. 'A man is right to defend his honour.'

'Not where I come from, mate.'

Was that a false move? Nancy held her breath, but Ramos

appeared not to have heard. He reached out and pulled a low bedroom chair towards him, sinking into it as though every fibre of his body had lost the desire to live.

'She is a bad woman with this, this *cachorro*, this dog... but do you know,' he said almost amiably, 'she has done many more bad things? Many more,' he repeated dully. 'I have a good future and she has ruined me.'

'You mean by taking a lover?' It might be a forlorn mission, but she must try to distract him as well. 'You could have recovered from that—in time.'

'She made me bad. Made me a *criminoso*.'

'A criminal? But you are one,' Nancy said softly. 'Surely you can see that. You made yourself one when you killed your wife.'

Seemingly intent on following his own disordered train of thought, Ramos ignored her comment in the same way as he'd ignored Archie's. It was as though he was in another world, one inhabited by him alone. Nancy was sure that he hadn't heard the noise she had picked up. A soft crunch of the gravel. She looked across at the window, realising the room must overlook the rear garden—a large palm tree half-covered one side of the window pane—the same garden through which she and Archie had crept only minutes ago. Was someone else creeping through it at this very moment?

'This house,' Ramos said suddenly, waving his free hand vaguely in the air. '*Tão lindo, tão caro*. Beautiful, expensive. It is for Jessica. She has everything she wants—everything is for her. For me, nothing. But then she made it dirty. Made it a bad place.'

'How did she do that?' Nancy asked quickly, and this time it wasn't just to keep him talking. Whatever secrets were hidden in this house, Ramos was about to spill them.

'You mean the children?' Archie said. It was an

inspired guess.

Ramos nodded. 'I don't like it but I can say nothing. I am the poor one. Jessica decides. *This is my business*, she said. *You go and be manager at the Tivoli and earn nothing. For me, I earn ten times more in a day.*'

'Are you saying that your wife was responsible for kidnapping children?' Nancy fixed him with a ferocious stare.

'Not her. Not Jessica. The men her father pays. They bring the children here.'

'Why is that?'

'They wait until they have four, five, then take them away. I told her this is bad, this will make big trouble for us. But she said it is only for a day, maybe two. *What is wrong?* she asks. *They are fed, they have drink. I do not beat them. And they make me money.*'

Nancy stared blankly at him, hearing the words but trying to grapple with their meaning. Had it really been Jessica Ramos behind this terrible exploitation? She questioned as much aloud and Jessica's husband moved his head slowly up and down, as though he, too, could hardly believe it.

'It was her idea,' he said sadly. 'She was proud she thought of it. Papa told her she has done well, she is his true daughter. This is all Jessica wants. For him, the business is too small. Not enough money. But for his daughter, it is a little job to keep her busy.'

Nancy felt Archie move closer, then the warm clutch of his hand. He would know what she was thinking: how could a woman do that? Acquiesce in the theft of other women's children, knowing the kind of life she was consigning them to? Yet Jessica Ramos had stood in Ester's sitting room and denied all knowledge of the missing Livia. The woman's wickedness knew no bounds.

But Livia—Nancy was forgetting Livia.

'Are there any children here now?'

He shrugged. 'How do I know? It is nothing to me.' Suddenly, he lurched forward in the chair, almost doubling in on himself, a keening noise coming from his crumpled form. 'Why did she take my honour? Why did she make me kill her?'

Archie's ears had picked up the sounds, too. His grasp on her hand had become painful. Feet, she thought, feet on the wooden flooring below.

'I did everything for her,' Ramos panted. 'I said nothing of the children. I said nothing of the maid. Of Vitoria. And look how she repaid me!'

Nancy forgot the noises and started forward. 'The maid. You killed Vitoria Dias, too?' At last, the confession she had always known was there.

'No, no. Vitoria was a good worker. Difficult. Noisy. But a good maid until she asked about the girl.'

'You quarrelled, I know. I heard you the first evening I was in the hotel. What happened afterwards?'

'I did not know the girl she spoke of and I thought it bad if she goes looking, making a big fuss. Then one of Sousa's men came to the Tivoli to tell me that the warehouse has gone and the children, too. I must tell Alvar Monaro, he said, tell him his property burns and the children escape.'

'So you went to *Buffet Bonito* to find him?' Ramos nodded. 'Why didn't the man who told you the news go himself?'

'People know him. Know he is a bad man. The owner will turn him away from the restaurant. I have to go instead. On the way, I panic. I think that if the children escape, then tell people where they have been, they will say Leblon. They will say my house. Then my job goes. My life goes.'

'Did you say all of this to Monaro?'

'I panic, I tell you.'

'Yes,' Nancy said impatiently, 'but how did Monaro respond when you told him? What did he say to you?'

'He said the children will not speak. They are too young to know the house. But then I told him about Vitoria. The girl the maid looks for may be in my house right now, I said, and this woman is making trouble. He told me I must get rid of Vitoria.'

'He told you to kill her?'

'But I cannot kill.' Ramos looked bewildered at the thought.

'You just have, mate,' Archie put in.

'No.' He pointed to the lifeless figure lying between them. 'Jessica must die. But Vitoria did no hurt to me.' Ramos stopped speaking and, for the first time, seemed aware they might not be alone.

'And then what?' Nancy asked quickly.

'I telephoned Jessica and told her that if the child is in the house, she must send her back to the *favela* straight away. *Keep calm*, she said. *It will be okay*. Then she came to hotel and made me call Vitoria.'

'It *was* you who called her from the housekeeper's office. You told Vitoria you had information?'

'I pretend. She wanted to know everything but I said I cannot speak on the telephone, we must meet. A secret meeting.'

'But it wasn't you who went to meet Vitoria?'

He slumped further into the chair. 'No, not me. Jessica.'

Chapter Twenty-Nine

Jessica had killed Vitoria Dias! Nancy could see it was possible. Vitoria would be eager to have any information that could help her find her niece and, when she saw a woman's figure approach her in the cellar, she'd be lulled into a false sense of security. Particularly if she didn't recognise Jessica and the family she came from. If Jessica had managed to distract the maid, told her to turn around say, look the other way, she could have looped a scarf—or a stocking or a length of tape or whatever she'd brought with her—around Vitoria's neck and strangled the poor woman. Jessica was tall and athletic, the chambermaid older, smaller, and far less fit.

It would be over in a moment, then Diego summoned to the cellar to clear up the mess. He'd be frantic. How to dispose of the body? How to get away from the nightmare overwhelming his life? He'd look around for escape, but there would be nothing but wine. In a panic, he'd push the dead woman into a barrel and in his haste leave the lid unsecured. Poor, poor Vitoria.

Now it was she, Nancy thought, that was facing death, but it wasn't going to end like this. She was determined to survive long enough to find the little girl that her aunt had died for.

'She killed her,' Ramos was continuing dolefully, 'and I must get rid of the body and say nothing. It is too much. And how has she repaid me for this great service? She has broken my heart. Is it possible for a woman to be so bad?'

Ramos seemed to have exempted himself entirely from blame. He had covered up a murder, then killed on his own account, but in his eyes he had done nothing wrong. It was only what he'd had to do.

'You have been misled, Diego,' she said in a gentle voice, and felt Archie stiffen beside her. He would be wondering where she was going with this. 'It's time now, though, to make things right. Let's go downstairs together—to the cellar. If the child we've spoken of is still there, we can rescue her. *You* can rescue her. That will surely count in your favour when we go to the police station.'

Ramos did not respond, but sat the gun in his lap, staring at the floor. The noises Nancy had heard earlier seemed to have stopped and her hopes of a possible rescue began to dwindle.

'You can tell Inspector Alvarez the story you've just told us,' she urged. 'He will see that you're innocent of much of this trouble, and though you'll be punished for your wife's death, I don't think your punishment will be heavy.' Nancy was fairly certain that in this country a crime of passion would not be judged too severely.

Ramos shook his head and staggered to his feet. 'It is too late. I have lost everything. All I have now is my life and I will keep that. I will go—to Venezuela, Argentina, Paraguay. Wherever.'

'Good plan,' Archie said. 'It's just a shame we can't let you do that.'

'But yes, I think you can. I have the gun.'

For the first time, Diego smiled, a horrible facsimile of a smile. He stretched out his arm and grabbed at Nancy's dress, dragging her roughly to his side. Archie started forward, but

Ramos pointed the gun quite deliberately at Nancy's head.

'You will stay here,' he said to Archie. 'Senhora Tremayne and I will leave. She will make sure that I stay safe. I am not stupid, you see. There is someone here, maybe the police, maybe not. But whoever it is, they will not shoot me while she is with me. And if she is good, I will send her back. If not, it will be sad for you.'

The touch of the pistol on her temple had Nancy's legs weaken beneath her and the breath tangle in her throat so badly that she couldn't speak. Her kidnapper was holding her close, rammed against his body, giving her no chance of wriggling free. She looked across at Archie, whose face had hardened into stone, and tried to signal to him that he should let Ramos go. She could sense the man's tiredness, the way his body seemed to have shrunk into itself. He was desperate, and the gun could go off at any moment.

Archie could not have been listening to her silent message. As Ramos, Nancy pinned to his side, shuffled backwards making for the staircase that would take him to the front door, Archie crouched down by Jessica's body.

'Are you sure you killed her?' he asked, pretending to feel for the dead woman's pulse.

Momentarily taken off guard at the thought that his wife might still be alive, Ramos lowered the gun. In an instant, Archie jumped into a crouch and, summoning every ounce of strength to his cause, made a dive for the man's feet, bringing him crashing to the floor. The weapon was knocked from Diego's hand and fired wide, hitting the ceiling and showering them with broken plaster. As Ramos fell, Nancy toppled over and, struggling free from the man's grip, she jumped to her feet and grabbed Archie's hand. Together they fled towards the stairs.

Even before they reached the first step, a line of uniformed police confronted them, Inspector Alvarez at its head.

*

A handcuffed Diego Ramos had been bundled down the stairs to a waiting police van and the inspector had given orders for an ambulance to remove the body to the morgue. Now it was their turn.

Alvarez let out a weary puff of breath as he faced them. 'Senhora Tremayne, perhaps you will tell me why you are here.'

'I'd be much more interested in knowing why the police are,' she said.

'Though it's always good to see you,' Archie put in.

'That is easy. I am here to investigate the death of Mateus Cariba. You already know of it. Senhor Cariba was said to be… to be friends,' he finished, 'with the young woman who lives here. I come to interview her.'

'Tough luck,' Archie said. 'I don't think she'll be doing much talking.'

Nancy wrinkled her forehead. 'You came to interview Jessica Ramos with ten armed policemen?'

'It is a precaution.' The inspector spread his hands. 'I am aware who is the father of Senhora Ramos.'

'So you didn't come to look for the child?'

'Should I have done? Yesterday, you show me a shoe, but why? What does that tell me?'

Nancy wanted to say that if it didn't tell him what was so clearly obvious, he wasn't much of a policeman. But they were wasting time. She had to get to that cellar, had to make a search. She was feeling stronger now, her legs only slightly wavering. They would carry her as far as the cellar at least.

'I am afraid,' the inspector was saying, 'you must come to the station with me. Explain how you are here with a dead body.'

'That's simple enough. We came to find the child,' Archie said. 'Instead, we found a dead woman and a lunatic with a gun. If it would help, we can give you a written statement. Or I can come back to the station with you. I don't see the need for Mrs Tremayne to come as well.'

'But it is not so simple... Senhor Jago? I must insist you both come with me. The ambulance will be here soon and then we will go.'

This was the worst of both worlds, Nancy thought, to have failed to find Livia and at the same time angered her husband, once Leo knew she had been escorted to the police station. He would know, too, since there was no way she would be able to explain a protracted absence this morning. He'd be incensed by the fact that she'd once more involved herself in the 'poking and prying' he hated, and this time made much worse by the new beginning they had promised each other only last night.

'Allow me to escort you to my car.' The inspector made a shepherding gesture with his arms. 'You will not wish to witness the ambulance men at work.'

'You think that bothers me?' she challenged him. 'There's something far more distressing than the dead body of an evil woman, and it's down two flights of stairs. We need to get to the cellar. Why don't you come with us?'

Before Alvarez could prevent her, Nancy had started down the first flight, Archie jerked into action close behind.

'After this, I hope to God we can find a cellar,' he muttered.

'We'll try the door you mentioned,' she said over her shoulder, 'the one that's in the room with the blood.'

The graphic description was underlined just then by two white-suited men who had come through the front door, carrying a stretcher between them. Morgue attendants, Nancy thought, swerving past and only just ahead of the inspector panting in their wake.

Alvarez was forced to a halt, needing to issue the men with directions to the body, and by the time he'd disentangled himself, Nancy had reached the drawing room and the door that Archie had spotted earlier. She pulled on the handle, thrilled that at last they might be close to Livia, but the door refused to open. She tried once more, and then again, her desperation increasing.

'Here, let me.' Archie gave the door handle an almighty tug, but had no more success. 'The door must be locked,' he said, 'and there's no key.'

'Is there any way—'

Before she could finish, Archie had pulled a business card from his pocket and, with its sharp edge, was forcing the lock when the inspector caught up with them.

'You cannot damage property,' the policeman started to say, his words coming in stutters.

There was a loud click as the lock gave and Nancy held her breath. Archie had been right. A winding flight of stone steps lay beyond the door, leading downwards to whatever secrets the house held.

'You should go no further, Senhora Tremayne, Senhor Jago,' the inspector began, but with one accord, they had plunged forward and were already on the twisting staircase.

Halfway down, they came to a wide landing, with a door leading into what must be the elusive kitchen—a room, it seemed, wholly illuminated by artificial light. Ignoring the kitchen, they scrambled down the remainder of the staircase. Hardly any natural light penetrated this far and it felt to Nancy increasingly hazardous. Reaching what she took to be the final step, she fumbled a hand against the wall, hoping to find a light. It was Archie, close behind, who hit the switch first.

The inspector was now beside them, and all three gazed in wonder at the enormous space that had opened up, spreading not just beneath the house but the garden, too. Alvarez jabbed at his moustache, plainly stunned. A line of shabby doors filled one side of the cellar. Nancy pushed the first open. A cell. A prison cell.

'Livia,' she called out. 'Livia Barreto. Are you there?'

Not a sound. The inspector gave a small huff and grasped Nancy's arm, ready to march her back up the stairs.

She twisted out of his grasp. 'Livia, we are friends. *Amigos*,' she added hopefully, wishing she had her dictionary with her. 'Your mama, Ester, sent us.'

It was the name that did it. At the sound of "Ester", there was a small scuffle from the furthest corner of the cellar.

'Here! She's here!' Excitedly, Nancy ran towards the room at the end of the line.

This door was locked, but there was a small grill cut into the wood and Nancy went on tip-toe to peer through. At first, in the dim light, she could make out nothing more than the earthen floor and concrete walls, but then her eyes travelled to one of the corners of the room. A stained blanket, several blankets, in fact, an empty dish and a water bottle, and huddled into the smallest shape possible, a little girl, her knees drawn up and her head buried.

'Livia,' she called softly through the grill. The child slowly raised her head, but refused to look at the door.

'You must speak to her,' Nancy said to the inspector. 'In her own language. Tell her she is safe, that we have come to take her home to her mother.'

In the muted light, the inspector's face had turned ashen. Seeing the child's dreadful plight in this filthy place had evidently been a grievous shock to him. She was the same child that earlier he had dismissed so lightly.

Alvarez spoke gently in rapid Portuguese, and the little girl finally looked towards the door. Nancy saw the tear-stained cheeks and the matted hair and her heart ached.

One of the uniformed policemen had followed them down to report to the inspector that the prisoner was now on his way to the station and the body on its way to the morgue. With a swift glance, he took in the scene and, striding to the door, unclipped the baton from his belt and struck the padlock a hefty blow. The door of the cell swung open.

Nancy approached the child very slowly, holding out her hand to the little girl and keeping it there for some time. Then lifting her clear of the dirty blankets, she cuddled her close.

'It's okay, now,' she said. 'It's okay.'

*

The police car dropped them outside the hotel. A silent agreement seemed to have been made. The inspector would forget they were ever at the house in Leblon and they would forget that he had not acted earlier to rescue the child. Whatever the truth of it, there had been no further talk of them accompanying Alvarez to the police station, but there had been a promise on his part that he would drive immediately to Santa Cecilia and restore Livia to her mother.

Nancy gave her a last hug before she got out of the car. 'I don't know if we will see you again, Livia—we go home to London this evening—but tell your mama that we wish you both happiness.' The inspector obligingly translated.

Together, she and Archie stood watching the car as it disappeared into the traffic of the Avenida Atlantica.

'Well, sleuth, what now?' he asked. Then breathed out deeply. 'I think we came out of that remarkably well.'

'We did, but only because Alvarez was mortified at how

badly he'd let Livia down.'

Archie pulled a face. 'Maybe. The reason doesn't matter. The child is safe, thank the Lord. Alvarez is happy he's solved two murders within a week. It's us that's left with one teensy little problem.'

'Leo?'

'Exactly. How do we explain your absence this morning? Not to mention mine.'

She felt herself crumbling at the need to explain, at the inevitable anger, the likely estrangement ahead. 'I have no idea. I'm just so tired...' Her voice faded and suddenly she was shaking and tears were tumbling down her face.

Archie pulled her into his arms and, regardless of who was watching, held her close, rocking her back and forth, nestling his face against hers.

When she pulled away, he handed her a handkerchief.

'I should stop snivelling,' she said. 'Livia is back with her mother. Jessica is dead and Ramos will be found guilty of murder. There's only Monaro and Sousa to deal with.'

'Don't even think of it. Just concentrate on getting through this morning. It won't be easy.'

'Good grief, is it only morning?'

He looked at his watch. 'Eight-thirty precisely. How time flies when you're having fun. So... you got up early and went for a walk along the beach, didn't you?'

'I did?'

'You did. And now you're about to take a quick shower before you go to breakfast.'

'That's my story?' She gave him a weak smile.

'It's as good as any. And you need that shower, believe me.'

Chapter Thirty

L eo was already washed and dressed when Nancy walked into the bedroom.

'Sorry I wasn't here when you woke,' she said. 'I couldn't sleep and went for an early walk on the beach.'

He walked over to the dressing table and picked up his hairbrush. 'You should have woken me. I would have come with you.'

Nancy saw his eyes in the mirror studying her, holding her in their gaze. She felt a sudden emptiness as though she had walked over a precipice into thin air.

'I didn't want to disturb you.' Her voice was flustered despite her best efforts. 'You need as much sleep as you can get.'

'There'll be plenty of time to sleep once we're back in London, but not the chance to walk on Copacabana beach.' He straightened up, replacing his hairbrush on the silver tray with a deliberate precision. 'You look a little frazzled. Anything happen on your walk to upset you?' He was smiling, but the smile didn't warm her.

'No, nothing. It was pretty humdrum.' She was a poor liar and to cover the fact began to gabble. 'Except that I realised I'd been walking far too long and decided to run back. Tried to run back,' she amended. 'Those athletes on the beach put me to shame.'

Leo lowered himself into the easy chair and sat, hands steepled, his eyes never leaving her. Nancy felt herself examined, dissected. Had he made up his mind? Decided she was deceiving him? If he had telephoned Archie's room, and found his assistant absent, too…

'I'm glad it was nothing more than that,' he said, his voice devoid of expression. 'It always worries me when you disappear without a word on one of your little jaunts. It usually means you're doing something I wouldn't like.' He straightened himself in the chair. 'If we're to go to breakfast looking half presentable, you'd better get busy.'

Closing the bathroom door behind her, she let go of the breath she'd not realised she had been holding. Her pretence would stand, for the moment at least, but it would only take a loose word from her, from Archie, maybe from Francisco if he'd had news from the inspector, for the truce between them to be shattered. It was clear that Leo was suspicious, but had chosen not to voice his doubts. Not yet, at least.

Nancy made sure she was quickly in and out of the shower but, even so, most of the guests had already breakfasted by the time they reached the roof terrace. There was no sign of Archie—he would be keeping his head down, she was sure. The table they were shown to had a magnificent view of the bay, of a string of bays, and she took her time savouring the scene below, laid out like an unwrapped gift. It was unlikely she would ever return to Rio again and she hoped to fix in her mind the extravagant loveliness of the city: the white sands that stretched for miles, the glistening turquoise water, the twin mountains of Dois Irmãos, hazy in the background.

It was only when two waiters, both carrying laden trays, arrived at their table that she looked away.

'What a spread,' she remarked brightly, as the table

gradually filled to overflowing. 'Our last breakfast here. We should make a toast.' She raised her glass of papaya juice. 'Let's drink to a safe journey home and a less worrying holiday next time.'

Leo touched glasses, but the gesture felt faint, mechanical.

'I must admit I won't be sorry to get on the flight this evening,' she said, hoping to lighten the mood. 'How about you?'

He helped himself from the platter of sliced fruit. 'I'm looking forward to getting home, certainly. It will be good to see Cavendish Street again.'

She nodded agreement, but somewhere, deep within, there was a pain so deep it had ceased for the moment to hurt, like the cut of a sharp knife when it first wounds. Archie had said no more about leaving, but he wasn't a man to make idle remarks. Once back in London, he would walk away and she would never see him again.

Had he already told Leo of his plans and her husband was keeping tight-lipped? She gave him a swift glance, thinking what a relief it was to see him looking so much healthier. Almost the handsome man she had known before his winter illness and before that wretched attack on the beach. He was making solid inroads into his breakfast and seemed unperturbed by any worries, but she knew he would be turning over in his mind what exactly she'd been doing this morning and how far his assistant had been involved.

As though aware of her scrutiny, he picked up the plate of small cakes and offered it to her. 'These are very good. You should try one. I imagine you'll be glad to get back, too — to the studio.' He could never speak of her work at the art restorers without a certain stiffness, but Nancy was glad of the overture.

'I'm looking forward to the end of my apprenticeship, for

sure. Only a few months and I'll be a fully fledged restorer, think of that!'

'It's about time. It seems to have gone on for years.'

'It *has* gone on for years,' she said more forcefully than she'd meant to. Years of hard work, which Leo would never acknowledge, but also years of deep pleasure.

'Once it's done and dusted,' he said, filling their coffee cups, 'perhaps we can get back to a more normal kind of life.'

She could feel herself bristling, though she tried not to. A quarrel was the last thing she wanted, but couldn't stop herself saying, 'More normal as in my not working?'

Leo put down the *pão de queijo* he'd been about to attack. 'More normal as in how most couples live their lives. I know last night you mentioned working part-time, but art doesn't fit that kind of schedule, does it? You'd inevitably be drawn into staying longer at the studio. Remember, you were keen that we spend more time together? If you don't work, there'll be a far greater chance of doing that.'

'And if you don't work so much, an even greater one,' she said brightly. 'I think I'll go and pack before it gets too hot.'

'But you've hardly eaten,' he protested.

'I've eaten enough.' She had to get away before she said something she'd regret. 'It must be all that running I did!'

'Isn't exercise supposed to increase your appetite?'

'Obviously, I'm an oddity, but you must enjoy the rest of your breakfast.' She jumped up and, collecting her bag, started towards the lift.

'Nancy,' Leo called after her, 'I forgot to mention... I'd like to go back to the hospital this morning, take a taxi over there and see some of the doctors. I didn't really thank them properly yesterday for all they've done for me. Is that okay with you? You could come, too, but don't feel you have to.'

'I think I'd better spend the time packing — for both of us!'

When she walked back into the bedroom, though, Nancy made no attempt to pull their suitcases from under the bed. Instead, she drifted aimlessly from bed to chair to window and back, listless and unfocussed. It seemed impossible to get moving. Eventually, she crossed to the wardrobe and opened the doors, pulling out swimsuits, slippers, blouses and skirts she had hardly worn, and piling them in a jumble on the bed. She tried to fold one or two of the garments, but then gave up, leaving them to one side and walking to the window to stare down at the road below. For long minutes, she stood there, simply staring, lacking the energy to go on.

And then suddenly her legs weakened and her breathing became irregular. With a small groan, she tottered back. The fear she'd felt a few hours ago was hitting her anew. She thought she had coped well, but now what felt very like a panic attack was overtaking her. She stumbled to the easy chair and sank down with a heavy thump, looking blindly ahead, her mind filled with the terror she thought she'd put behind her. The blood-soaked body of Jessica Ramos hardly impinged—it was the child, dirty and half-starved, that she couldn't forget. And Ramos, madness chasing across his face. And the gun. The gun against her temple. She lifted her hand to rub the place where the cold metal had pushed into her skin, as though by doing so she could erase the memory.

She had been in tight corners before, but until that moment she had never truly believed she would die. She and Archie together. But they had survived, both of them, thanks to him. His courage had saved her life once more. In future, he wouldn't be kept quite as busy, she thought wryly. She would never again lead him into trouble. And never again, she vowed, find herself in such a desperate situation.

It was time to end this: her obsession with justice, with righting the wrongs that others had ignored. Leo had been partially right when he'd said the terror Philip March had wreaked on her, the feelings she'd experienced then of powerlessness, of lacking any help or support, had turned her into a woman who could not pass by when she saw it happening to others. But with luck, March had gone for good, and her own life was no longer on the line. She must finally forget those dreadful months she'd spent battling his depravity alone. Forget and move on.

It was moving on that she needed to do now or Leo would be coming back to an empty suitcase. Heaving herself out of the chair, she walked back to her wardrobe to clear the remaining clothes, folding them slowly and carefully into neat piles. She had just begun on Leo's wardrobe when there was a knock on the bedroom door. She was surprised. Taken aback. It wouldn't be her husband knocking and it was unlikely to be Archie—he had no idea Leo was at the hospital and, after this morning's exploit, he'd be careful not to intrude.

So who was on the other side of the door? There were still enemies out there, she recalled. Monaro, Sousa. Enemies with a grudge against her. She had helped the police track down Sousa's son-in-law, unmasked the terrible racket his daughter was running. Nancy felt her heart begin its pounding again. This is ridiculous, she scolded herself. Was she to fall into a panic every time she heard a knock?

Chapter Thirty-One

Opening the door a fraction, Nancy caught a glimpse of a round cap and felt foolish. It was one of the bell boys. Solemn-faced, he handed her a piece of paper and, without saying a word, disappeared down the corridor towards the lift.

She sat down in the chair to read, puzzled as to who could be sending her a message. It must be Francisco, she decided, there was no one else. For the last day or so, he had been at one of his mines in Minas Gerais, but had promised to return to the hotel in time to wave them goodbye. They'd been expecting him this evening, but had he returned early, perhaps at the behest of Inspector Alvarez? It was a worrying thought.

The inspector might have telephoned their host in Minas Gerais, relaying the news that one of Francisco's senior employees was under arrest. If so, her name and Archie's could well have been mentioned, meaning that it wouldn't be long before Leo knew the worst. Frowning, she scanned the very brief message. Just four words, but words that brought relief. Not Francisco, but Ester!

I WAIT ON BEACH was printed in capital letters.

Nancy felt admiration. To have mastered English well enough to write such a message! If the roles were reversed, she would have found Portuguese almost impossible. In another world, Ester would have thrived. She deserved so much more than she'd been given, the chance to use her energy and intelligence to build a better life for herself and her daughter.

But why was Ester wanting to speak to her? To say goodbye perhaps? Or was she concerned about Livia? Panic gripped Nancy again. Was the child safe? Was she even with her mother? She must find out and quickly. Unearthing her handbag from the jumble on the bed, she was out of the door in seconds and walking swiftly to the lift, her fingers tightly crossed that she wouldn't meet Leo on his way down from the roof terrace.

Thankfully, there was no sign of her husband and, escaping the hotel unnoticed, she crossed the Avenida Atlantica with a lighter heart. Just ahead of her, beyond the promenade, she spied a familiar figure. Archie was making for the beach, too. Ester must have written to him as well. He was striding towards a woman dressed in bright pink, standing close to the water's edge. Increasing her pace, Nancy caught up with him before he reached the sea.

He turned as he sensed her approach. 'What do you think Ester wants?' he asked.

'I've no idea. I was worried when I got the message, but perhaps it's something good. I've had enough bad news since we've been here.'

Archie's deep blue eyes searched her face. 'Did it go all right? He inclined his head towards the hotel.

She didn't pretend not to know what he meant. 'I think so,' she said cautiously, scuffling the sand with her shoe. 'For now, at least.'

'Fireworks later?'

'Probably, but they're ones that you'll escape.'

Her voice faded away. She hadn't meant to sound so broken. Archie had started towards Ester, but that stopped him in his tracks. He put out his hand and traced a finger along her cheek.

'It's the right thing to do, Nancy. You know that in your heart.'

'Do I?' She stared miserably down at the wet sand.

'I'm doing you no good by being around. And as long as I'm working for Leo, that's not going to change.'

'And you?' she asked sadly.

'I have to make a different life for myself and you have to remake the one you already have. It will be easier—for both of you—when there's only two in your marriage. Not at first maybe, but give it time and you'll see. Much easier.'

She shook her head not wanting to believe him, but nothing now would change his mind, she knew. Fixing her gaze ahead, she walked towards the pink sundress, a splash of colour against the white of rolling waves.

'Promise me one thing, though,' he called after her. 'You'll give up being a warrior for justice.'

She half turned to face him. 'I've already promised myself that. I can't be a warrior without someone to fight by my side, can I?'

Ester must have recognised them as they drew closer, and ran to greet them. To Nancy's alarm, the little girl was nowhere to be seen.

'How is Livia?' was her first question. She was trying to subdue a wash of fear.

'Good. Livia good. I bath, ' Ester made a dunking action with her hands. 'Then make *canjica*. Liva like. Then she go bed.'

'Alone? Livia is alone in the house?'

The woman had understood the frightened tone, if not all

the words, and was quick to stroke Nancy's arm. '*Amiga* with Livia.'

Nancy closed her eyes briefly in grateful thanks, her worries partly assuaged. A friend was in the house in Santa Cecilia. Livia would be safe until her mother returned. After that, Nancy dared not think.

'I come,' Ester said. 'Say thank you. For Livia.'

Nancy reached out and hugged the woman's thin shoulders. 'Please, no thanks. We are so happy you have your little girl home again.' She looked back at Archie, lingering a few paces behind, and he gave a simple nod.

'Vitoria love Livia much, but no find her,' Ester said. 'You find her. I thank you.'

'I hope she will be safe,' Nancy murmured. It wasn't the wisest thing to say, perhaps, but she couldn't rid herself of the knowledge that the child might still be in danger.

It seemed that Ester shared the same fear. 'I go,' she said, 'I go when Livia *na escola*.'

'Do you have the magic book?' Archie asked, coming to stand by Nancy's side.

She rustled in her handbag for the dictionary. 'When Livia goes to school,' she translated. 'I remember that Vitoria told me she was taken when she was walking to school.'

'*Escola, sim*.' Ester nodded.

'You will keep her safe, I'm sure—now that Jessica Ramos is dead.' She tried to sound encouraging, as much to rally herself as Ester, but couldn't prevent the creeping fear. 'It was Jessica who was guilty,' she went on. '*Jessica culpada*, and now Jessica *morta*.'

'*Sim, sim, mas Papa viva. Papa aqui*. Papa still here,' Ester spelt out slowly.

'Sousa is still here, it's true, but I don't think he'll have any interest in carrying on the business. According to Diego

Ramos, it was Jessica's own scheme.' Nancy riffled though the pages of the dictionary. *Papa não interessado.*'

Ester seemed unconvinced, her foot digging hard into the sand and sending grains flying.

'*Veja!*' She raised her hand suddenly and Nancy followed where she was pointing—two figures that she'd barely noticed before. Two men walking further along the beach, by the edge of the sea.

'I think this could be our friends again,' Archie muttered.

Shielding her eyes from the sun, Nancy stared across the intervening distance. Archie was right. She recognised the bulky outline of the figure nearest them and, when he turned to face his companion, she saw again his pudgy cheeks and hanging jowl. Leandro Sousa. And who else would be with him but Alvar Monaro?

'Sousa bad man. Monaro bad man. *As crianças em sua prisão.*'

'In his prison?' Archie guessed. 'The children were in his prison? Yeah, we know. We saw it,' he said, 'or what was left of it. Have all those kids come back to Santa Cecilia?'

Ester pointed to the dictionary and Nancy translated as best she could.

'*Muitas meninas vêm,*' she answered. 'Many girls come. But bad men still in Santa Cecilia,' she managed in English.

A stiff breeze had begun to blow and the waves, Nancy noticed, were higher than ever. Squinting against the sun, she picked out the men's figures once more. They were wandering along the water's edge, deep in conversation, seemingly unconcerned by the sudden change in the weather.

'Look at them,' she said to Archie, 'Two of the most evil men I've ever seen. And planning more wickedness, I'm sure.' A sudden thought had her say, 'Do you think Sousa knows his daughter is dead?'

'And his son-in-law in gaol with a charge of murder hanging over his head? I doubt it. The bloke wouldn't be walking as easily if he did.'

While they had been talking, Ester hadn't moved. Her gaze was intent, fixed unnervingly on the distant figures. 'It not right,' she said at last, '*mas*… She gave an expressive shrug of her shoulders.

'None of it is right, but what in particular?' Archie asked, sounding puzzled.

Nancy thought Ester must mean the way these two brutal men, with blood on their hands, endless blood in the case of Leandro Sousa, were able to talk together without concern, enjoy their surroundings, stroll carefree along a beautiful beach.

'*Avó da minha mãe…*' Ester began.

This took some translating, but after a few minutes, Nancy said, 'Your mother's grandmother?'

'*Sim*. She slave. From Haiti. I have *spirita*.'

'What does that mean?' she asked, as puzzled as Archie.

'*Poder. Poder sobre a vida.*'

'Power over life? I don't understand.'

Archie frowned. 'I don't think—' he started to say, but Ester wasn't listening. Her eyes were blank and she seemed to have fallen into a trance, her body tense and concentrated.

In the distance, Nancy saw Sousa stumble, then fall slowly to his knees, as though paralysed. Monaro was stooping, holding out a hand, seeming to help his companion to his feet, but then he, too, lost his balance and fell heavily. Their prone bodies lay perilously close to the waves that continued to soar and thunder onto the beach. In seconds, one enormous breaker of hissing, bubbling water had crashed to shore and covered them completely.

'They'll drown,' Archie said, 'if they're not already dead,' and started to run towards them.

'No.' Ester's voice was shrill and, at that moment, a heavier wave hit, towering over the limp bodies and drawing them into its maul. Once the wave retreated, there was nothing to be seen. It was as if the men had never existed.

'I go now,' Ester said in her normal voice. 'I go home—to Livia.'

And with that, she turned and walked up the beach towards the promenade, leaving them motionless and open-mouthed.

Several minutes passed. Minutes of complete silence. 'Did I see what I thought I saw?' Archie asked at last.

Nancy was too shaken at first to speak, but eventually said slowly, 'I think you did. But, no, it couldn't have been. Could it?'

'Ester cursed those men before, remember?' Archie said. 'She ran after us in the favella, saying we weren't to worry, she'd make them go. I asked you then what you thought she meant. Neither of those crooks were there at the time. Monaro was in the favella—we discovered that to our cost—but Ester didn't know that. This time, though, she did. She had them both in her sights.'

'They seemed suddenly to be paralysed.' Nancy was still grappling with what she'd seen. 'Ester couldn't have done that, could she?'

Archie's eyebrows rose. 'I dunno. It might be better not to ask too many questions.'

'Those men. They just disappeared.' Nancy couldn't stop babbling.

'So would you in that sea.'

'One minute they were talking together, the next...'

'Why don't we forget what we think we saw, and just be glad. Their disappearance is good news all round. Certainly for Francisco. He might have a chance now of getting the licence he's chasing. And good for Leo, too—it's not likely anyone will ever be charged for the attack he suffered, and those men were implicated.'

Nancy gave a small shake of her head. 'The cartel will have got away with it, though. I don't think Francisco's policeman has found any evidence. But Ester…'

'Whatever Ester did or didn't do, they were evil men and deserved to die. Their deaths won't mean an end to crime in Rio, but there should be a good deal less. That has to be welcome.'

'And the gang? The men in black—what about them? They're still around.' Amazingly, she sounded rational, which was strange since the shock of what she'd witnessed was still reverberating.

'Still around, but crucially without a leader.'

'They'll find another, I'm sure.' The thought was depressing.

'They'll try, I guess, but there'll be massive rows. Endless fights to see who comes out top dog. Even better, they could end up killing each other!'

It was a streak of hope, but a tenuous one. Nancy looked towards the spot where the men had disappeared, the waves ceaselessly battering the shore. There was nothing to see, only empty sand. Was that an omen for the future? She hoped so, but couldn't truly believe it.

'While that gang is around, in whatever form, the favella children won't be safe,' she said gloomily.

'I think you're wrong. Child kidnap isn't going to interest them. That was Jessica's racket. These blokes aren't likely to adopt a woman's leftovers, not when they're having to rebuild a whole empire. Monaro's warehouse is destroyed, Sousa and his daughter are dead and the house in Leblon will be sold. When you think about it, there's not much left.'

'Maybe then Santa Cecilia *will* sleep more easily.' The beginnings of a smile was in her voice.

'I'll say amen to that.'

Together, they turned to walk side by side up the beach until they reached the promenade.

'I'm supposed to be packing. I better get back to it,' she said forlornly.

'Me, too. It should take me all of five minutes—plenty of time to prop up the bar. It's just as well Brazilian beer is weak, I've taken quite a fancy to it.'

'The taxi is booked for five o'clock,' she reminded him.

Such a mundane thing to say when this was the end, the very end, but what else was left? On impulse, she reached for his hand, knowing she should not.

'Archie,' she said. 'Do you have to leave?'

His smile didn't quite reach his eyes. 'Go and pack, Nancy. I'll see you at five.'

If you've enjoyed this novel, do please leave a review—a few lines is all it takes. It's helpful to readers and makes authors very happy! I'll be sure to read every review.

Where next for Nancy? *The London Reckoning* brings Nancy full circle—or does it? Make sure you find out!

And follow me at
https://www.bookbub.com/authors/merryn-allingham
to be the first to know whenever there's a new release, pre-order or new discount!

FREE COPY OF *THE DANGEROUS PROMISE*

Sign up to Merryn's newsletter and, as a special thank you, claim your FREE book.

The Dangerous Promise introduces Nancy Nicholson, the feisty heroine of the Tremayne Mysteries Series, setting her on a journey that sees her become an amateur detective and find the love of her life.

Merryn's newsletter is sent only when there is something special to communicate—such as new book releases, special promotions, and price reductions.

Use the URL below to be taken to the sign-up page. Your details will not be shared and you can unsubscribe at any time.

https://merrynallingham.com/free-book/

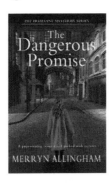

Other Books by Merryn Allingham

A Tale of Two Sisters (2019)

House of Lies (2018)
House of Glass (2018)

The Buttonmaker's Daughter (2017)
The Secret of Summerhayes (2017)

The Girl from Cobb Street (2015)
The Nurse's War (2015)
Daisy's Long Road Home (2015)

Printed in Great Britain
by Amazon